Jake & Clara

OTHER BOOKS BY THE AUTHOR:

The Shooting Salvationist
Camelot's Cousin
November Surprise
Capitol Limited
In the Arena
How to Keep Calm and Carry On
The Simple Life

Jake & Clara

DAVID R. STOKES

Jake & Clara
Copyright © 2015 David R. Stokes

Critical Mass Press
Fairfax, Virginia
Critical Mass Press
ISBN 978-0-9969892-0-6 (softcover)
ISBN 978-0-9969892-1-3 (ebook)

Cover Design by Mark Moorer
Interior Design by Penoaks Publishing,
http://penoaks.com

For more information, visit the author's website:
www.davidrstokes.com

To Betty Holland—
the best mother-in-law in whole wide world.

"Can one go upon hot coals,
and his feet not be burned?"

— *Proverbs 6:38*

FROM THE AUTHOR

This is a true story, but I have written it in the style of a novel. I have taken certain storytelling liberties, including the invention of some of the dialogue. Where the narrative strays from strict nonfiction, my intention has been to remain faithful to the characters and to the essential drift of events as they really happened.

Cast of Characters

CLARA SMITH HAMON: She was just seventeen when she met the handsome and charismatic man twenty years her senior. Jake Hamon swept young Clara off her feet and into his whirlwind of a life. He talked big and dreamed bigger. He promised Clara that she would be at his side for all the glory to come. And she was responsible for a substantial amount of Hamon's success.

JAKE HAMON: With the nickname "The Oil King of Oklahoma," Jake had the world on a string. Rich, powerful, and hard living, he seemed to be the embodiment of the new decade at its dawn. He used people. Sometimes abused them. And he tended to get away with it. He was poised to become the most powerful businessman in America.

GEORGIA HAMON: Georgia Hamon was Jake's wife. She had been with him from the beginning, when they didn't have two dimes to rub together. When prosperity came to her husband, their relationship turned into a marriage of convenience. This went on until Jake began to set his eyes on Washington. Georgia liked the idea of living in the nation's capitol. She looked forward to spending time with her relative and friend, the new First Lady of the United States.

WARREN G. HARDING: The man who would become the President of the United States in 1921 loved whiskey and women. When he met Jake Hamon, he knew his new friend was wired like him, at least when it came to the ladies. Harding had mistresses of his own, so Hamon's "arrangement" didn't really bother him. But when his wife, Florence, spoke, Warren listened.

FLORENCE HARDING: The future First Lady of the United States was referred to by many as "The Duchess," though never to her face. She was ambitious and controlling, which worked fine because someone had to look out for Warren Harding's career. She was intrigued to meet Jake because, though he did not know it, Florence was related to Jake's wife, Georgia. Georgia and Florence were cousins who spent much time together during their childhood.

FRANK KETCH: Jake's long time business manager knew where all the money was and all the bodies were buried.

JOHN RINGLING: The owner of the famous circus bearing his name, Ringling became Jake Hamon's partner in a railroad venture. Ringling would get an Oklahoma town named after him for his efforts. Jake would get more wealth and power. And it all began one day at the Waldorf Astoria Hotel in New York when Clara "accidentally" spilled a drink on the famous circus man.

BUCK GARRETT: The longtime sheriff of Carter County, Oklahoma was said to be related to Pat Garrett, the man who killed Billy the Kid. He knew the story wasn't true, but he seldom discouraged such talk. He enjoyed the legend. But he created a real name for himself when newspapers around the world covered his nationwide search for Clara.

BUD BALLEW: Sheriff Garrett's chief deputy was a colourful and sometimes violent man. He prided himself on the fact that he had killed many men. He shot first and asked questions seldom. He joined his boss as they searched far and wide for Clara Hamon, becoming famous in his own right.

SAM BLAIR: A Chicago reporter with a hunger for the big scoop, Blair made a name for himself via the Clara Hamon story. His big break came one day when he found something extraordinary in her long lost luggage. Soon millions were reading every word he wrote.

W. P. "WILD BILL" MCLEAN: Already famous in Fort Worth, Texas, where he lived, McLean joined Clara's defense team in Ardmore, Oklahoma. He made a national name for himself as one of the premier defense attorneys of the day.

JAMES "JIMMIE" MATHERS: Though he had only recently won election as Carter County Attorney—the office investigating and later prosecuting Clara—he put that aside to work on the defense team. Was it because he believed so much in her innocence, or that he simply had hated Jake Hamon for years?

JOHN GORMAN: A veteran Hollywood producer by the time 1920 rolled around, Gorman saw in the story about Clara something fit for the big screen. He decided to track her down. Not only did Gorman get to make a big movie, he got the girl, as well.

ONE

SAN FRANCISCO — SEPTEMBER 1921

It was a moment made for Hollywood, though it took place 375 miles to the north. The scene was the palatial lobby of the St. Francis Hotel on Union Square in the heart of San Francisco. A large crowd gathered there that afternoon. Some had been there for hours, moving in and out of the hotel and monitoring the situation.

Most of them were just plain old curiosity-seekers, but a few were there in "official" capacities. Some were cops. There were also at least a couple of Pinkerton operatives, including one Samuel D. Hammett (eventually to be known by his famous middle moniker, Dashiell). But he wasn't there on agency business. He wanted to be a writer and was looking for a good yarn. Seeing as the still-a-bit-new decade was already beginning to be known as the age of celebrity, he thought the potential for a monumental convergence—two very famous people bumping into each other—that day at the St. Francis just had to contain a story.

Of course, Sam wasn't the only scribe on the prowl on that day and in that place. The detective in him observed many men, and a couple of gals, who looked to be hunting a scoop as well.

The city was rife with rumors—had been since the night before. Word was that the St. Francis, which had mostly survived the big earthquake back in '06, would be the stage for the appearance of not just one, but two, big names. One was a star—the guy was making a cool million bucks a year for being fat and funny. He was driving his $25,000-Pierce Arrow touring car up the coast from Los Angeles.

The other attraction that day was a lady, although some called her other less flattering things. She wasn't a star, yet. But she wanted to be, and it looked like she just might make it. She was famous for a sensational story, complete with a high-profile murder trial, and was doing her best to leverage that notoriety into box office gold.

In fact, even without the famous comedian motoring toward San Francisco, the lady (though, again, I must belabor the point that some would simply not refer to her that way) was pretty big news herself. Had been for quite some time.

Then, of course, there was what happened the night before at The College Theater over on Market Street. Sure, it was a minor venue compared to the Majestic, or the Rox, but that prior night—Friday—it was the place to be in town.

Sam was there, too. Not officially, but just to see the show. Not just the movie, but the other show. The event. And he wasn't disappointed, which was why he was willing to hang out with this crowd in the hotel lobby trying to figure a way to get close to the famous (yes, yes, some said, infamous) gal.

When he had returned home after the big show the night before, he ignored his eight-month-pregnant wife, Josephine, annoying her to no end. Wouldn't even talk to her. Just pounded away on his infernal typewriter, that ugly (Josephine thought) Underwood number five model. He referred to page after page of notes made earlier that night. He wanted to write it all up while the scene was fresh in his mind.

It was while he was tormenting the Underwood and oblivious to everything else that he had the idea, well, more of an urge, to try to catch up with the famous lady the next day. Now, as he looked around the St. Francis lobby, it was apparent to him that his urge was part of a contagion.

Sam reached into his jacket pocket and pulled out several pages, the ones he'd written the night before. The words on paper introduced what was obviously an unfinished story. A movie premier had been scheduled—grand premier—right there in San Francisco. That itself was big news. The production had received publicity for many months.

Some cities refused to allow it to be shown. The censors were out in full force with their scissors and placards. Speaking of the latter, he was amused when they showed up on Market Street, long before the film's star and producer appeared. Poor gal, he thought. On her big night, she'd have to see signs saying things like, "No Filth in Our City!", "Adultery and Murder are Not Only Sins, They Are Crimes!", "Ban this Film!", and "Clara, Go Home!"

Clara. That was the lady's name. Clara Smith Hamon. She was just about the most famous woman in America at that moment. Famous for killing a rich and powerful man and getting away with it. Famous for bankrolling her own movie about it, starring herself. Famous for marrying the film's director while the picture was being filmed at Warner Brother's Studio in Los Angeles.

As Sam waited in the lobby that Saturday afternoon, he rehearsed the scene from the night before in his mind. There was a big crowd then, too. The theater's marquee bore the movie's title in big letters: "FATE," then, in smaller font: "Clara

Smith Hamon as Clara Smith Hamon … also starring John Ince as Jake Hamon."

He remembered watching a big car make its way slowly through the massive crowd. Sam winced when he realized that he forgot to note what model it was. Details. People—mostly girls of all ages—swarmed the machine. "Clara!" The word was uttered, complete with exclamation point, hundreds of times.

"There she is!"

Then the car stopped in front of the movie house, right at the end of a long red carpet. An usher opened the car door, and Clara gracefully exited the vehicle, her husband, Mr. John Gorman, falling in behind her.

She was attractive, though not what Sam thought of as gorgeous. "Not quite a beauty," that's what his notes said. Her brown hair was bobbed—that's how they all wore it, he noted. She was not as tall as he had imagined. She looked self-assured, as if used to the attention, yet every move was cautious and slow.

Again came the swarm, almost engulfing her. Shouts. Flashbulbs. "We love you, Clara!" "We believe in you, Clara!" Clara and her husband moved quickly down the red carpet, and, in an instant, they disappeared into the theater, which wasn't scheduled to open to the public for another fifteen minutes. Meanwhile, the crowd grew in size and impatience.

Sam recalled wondering where the couple would be sitting in the theater, when, all of a sudden, that thought was interrupted by the piercing sound of whistles—police whistles. Annoying things. Lawmen converged on the scene from every direction, forming their own ominous swarm. Sam recognized many of them from his Pinkerton work. Had to be at least two dozen cops.

There was a lot of shouting and a mild sense of panic. After a few moments, Sam figured out what was going on. The box office was told not to open, and the movie was being banned. Simple as that.

The moviegoers were not happy. But the police formed a line and made it pretty clear that the show was over—literally.

Sam lingered, though from a safe distance across Market Street. He wanted to try to catch Clara and John when they came out. But they never did. He figured they had ditched out a back exit.

✻

Clara Smith Hamon was both humiliated and enraged. They had done it. The threats had been there since she announced that she was making a movie. That was back in March, right after the trial. Sure, there had been some problems getting workers to do some things, and production delays abounded. But the film was made—costing $200,000, which included $75,000 from her own bank account. And clearly customers wanted to see it—to see her—if the crowd on Market Street was any indication.

But she retreated to her suite at the St. Francis. Her husband tried to console her. "Honey, tell you what, instead of the train back to Los Angeles, let's take the ship. The Harvard leaves San Francisco Bay tomorrow afternoon at four o'clock from Pier 7, and I'll book us a suite—first-class all the way. It'll be relaxing. We don't ever have to leave the room," he said, with a mischievous smile.

"Oh, John, it's so unfair. There's nothing wrong with my movie, and people should be allowed to see what they want," she replied, ignoring his suggestion with a pout. "Will they be doing this same thing in other places?"

"Dunno, doll. I just don't know. But if they try, we'll fight 'em. This is supposed to be a free country. That's what they told us we were fighting for when Wilson sent our boys to war over there."

"I love you, John. I'm sorry to be such a baby. I'm pathetic. Let's do that cruise home tomorrow. It'll be a hoot," she said, smiling through her tears. And then she hugged her husband and held on to him for a while.

John went over to the telephone, and when the operator came on, he said, "Get me Douglas 2576," reading the number from the advertisement in the evening paper—the one that was outside the door of their suite when they returned from the theater. In a few moments, it was set. Suite reserved. Champagne for the room. Deluxe all the way. They'd be in Los Angeles Harbor by ten o'clock Sunday morning, refreshed and ready to take on the world.

Saturday afternoon Clara and John were on the lift heading down to the lobby, their ample assortment of luggage having been sent down earlier, safe in the custody of the bellman.

"That's interesting, what the bellman said," John remarked to Clara as the lift stopped at another floor without anyone getting on.

"What?" Clara asked. She'd been distracted all day and had slept lousy the night before.

"Arbuckle. He said that they expect Fatty Arbuckle any time. He was checking in today."

"Oh, oh, yes. I heard that."

"Remember that party in Los Angeles? He seemed like a nice fella when he came over and talked to you for a while."

"Yes, he was. Nothing like I pictured. And not nearly as big as he is in the movies. Think we'll see him?"

"Dunno. Maybe."

"What was his real name? Can't call him Fatty, just wouldn't be right. What was it ... Ronald ... no, Roscoe. That's it!"

Roscoe "Fatty" Arbuckle, that was his name. The guy was big in more than one way. At that moment, he was starring in six new motion pictures in theaters across America. Paramount was making money hand over fist with him. He was a funny guy. Pie in the face and fall down laughing funny. He also lived large. He carried a party with him wherever he went.

They loved him at the St. Francis, but they also knew that they were in for a few challenging days. And they'd have to do a lot of looking the other way. Some of Fatty's parties were, well, known for booze and sex. Lots of both. Prohibition? What Prohibition? No such thing in the world of Fatty Arbuckle.

But he was a great tipper. And when he stayed at the hotel it was always great for business. Which brings us back to that moment made for Hollywood ...

As the title word of Clara's forbidden movie, "FATE,"would have it, Fatty Arbuckle walked into the lobby of the St. Francis Hotel at the very same moment Clara Smith Hamon exited the lift. She saw him first. He was pretty hard to miss. Within just a moment, though, her presence in the lobby became gravitational as her name was whispered around and then shouted out.

He saw her and smiled. "Clara! Honey, what the hell are you doing here?" Somehow, the crowd parted, and the resulting void seemed to draw the two celebrities together. They embraced. Flashbulbs popped. Sam Hammett tried to elbow his way toward them, with marginal success. But he would not be denied.

"Where ya headed, baby?" the comedian asked Clara.

"We're going over to the wharf to board the Harvard back to Los Angeles. I've had enough of San Francisco."

Arbuckle had a puzzled look on his face. "You don't love this town? Why, it's the greatest, a real gasser."

"You, sir, can have it after what happened last night."

Fatty Arbuckle had been in his car all day and was never much for newspapers unless they had something in them about him. "Sorry, kid, no clue what you mean."

"The censors banned my movie; they sent the police and everything. It was horrible," she said as she started to weep. Arbuckle felt awkward and tried to make a joke, mostly to run interference for Clara as a couple of reporters positioned themselves to get a photograph of her in tears.

"Hey, fellas, next one who pops a bulb gets a pie in the face!" Laughter. He smiled and passed a few expensive cigars around. Then he leaned close to Clara and whispered, "Let me drive you folks over to your ship. My car's right out front."

She looked up and nodded, and in an instant they were out the door and climbing into the car. Arbuckle gave the bellman a hundred-dollar bill and told him, "See that their luggage makes it to Pier seven on time." The hotel worker sprang into action. Sam managed to position himself close to them and followed them out onto the street where the funny man's car was parked.

He decided to give it a shot. "Mr. Arbuckle, I'm a Pinkerton. Happy to ride along with you, in case you need someone to keep the crowd at bay, so to speak."

Arbuckle took a moment, only a brief moment, to size up the guy with the nerve and made a snap decision. "Sure. That'd be great. Hop in. This is Clara. Clara, this is … ?"

"Sam. Sam Hammett, with the Pinkerton Agency."

"Pleasure. Now let's get moving." Clara smiled. Then she climbed in and sat in the front passenger seat, leaving a back seat for John.

As the crowd began to pour out of the hotel, Arbuckle pulled his Pierce-Arrow away from the hotel, taking Powell to Geary and then turning left toward Market Street.

"Quite a machine," John said from the back seat. But he wasn't heard. Arbuckle was clearly interested only in Clara.

"So, baby, tell me more about what happened last night. Sounds just plain awful."

"It was. I worked so hard on that movie. Put some of my own money behind it. If they stop it from being shown, I don't know what I'll do," she said, starting to tear up again.

Roscoe put his beefy hand on her knee and stroked it. "Hey, doll, no worries, okay? I've got a lot of friends in this business, and I'll see what I can do for you. How's that?"

"That's swell, just swell," she said, smiling through the tears.

They continued the conversation as Arbuckle steered the Pierce-Arrow left onto Market Street and neared Pier seven. "As soon as I get back to Los Angeles, I'll get on it. You can count on your friend Roscoe. How about we get together next week after I get back from Frisco? I'm here to relax. Have some friends coming by the St. Francis, and we're going to have a good time—but after that ..."

"I'd like that," Clara said.

Clara and John thanked Arbuckle—she hugged him tightly—and waved as he began to drive off. Clara told her husband, "He's a swell guy. He's going to help us. He has friends all over. Nobody says no to Fatty Arbuckle." For the first time since before the debacle the night before, she actually allowed herself to feel hopeful.

Poor Clara. She couldn't catch a break. In fact, Roscoe "Fatty" Arbuckle wouldn't follow through on his promise. Not because he forgot Clara, mind you, just that he had other things on his mind.

San Francisco turned out to be a nightmare for the big Hollywood star that weekend. And by the time he was supposed to get together with Clara back in Los Angeles to report on how he was working to fix her problem with the censors, he had problems of his own. Big problems. With the police and the public, at large. Fatty Arbuckle's story became the first sordid Hollywood scandal of the decade—ever, for that matter.

Frankly, Clara Smith Hamon and her film never had a chance. Not once Arbuckle's famous fat hit the fire.

It was indeed a matter of fate.

TWO

LAWTON, OKLAHOMA — 1910

One day, in the autumn of 1910, Jacob "Jake" Hamon walked into a store on the main thoroughfare of town in Lawton, Oklahoma. He was hunting a new pair of shoes. He went through a lot of shoes out in the fields. No, he wasn't a farmer—he was an oil man, and Carter County was the home of some nearby oil fields, where Jake was beginning to make a fortune.

Miller's Store, located near the center of town, was your average, run-of-the-mill enterprise, where local citizens could find most anything they needed, and usually at a fair price. They had a modest selection of shoes, but what they didn't have they could get from a catalogue.

It was late afternoon, and business was slow. Old man Miller had gone home for dinner—he just lived a block or so away—and left a young lady in charge of the store. She was just seventeen and in her final year of high school. She was a very good worker, with a pleasing personality and a keen mind.

Her name was Clara—Clara Smith. The daughter of James and Margaret Smith. They owned a pool hall down the street. She stood just over five feet tall. Her brown hair had a reddish tint that was more pronounced in the sunlight. She had brown eyes that sparkled, and a cute, slightly round face. There were freckles, but just a few—remnants of her childhood. She exuded confidence and was good at the art of conversation.

She had been working for Miller for less than six months. But he would tell people that his girl Clara knew more about the merchandise in the store than he did. He was probably right. She was ambitious and gave all the energy she could muster to everything she did.

On this particular day, she was measuring a piece of cloth for a customer. She looked up from her work when Jake Hamon walked in and smiled his way. "Be right with you, mister," she said. She recognized him. Everyone in town knew Jake Hamon, though not everyone liked the guy.

"Oh, darlin', take your time. I'm fine. You look busy," he said.

"Almost done." She smiled his way again.

There was something in that smile that was both inviting and unsettling to Jake. It hit him instantly. He would always remember the moment and how he felt. He watched the girl while she worked. Then he caught himself and looked away. He had just celebrated his thirty-seventh birthday, after all, with his wife and two children. He reminded himself that he was old enough to be the girl's father.

Jake was originally from Kansas, born there in 1873. Educated there, too, a graduate of the University of Kansas Law School class of 1898. But he had long ago lost interest in the law, and

Kansas for that matter. He and his wife, the former Miss Georgia Perkins from Cincinnati, Ohio, moved west a few years later and started a family. They had a son in 1901—named him Jake Jr.—and a daughter named Olive Belle, who was a year old.

Oklahoma—largely Indian Territory then—was a land of opportunity, that's what he told his wife to convince her to leave her kin. Hamon opened a law practice in Lawton and had modest success. He leveraged his knowledge of the law and his natural political instincts into an appointment as Lawton's first city attorney—this at a time when the town was reorganizing its civic life.

Jake Hamon helped organize the city government for future growth. He tried to get support for floating a paper bond issue to finance a railroad from Lawton to Ardmore, and from Wichita Falls, Texas, to Oklahoma City, but he couldn't get the backing. He put that idea on the back burner, where it would simmer for a few years.

Many thought that City Attorney Hamon was on the take, that he was extorting money from local gamblers in exchange for his legal protection. Though never proven, the allegations were enough to get local voters to oust him in 1903. But he took it all in stride. He donated a tidy sum of money to Lawton's First Presbyterian Church—highly publicized, of course—though no one could ever remember him actually sitting in its pews. He had a reputation as a womanizer, and the rumor was, one of the girls who worked at the Midland Hotel was his mistress.

In spite of his notoriety and political defeat in 1903, he was eventually elected as Mayor of Lawton. He was on the ground floor of Republican politics in the state while fellow Republicans Theodore Roosevelt and then William Howard Taft ran things in Washington. But his political party repudiated him in early 1910, after he was accused of attempting to bribe United States Senator Thomas P. Gore. Hamon did his best to talk his way out of that trouble, but Oklahoma Republicans gave him the boot.

He managed to wrangle an invitation to the Republican Convention in Chicago, even though it was still two years off, but had no stomach for the schismatic politics of the Roosevelt and Taft forces as they feuded. His bias was more for Taft than Teddy, largely because Roosevelt was not a fan of oil or the kind of wealth Jake longed for, but none of that mattered. No one was interested in Jake or his opinions.

No matter—he already had his dream-filled eyes on other things—particularly the oil business. He began to quietly acquire leases and partnerships in Carter County, particularly in the area where the Healdton and Ragtown oilfields would eventually be developed. His hunches paid off, and his timing was perfect. These investments would form the foundation of what would eventually become a vast business empire and personal fortune.

Jake had a magnetic personality and unbridled ambition. He dreamed big dreams about money and power. He believed he could accomplish anything he tried to do and could have anything he wanted. He had a swagger about him, and maybe that's what young Clara saw when Jake came into the store that day.

She had grown up in Lawton and though very smart— she'd always done well in school—she hadn't found an ambition yet, beyond the normal dreams of a young girl. She assumed marriage and family would be her lot in life. And that was just fine.

She didn't know it at the moment, but all that was about to change. Jake Hamon did more than walk into a store that hot day, he walked into her life—and she into his.

They'd eventually break all the rules and make up new ones of their own, and, together, they'd shoot for the moon and almost get there.

But the price they'd pay was something neither of them could possibly fathom that day back in 1910.

Jake Hamon was browsing the scant few titles in the store's tiny book section when Clara came over to him.

"What can I help you with, sir?"

"Oh, I wanna look at your shoe catalogue. I doubt you have what I want in stock."

"Oh, really?" Clara replied with a mocking tone that was a slightly coquettish. "Well, I accept the challenge. Why don't you sit down over there, and I'll show you what I have," she added with a smile.

"Well, aren't you the little charmer. All right, show me."

Ten minutes later she was wrapping up a pair of black dress shoes that Jake didn't really want—or need—but couldn't resist.

"What kind of books do you like? I saw you were looking at what we have; sorry there aren't more," Clara said, clearly wanting to continue a conversation.

"Oh, I like biographies—biographies of famous men."

"Like who?"

"Napoleon Bonaparte is my favorite—he's a hero of mine. Great leader and warrior. Inspired those around him."

"You want to inspire people, do ya?" Clara asked with a chuckle.

Jake gave her a serious look and said, "Young lady, I was being serious. I thought you were asking a serious question."

Clara was horrified. "Oh my, I'm sorry, mister—I was just having some fun. Didn't mean to make you mad."

Jake paused and then smiled and said, "How could anyone stay mad at a pretty girl with such beautiful eyes?"

Clara blushed. "Oh, mister, I ... er ... I ..."

"Call me Jake; what's your name?"

"It's Clara, Clara Smith. Pleasure to meet you, Jake."

And that was how they met. Simple as that.One of the few simple things about their relationship.

Over the next several weeks, as autumn gave way to winter, Jake found a reason to stop by Miller's Store whenever he was in town. He usually timed his visits to when there were few customers around and when the old man went home for dinner. He bought many things—none of which he needed. He smiled one morning while shaving when he realized he now owned five safety razors.

And he always lingered to talk to Clara.

As for her, she was flattered by the attention and found herself looking forward to Jake's "drop-ins." She'd watch the clock and fix her hair and makeup before his visits. But she never told anyone about the attentions and intentions of the older man who had found a place in her young heart. Frankly, she wasn't sure herself what they were.

Their conversations were about a wide range of subjects, but more and more turned to Jake's big dreams for the future.

"Little darlin', I'll be running things round here one day."

"Lawton?"

"Hell, the whole state. I'm gonna make so much money that I can't be denied. Money is power, I tell you. I may be Governor of Oklahoma, and maybe one day I'll be living in the big White House in Washington, DC. Whadaya think about that, sweetheart?"

"Oh, Jake, I love to hear you talk big. Never heard anyone talk like you."

"Well, how would you like to be First Lady of this country one day?"

"Me? How? What about your wife?"

"Oh, she's a fine woman, but we're not really living as man and wife. One day, I'll divorce her and marry you—how 'bout that?"

"Oh, Jake, you're so silly."

Their conversations were filled with teases and flirtations, but Jake was always the perfect gentleman. Clara grew to trust him. She looked up to him. And somewhere along the way, those dreams Jake always talked about began to get more serious and detailed, and they all included young Clara Smith.

One day, Jake said, "Clara, I'm thinking of buying an automobile."

"Do tell, Mr. Hamon."

"Would you like to go riding with me?"

Clara giggled and replied coyly, "I wouldn't go riding with you if you had a string of automobiles."

"Oh, we'll see about that," he replied with a tone of determination. A few days later, he bought a brand new Packard.

On another day, as Jake came by for a visit, Clara was looking through some furs that had been delivered. "Mr. Hamon, maybe you should buy one of these for your wife," she said with a wink.

"I don't think so, honey. But I'll buy you all the furs you can wear, if you come for a ride in my new automobile."

THREE

"Old Jake will pay for it ..."

It was the next spring when Jake talked seriously with Clara about her future. "Clara honey, what do you want to do with your life?"

"Well, I 'magine I'll keep working here at the store—only I'll get more hours, and it'll be more permanent. I think Mr. Miller likes me and will give me more responsibility."

"Well, I have an idea you might like."

"What's that?"

"I could use an assistant, a secretary to help with my business, someone I can trust."

"Aw, Jake, I don't know a thing about oil. I wouldn't know what to do."

"Well, honey, I was thinking of you going to a business school to get some training."

"Business school, where?"

"There's a fine one over in Ardmore called the Selvidge Business College. They have a great program."

"Ardmore? That's almost a hundred miles from here. I've never been away from home—and there's no way my folks would be able to afford something like that."

"They wouldn't have to. Old Jake will pay for it."

"Daddy would never go for that, Jake."

"He'd never have to know. I'd set it up with the school—I know someone there—it'd be a scholarship, one that I'd pay in full anonymously,'" he said, flashing a mischievous smile.

Clara smiled back and ran around the counter she'd been standing behind and gave him a big hug, but just for a moment. Their embrace was interrupted by the noise of the store door opening.

Before he left Miller's Store that day, Jake mentioned, almost casually, "Oh, I've got an office in Ardmore. It's a great town—probably gonna make my headquarters there eventually."

He was out the door before Clara could say a word.

True to his word, Jake made an arrangement with the school in Ardmore for them to offer Clara Smith a "scholarship," one that he completely funded. There would also be expenses provided for Miss Smith to have a room at a local boarding house—one run by a widow woman named Violet Morrison.

Clara traveled with her parents to Ardmore shortly after Easter for an interview at the school—a formality—and to look everything over. This was more for her parents' benefit than anything else. They stayed—all expenses paid for by the "school"—at Ardmore's Randol Hotel on Main Street. Of course, Jake paid that bill, too.

Their last night in town before heading back to Lawton, Jake saw Clara having dinner with her parents in the hotel's dining room. She saw him across the way and became nervous. Hamon noted the concerned look on her face, but made his way toward their table anyway with a smile on his face.

"Well, hello, young lady. Aren't you the girl from Miller's Store over in Lawton?"

Clara gathered herself and did her best to play along. "Why, yes, how kind of you to remember me, Mr. Hamon. I'm Clara Smith. Mommy, Daddy, this is Mr. Hamon, he's a regular customer at the store. I think I sold him the shoes he's wearing." They all laughed as they shook hands.

"They treatin' y'all right here at the Randol? They're good people. If you have any problems, let me know."

"Oh my, everything has been wonderful," Clara's mother spoke up. "Clara's gonna be coming here to school in a few months."

"Is she now? Well, that's great. What're you going to be studying, young lady?"

"Um, business and secretarial."

"Very good. Well, when you're done, if you need a job, come see Jake, okay, dear?"

"Why, what a nice thing to offer, Mr. Hamon," her mother replied. "Isn't that nice, Clara—say thank you to the nice man."

"Thank you, Mr. Hamon," Clara said with a smile her parents didn't see, nor would they understand. Jake made his way upstairs to room twenty-eight, where he stayed whenever he was in Ardmore. A bit later, Clara and her parents occupied the room next door, number twenty-nine.

She drifted off to sleep thinking about the man in the next room.

With the business school's term scheduled to start in September, Clara went back home to Lawton and her job at Miller's Store. She broke the news to her boss that she would be leaving by summer's end, and the old shop owner was sad, but understanding. He smiled and told her that he had known she'd be a hard one to keep. She was flattered by that and also a little sad.

Jake kept coming in, but by this time, he was finding other ways to spend time with young Miss Smith. There were drives in the country in his Packard touring car, picnic lunches, long walks, and lots of conversation about Jake's dreams.

One day Jake pulled out a bottle and took a swig of something. Clara asked, "What's that, Jake?"

"Oh, darlin', this is good old Redbud Rye Whiskey from over in Moore. Just about the best thing on Earth. It's good for what ails ya."

"I didn't know you were a drinking man," she said with a hint of disappointment in her voice.

"Aw, hell, honey, just a bit now and then. Nothin' to worry your pretty little head about."

"What's it taste like?" she asked.

Jake was a bit surprised by the question and her curiosity. "Well, it's like nothin' you ever tasted before, I can tell you that. Wanna try a sip?"

"Sure, why not?"

He poured a small amount of the whiskey into a cup and passed it her way. "Now, you sip that, honey—don't gulp it."

She drank it down in one swallow and began coughing and gagging. Jake laughed. But after she had caught her breath, she said, "Not funny, Jake."

"I told you to sip it!"

It would be a while before she'd share a drink with Jake again, but on their last outing before her move to Ardmore to begin school, she tried the Redbud Rye again—this time she sipped. And then she sipped some more.

And as the stars started to pop out in the Oklahoma sky that night, Jake and Clara made love for the first time in the back seat of the Packard—and it was the very first time for her. Clara became Jake's mistress that night, and for the rest of his life.

When Clara moved to Ardmore, she never quite made it to Mrs. Morrison's rooming house. Instead, she took up residence in room twenty-nine of the Randol Hotel, paid for by good old Jake. He had an arrangement with the proprietor, and every precaution was taken to keep his relationship with young Miss Smith a secret. He spread money around to the hotel's staff— anyone who'd be in a position to see and tell. His generous tips accomplished their purpose.

Clara explained the last-minute change to her parents by telling them that a few of the girls from the school were at the hotel with her, but it was a lie. It was just her. Jake even paid for some remodeling for the hotel—he had rooms twenty-eight and twenty-nine turned into a suite, with a door adjoining the two. But this never appeared in any records, the money for the work all moved under the table, complete with bonuses to buy silence.

After all, Jake was a married man.

Georgia Hamon remained in Lawton while Jake was ramping up his relationship with Clara. If she suspected anything, she didn't let on—to Jake or anyone else. She was enjoying the ever-increasing fruit of her husband's wealth.

Jake's oil business took him to Fort Worth, Texas, on occasion, and this was one place Georgia liked to travel with him. The city was booming, and because so many millionaires called it home, there were amenities that didn't exist in Lawton. Georgia Hamon even made some friends—wives of other wealthy men. And the schools were better there, too.

It was an interesting place. Fort Worth, in those days, was filled with stories about fights between a moral crusader by the name of Reverend J. Frank Norris and anyone who dared to cross him. Georgia would attend his First Baptist Church on occasion. Her children loved its Sunday school.

It was the education system that became the stated reason for Jake to move Georgia, Jake Jr., and young Olive Belle to Fort Worth in 1912. But the real reason likely had more to do with her taste for the finer things in life, not to mention Jake's taste for young Miss Smith. By this time, the marriage between Jake and Georgia had become one of convenience. But his wife let it be known to him on many occasions that she didn't believe in divorce.

Norris's sermons appealed to her moral sense. She was not a fan of booze, gambling, and vice in general. She even gave money to support the Fort Worth preacher when he was indicted on charges relating to the burning of the church. She joined the local chapter of the Women's Christian Temperance Union and rallied to Norris's support.

Jake ignored all that. He had little use for Norris or others like him. But he saw Georgia's involvement in Fort Worth life as a way to keep her busy, and therefore away from him. He'd visit every few weeks, just for a day or so at a time. Then it was back to Oklahoma.

Before long, he moved his entire operation to Ardmore, just as he had promised Clara. And while he waited for her to finish her program before employing her full-time, she began part-time work for Jake while still in school. Clara was a quick study and learned every aspect of the oil business. She was determined to make herself indispensable.

And she almost succeeded.

Clara finished her studies ahead of schedule and received her diploma. Her transition from student to full-time girl Friday was seamless. And their romance continued and grew. She was in love with him and wanted to be his wife.

"Jake," she'd beg, "when am I gonna get that ring you keep promising me? You don't live with Mrs. Hamon. You're practically separated, so why haven't you left her completely? I want us to be married."

"I do, too, darlin'. You know I'm crazy about you, but it's complicated."

"It's the money, isn't it?"

"Hell no, honey—it's not that. I could set her up comfortably and have more than enough for us. It's just that the lady is stubborn as a Missouri mule. She don't believe in divorce. She's a church goin' woman and takes that stuff seriously. It's gonna take time. But I have a plan to push it along. I'm gonna get her out of Fort Worth and the grip of her temperance friends and that damn preacher, and move her and the kids to Chicago."

"Chicago? Why there?"

"She has some family up there, and she loves the city."

And before long, Georgia and the children indeed took up residence—and what a residence it was—at 4901 Sheridan Street in Chicago, among the wealthy citizens of the Windy City. But, even being farther away didn't bring Jake any nearer to making the break with his legal wife and making an honest woman out of poor Clara Smith.

FOUR

"MY NAME IS JOHN, JOHN RINGLING..."

By the time 1913 dawned, Jake found himself depending more and more on young Clara. She was a natural, quickly learning the details of Jake's business. He tutored her in the law—at least the part that touched his enterprises, and she learned the basics of prospecting.

One day he said, "Clara darlin', let's take a ride."

"Where to?"

"Gotta look at a couple of fields. Put some food together; we'll make a day of it."

Clara sprang to action with the giddiness of a kid buying a nickel's worth of candy from her back at Miller's Store. They traveled together to a prospective drilling site and had a picnic under the blue sky. Then they drove around some more.

It was too late to drive back to Ardmore, so they decided to spend the night under the stars in Jake's fancy car.

"This is so wonderful, Jake. Just the two of us. You make me so happy. Talk to me more about what our future will be like."

"Aw, Clara, you see those bright stars? That's our future. It's like the good Lord told old Abraham in that there Bible, those stars are our future, too."

"What do you mean?"

"Well, I'm gonna be a star. You're gonna be a star. And we're gonna shine."

She fell asleep in her lover's arms while he serenaded her—but not with song. His music was success, prosperity, big money, bigger power—he was Napoleon, Rockefeller, and P.T. Barnum all rolled into one. Her seduction complete, Clara now became increasingly intoxicated with Jake's potent brew of charisma and megalomania.

Her unshakable belief in Jake's star was reinforced as some of the oil leases he had acquired years before began to pay off big.

Way back in 1888, the United States Department of Interior had examined various lands west of the Mississippi, including what later became the state of Oklahoma. The conclusion was that there was a lot of oil below the surface. It would be years before a demand for crude oil would be sufficient to warrant the expense of tapping its potential. People still loved their coal. So did the big ships at sea.

But by the time Jake and Clara were well into their love affair, the world began to change. Most of the great warships—the Dreadnoughts that would soon feature prominently in a global war—had switched from coal to oil, increasing demand for crude significantly. And that meant that the quiet investments Hamon had made during his political days back in Lawton were beginning to bear fruit.

By the summer of 1913, the Healdton Oil Field began to boom. And a short time later, another area—less than three miles from the town of Healdton—seemed to be even richer in the resource. Almost overnight, a settlement took root. It was mostly tents. Thus the nickname "Ragtown" was affixed and never seemed to go away, even after the town was officially named Wirt.

Jake and Clara, from their base of operations in Ardmore in the Randol Hotel and a suite of offices across Main Street, were on the ground floor of this. Hamon made millions. He had been prosperous.

Now he was rich.

He was also a visionary and again had maneuvered to be way ahead of the competition. It was one thing to discover and drill for oil, quite another thing to find ways to get the commodity to dealers and consumers. The new oil fields were out in the middle of nowhere—there was no infrastructure. There were hardly any roads.

Jake had harboured the idea and hunger to be a railroad mogul for years. He had even tried to do something about it back in Lawton ten years earlier, but few listened to his grandiose plan. So he waited.

Then, one day, Jake and Clara traveled to Oklahoma City on business. They had a suite at the Lee Huckins Hotel. Clara was learning to love the finer things of life. A few other associates traveled with them—an entourage of sorts—including a fellow named Bob Hutchins. Jake had a nickname for him—Six-Shooter Man. Hutchins was Jake's bodyguard and fixer.

It was also his job to keep an eye on Clara when Jake was away.

Clara took a sip of her morning coffee from an elegant china cup. A half-empty plate of ham and scrambled eggs sat in front of her. She took another bite of toast, while reading that morning's edition of The Daily Oklahoman. Her eyes came to rest on a story about the famous circus man, John Ringling.

"Jake, isn't Mr. Ringling the man you want to find a way to talk to about your railroad idea?"

"John Ringling? Sure, but I haven't figured a way to get to him. You know, I worked once in his circus for a few weeks when I was a kid, saw him a few times. Never met him, though. Why?"

"Says here in the paper that he is in New York right now and staying at the Waldorf Astoria Hotel. Says he's there for the opening of the new Grand Central Terminal. That must be beautiful. Every part of New York must be grand!"

"New York's a great town," Jake replied. Then he paused for a moment. "Haven't been there in a while, though."

Clara put the newspaper down on the table and smiled at Jake. "Why don't you take your best girl to New York, Jake? We could stay at the Waldorf. Maybe we could run into Mr. Ringling. How about it?"

"You mean, just like that—hop on a train and head to New York? You're crazy."

"Crazy about you, Jake. And if you're crazy about little ole me, you could make me really happy by taking me to New York. Please? We could see the Ziegfeld Follies, or a play. I read in a magazine the other day that there is play there about Caesar and Cleopatra—you might like that, Jake. Oh, Caesar, please take your Cleopatra to New York, pretty please?"

She had him at Caesar.

An hour later they were on a train headed for Fort Worth, where they changed trains and headed to Chicago for yet another train. That one arrived in the brand new Grand Central Station thirty-six hours after Clara had begged Jake to whisk her away. She had one other request. She didn't want anyone else on the trip—no cronies, no bodyguards. Jake complied. And while en route to New York, they came up with a plan to get the important and wealthy circus man to take a walk on a risky high-wire business venture with them.

New York was everything Clara thought it would be, and Jake found himself surprised at how much he enjoyed showing his girl around. They saw The Ziegfeld Show, and Clara loved watching Ann Pennington.

"My magazine says that she's gonna be the next Mary Pickford."

"Who?"

"Oh, silly, you have so much to learn. Maybe I'll be an actress one day."

"Over my dead body, doll. I ain't sharing you with anyone." Jake smiled mischievously, as they ate lunch one day at Katz's Delicatessen. Clara just ignored him, while trying to figure out how to eat her mammoth pastrami sandwich. She nibbled on its edges and then just settled for a pickle.

They tried to find John Ringling and confirmed from one of the bellhops—via a sizable tip—that the showman was still in the hotel. But there was no sign of him—until day three of their visit.

"That's him," Jake said to Clara, pointing at a well-dressed man sitting alone at the bar. He was reading a newspaper and nursing a drink. It was just after three o'clock in the afternoon.

"Wish me luck," Clara said with a smile as she waited for the right moment. She watched Ringling pick up his drink for another sip, and she sprang into action—that spring being more of stumble, then a push, and a spilled drink.

"What the hell?" Ringling shouted before he turned around and saw Clara.

"Oh my, sir, I'm dreadfully sorry. I lost my balance, oh dear—did it spill on your suit? Oh, I am so very, very, sorry."

Ringling grabbed a napkin and smiled. "Nothing terrible, my dear, it comes right off. Not to worry."

"Are you sure? Please let me buy you another glass of what you were drinking?"

"Well, young lady, that's a nice thought, but it was very expensive. I'm not sure you can afford it."

"Oh, dear, I am so clumsy."

"But how 'bout I buy one for me and you, what do you say to that?" Clara asked, while smiling and pulling out a fifty-dollar bill.

"I'd say that was downright gracious of you," he replied, a bit surprised. "My name is John, John Ringling, and you are?"

"Clara Smith. Clara Smith from Lawton, Oklahoma."

"Do tell? Ever been to the circus in Oklahoma City?"

"Why, yes, my mother took me when I was about twelve, and … wait … Ringling. Are you that Ringling?"

"Indeed, I am."

"Oh my, I spilled a drink on a famous man; oh, forgive me."

"Clara, don't you bother yourself over it and please, please, stop apologizing."

Ringling ordered the drinks—expensive Irish whiskey. When they arrived, he raised his glass to hers. "To Clara from Lawton, Oklahoma." She smiled shyly. They chatted a while, and then Jake walked over.

"This lady being any trouble to you, mister? I told her I'd be here about twenty minutes ago. I guess if you snooze, you lose round here," he said with a smile that indicated he was not really upset.

"Um, well, yes—this wonderful young lady introduced herself to me in the most original way."

"Jake, honey, I bumped into him, and he spilled his drink on his suit. Jake, this is Mr. John Ringling—you know, the man who owns the whole circus?"

"Do tell, well, nice to make your acquaintance, Mr. Ringling. Sorry about my gal's mishap, can I buy you both another round and join you?"

"Certainly ... it's Jake?" he asked, extending his hand.

"Yes, sir, Jake Hamon."

"Hamon, Hamon, where've I heard that name?"

"Well, I used to work for you, and you never paid me," Hamon said with a smile.

"Pardon?"

"Yes, sir, I was 'bout fourteen and tried to run away with the circus, at least for a week, when you came to Kansas City back in '87. Your show was not nearly as big as it is now, but I worked putting up tents and such. My mother found me and dragged home by my ear," he said, while rubbing his left ear. "It still hurts today. Anyway, I never did get my pay for that week, so since we're talking, how 'bout my seventy-five cents, Mr. Ringling?" At that, Clara laughed out loud.

Ringling replied, "It's John—well, Mr. Hamon, that drink I want to buy you and your beautiful friend is worth twice that—how's that sound?"

"Deal," Jake said, while ever so gently patting Ringling on the back. He then gave Clara a wink—one that Ringling never saw. It was a gesture that said, "You done good, Clara—real good."

Jake and John talked for a couple of hours in the hotel bar that day. Clara lost interest barely into the second drink, but then again, that was the plan. She excused herself and said she was going back to her room for a nap.

The two men talked business. Jake was careful and crafty, not wanting to give away too much or push his quarry too far, too fast. He had done his homework, both about the railroad business and about Mr. John Ringling himself. Bob Hutchins had helped with the latter. Ever resourceful, Six-Shooter Man had worked in private security for years and knew how to dig things up. So Jake was always a step ahead of Ringling as he drew him out.

Jake knew, for example, that Ringling had owned—and probably still had connections to—a large section of property right where his envisioned railroad would go.

"Now, John, I guarantee you, that if we can connect Ardmore with those oil fields at Healdton and Ragtown, well, we'll have an economic boom. Just thirty or so miles of track— but it'll pay off a hundred times. Hell, a thousand times. Then …" At that, he motioned for the bartender. "You got a piece of paper I can write on?"

"Just some brown paper for wrapping."

"Fine, gimme a couple of feet of that."

The bartender complied.

Jake then took his fountain pen and drew a map of Carter and Jefferson Counties in Oklahoma. He drew barely recognizable oil derricks indicating the towns and oil fields. While Ringling watched him draw, Jake said, "Then the tracks would continue on to this point and beyond." He marked a spot and pointed at it again.

"I figure we could build a way station about here."

Ringling looked at the page, and then a smile gradually consumed his face. "Mr. Hamon, I actually know that place. We used to store some of our circus equipment near there in a warehouse. I own a large area of land there. Haven't thought about it in a long time."

Ringling was nibbling on the bait, then Jake worked to set the hook. "You're kidding? Really? My, oh my, ain't that somethin'? Hell, we could see a whole town grow out there, if the railroad went through. Could even call it Ringling!" Jake said, instantly fearing he had oversold it.

But any fear was chased away in a moment, as Ringling said, "Jake, my friend, I'm in. If I were to put up some of my money, would you run it?"

"I'd be thrilled to, sir. I've been dreaming about such a thing for years." At that, they shook hands, and both men signed the map drawn on the brown paper.

Clara walked back into the bar right then, fresh from her nap. "Well, you boys look like you're gettin' along just fine."

Jake told her the news. Then he said, "John, you free for dinner? I'm starved. How 'bout we go down to Delmonico's for a big, juicy steak?"

"Wonderful idea, but I insist on buying. We'll seal the deal even better with the best steak in town."

Jake and Clara spent one more celebratory day and night in the big city before returning to Oklahoma. And the first thing Jake did when he got back to his office was to mount the brown paper contract on his wall in a frame. He was now in the railroad business.

Soon, the partners received a charter from the state of Oklahoma to build their railroad. The initial cost was about $2.5 million. Construction quickly began, and a year later oil and everything else was flowing down the new tracks.

And in 1914, a new post office was built near a new rail station in a new town called Ringling, Oklahoma.

FIVE

"...THIS IS MY NEPHEW FRANK..."

As Jake's business empire grew, due in no small part to the diligence of young Clara Smith, so did his ambitions. He had not only made money, but he had also made a name for himself. His relationship with Clara was well known around Ardmore—and for whatever reason, most people turned a blind eye. After all, Hamon was the primary mover and shaker driving the area's economic engine.

Many local citizens honestly thought that Clara was, indeed, Jake's wife. They were always together. It all seemed so normal. Nothing scandalous about it. They were discreet enough to avoid making any kind of scene. But as Jake's profile rose, he became concerned about how people saw and thought of Clara when they traveled as apparent man and wife.

He remained adamant against any serious talk of divorce from Georgia—it just couldn't be done, yet. That's what he told Clara repeatedly, and it always disappointed her. She was hopelessly in love with the man and would do anything for him.

She sometimes wondered if his commitment to her was the same.

One day, Clara came back to the office after shopping at one of Ardmore's clothing stores—she'd been looking for a new dress, with no luck. She noticed a young man sitting in a chair, talking with Jake.

"Clara, honey, this is my nephew Frank. He lives down in Weatherford, Texas."

The young man stood and said, "Pleased to meet you, ma'am."

"Ma'am? You drop that right now. I doubt I am a day older than you, but nice to meet you too, Frank," she said with a smile. "What you fellas talkin' 'bout?"

"Oh, just chewin' the fat and catchin' up," Jake replied.

"How long you in town for, Frank?" Clara asked.

"A few days, I s'pose."

Clara thought nothing of it.

That evening, as Jake and Clara dined in the restaurant at the Randol Hotel, Jake spoke to her in hushed tones and with vague-for-him language. He was hemming and hawing, never seeming to make his point. He spoke of his love and concern for her. Frankly, his demeanor caused Clara to briefly wonder if Jake might be on the verge of proposing marriage.

She was right—well, almost.

After dessert, Jake and Clara went back up to rooms twenty-eight and twenty-nine. He poured himself a large drink and inhaled it in one pull. Clara watched with curiosity and a growing measure of concern.

"Jake, honey, something's on your mind. What is it? You can tell me. I love you, no matter what."

"Oh, sweet Clara, you're so good to me. And believe me when I say that I want to be good to you and for you. I'd marry you if I could, but Georgia will never give me a divorce."

"I know, Jake. I know. It's something I just have to accept, as hard as it is. I know I have your heart, if not your name."

"Sweetheart—what if you could have my name, at least in a way?"

"What the devil are you talking about?"

"The name. You could be Clara Hamon—legally."

"Well, maybe I'm not the smartest girl in town, but I know that having two wives is called bigamy."

"Not talking about bigamy, darlin'. I'm talking about the Hamon."

"Okay, well, you've obviously had more to drink than I thought, so maybe you need to sleep it off."

"I'm sober as a judge, Clara, honey. And I have an idea."

"I'm listening."

"You met my nephew today."

"That a statement or a question?"

"Both, I guess. Frank's a fine young man, a great guy."

"Whoa, horse, you pawnin' me off on your nephew?" Clara asked, visibly offended and annoyed.

"No, no, not that, honey … not exactly."

"Well, then, Jake Hamon, you need to put your cards on the table. What the hell are you talkin' about?"

"Well, I got to thinkin'—now, you hear me out before you start throwin' things, okay?"

Clara barely nodded yes and stared at Jake.

Jake continued, "What if you and Frank were to get hitched—not really—but legally at some courthouse?"

Clara crossed her arms to match her legs.

He plodded on: "…and then, say, a couple of months later, you get a divorce. All legal like. But you keep the name.

43

You'd forever be legally Clara Hamon, just as if we were husband and wife," he said. Then he paused and sat down on the bed and waited for her response.

Clara stood up and walked out of the room without uttering a word.

Clara drove Jake's Packard to Lawton that night. She didn't tell Jake that she was leaving, and she didn't tell her parents she was coming. She hadn't been to visit her folks in going on six months, so she was overdue.

It was after midnight when she pulled up to her childhood home. The place was dark. Her parents had likely been asleep for hours. She found the key in a flowerpot on the porch and let herself in, taking great care to be quiet. She found a pillow and some sheets in a hall closet and made a bed on the couch. She was exhausted and fell asleep about five seconds after her head touched the pillow.

About five hours later—it was still dark—Clara heard footsteps on the stairs. It was her mother. She didn't want to startle her, but there was no easy way to announce her presence. She half-whispered, "Hi, Mama ..."

Her mother shouted and ran toward her and hugged her. Clara never told her folks why she was visiting and why she had no luggage with her. And she told them that her boss let her borrow his car for the trip.

"That Mr. Hamon is a nice and generous man, Clara. You make sure to be good to him," her mother said.

She didn't reply except to say that it was good to be home, if only for a day or two. Soon she was sitting down to a massive breakfast—just the three of them.

There was no place like home.

The quick trip to Lawton was good for Clara. Spending time away from Jake, good food, better sleep. She called Jake from a phone at a store in town, after a trip to see Mr. Miller at her old workplace. Jake spoke in humble terms and with an apologetic tone. He asked her to come home soon.

She left early the next morning after yet another great breakfast. Her parents remained on the front porch, waving as she drove off in the distance. The drive home was therapeutic. Somewhere along the way, she made peace with Jake's idea. And when she returned, he was waiting at the Randol Hotel for her. Clara told Jake that she'd go through with the "marriage" to Frank and proudly take the Hamon name.

A few days later, Jake, Clara, and Frank drove down to El Paso, Texas. Clara became Mrs. Frank Hamon, and would be known from that day forward as Clara Smith Hamon. Frank received $10,000 from his Uncle Jake, plus a kiss on the cheek from Clara. The happy couple—that would be Jake and Clara, not Frank and Clara—drove down into Mexico for the honeymoon.

Frank and his money caught the train to Fort Worth. And three months later, in keeping with the arrangement, he filed for divorce in Weatherford, Texas, just as he was paid to do.

Six

"...PUT $30,000 CASH IN THE SATCHEL..."

With much of the world at war and America watching and waiting, the global demand for oil grew. The great ships of the sea were being retooled to use oil as opposed to coal. All this was good news for the oil business in general, and Jake Hamon, in particular.

By the time America entered The Great War in 1917, Hamon's empire was growing by leaps and bounds. Predictably, so was his ego. In June 1917, he became one of the founders of First State Bank of Healdton—adding banker to his already impressive résumé. Jake's behavior became more extravagant and erratic—evidence of a rapidly advancing case of chronic megalomania.

By this time, Clara was running many of the day-to-day aspects of Jake's business. She managed the office and his money, but always under the watchful eye of Bob Hutchins, Hamon's Six-

Shooter Man. Jake had several offices—one in Healdton, another in Oklahoma City. He'd kept the office in Lawton, but the offices conveniently located in a building directly across Main Street from the Randol Hotel in Ardmore served as the actual headquarters for Hamon's various enterprises.

Shortly after eleven o'clock one morning, Hutchins was sitting at Jake's desk at the Ardmore office with his feet propped up and smoking one of his boss's expensive cigars. The door was open so he could see Clara busy at work in the next room. The telephone rang and, as was his habit, he listened in as Clara answered the call. It was Jake.

"Clara," Jake almost shouted, "find Hutch, and both of you go over to the bank and see P. C. Dings." Dings was the President of Ardmore's Guaranty State Bank, where Hamon had several personal and business accounts as the institution's largest depositor.

Hutchins listened as Jake gave further instructions to his mistress. "Tell Dings I need him—now, this is very important, darlin.' Find an old satchel there in the office. There's one across from my desk. Take that down to Dings. Tell him that I need him to put $30,000 cash in the satchel."

"Jake, what's wrong?"

"No questions, Clara—just listen and do what I say!"

"All right, Jake. Calm down. What do I do with the satchel?"

"Bring it to me here in Healdton. My office. Now, honey, you gotta get here by three o'clock, you hear me?" Jake asked urgently.

"Yes, Jake—I think the whole office can hear you. Stop yelling."

Hutchins was taking it all in and wondering what the boss was up to, or in to.

"Three o'clock, or the deal is lost. Don't waste a second. I've gotta hot deal," he said as he ended the call abruptly without even a goodbye.

Clara walked into Jake's office to tell Hutchins about Jake's instructions. Of course, he didn't let on that he already knew. He grabbed the satchel, which was right where Jake said it would be, and they made their way down the stairs and out the front door.

Jake was a dealmaker. So they were not completely surprised, but the urgency was a little off-putting, particularly to Clara. She prided herself on knowing Jake's business and hated to be blindsided. They entered the bank and made their way back to Dings's office.

Hutchins spoke for the duo. "Mr. Dings? Jake just called with an urgent message. He sent us here to get $30,000 cash. We need it put in this satchel, and we need to deliver it to Jake over in Healdton before three o'clock. He gave us a deadline."

The banker looked at Bob and Clara—then at the well-worn leather satchel in his hand. "What kind of whiskey is Jake goin' up against now? He in some kind of trouble? That kind of cash right off the reel is a big undertaking with any bank today—particularly in a town the size of Ardmore."

Clara handled this one. "Mr. Dings, Jake's fine. You know him, always making deals. If he says he needs $30,000 today, then he needs it for business. Are you gonna help him?"

"Yes, of course. I'll do my best. You two go get lunch somewhere—come back in an hour. I'll have the money, okay?"

"Thanks, Mr. Dings, we'll be back about twelve fifteen," Hutchins answered. They left the office and bank and walked over to the Whittington Hotel coffee shop. They ordered sandwiches and coffee. Hardly a word passed between them. She hated how he hovered over and around her when Jake was away. She also resented the closed-door meetings—secret things Jake was sharing with Hutchins.

The feelings were mutual. Hutchins saw Clara as a gold digger. He had no respect for her. It wasn't that he was the most moral man—far from it. Just that he saw Clara as a certain kind of woman used for one purpose. He was sure that Jake had made a terrible mistake by allowing Clara so much latitude with his business affairs.

Hutch was convinced that Jake and Clara were destined for a nasty breakup down the road. Just how far down that road, he didn't know. One secret Hutch was keeping from his boss was that he didn't know how long he could stick around to watch the thing unravel. He didn't mind being bossed around by Jake. After all, he was the boss. But he didn't like Clara telling him what to do, and it seemed like that was happening more and more.

Clara left the table and began walking back to the bank, while Hutch paid the bill. He caught up with her just as she was entering Dings's office. The satchel was sitting on the desk.

"Did you get the money together?" Hutch asked.

"Yes, yes—took some doin', but it's all in the case— $30,000 in assorted denominations," the banker replied.

"Great!" Clara said, and she stepped forward and grabbed it. "Hutch, you sign whatever he needs. We'll take my car. I'll drive." With that she was out the door.

Hutch signed a single paper pushed his way by the banker. He then quickly left. By the time he exited the bank, Clara was approaching in her new cream-colored Hudson—a gift to her from Jake. Hutch thought of it as one more reminder of what he saw as Jake's poor judgment.

Hutch got in the car, and they took off for Healdton, about a twenty-five-mile ride on an unpaved road. Clara had the throttle open and seemed to hit every low and high spot on the road as the car bounced along at breakneck speed. Hutch held on for dear life.

As they came toward a waterway called Bayou Creek, they saw four cars ahead, parked alongside of the road. Clara slowed down. "Hutch, think this is a hold up?"

"Doesn't look good," he replied. "You've got two choices as I see it, my dear lady. You can turn around and head back to town and call Jake and tell him why you didn't get the money to him on time."

"Or ... ?"

"Well, you can tighten your guts and blaze on through. You know I've got my trusty six-shooter with me," he said with a smile as he pulled the gun out.

Clara smiled back and stepped on the gas. "Get ready for a showdown, Mr. Hutchins." As they approached the party up ahead, the men moved out of the way quickly and gave friendly waves as they drove by in a cloud of dust. Hutch later found out that the men were just discussing an oil deal.

They made Healdton about twelve minutes before the three o'clock deadline and raced into Jake's office with the satchel filled with money. Jake opened the case and dumped the money on his desk. It was then that Hutch and Clara noticed another man in the office. His name was J. F. Hollingsworth, a local businessman.

Seeing the money on the desk, Hollingsworth said, "Oh shit ...!" Then he took a piece of stationary from Jake's desk and wrote the words: "He wins. Give Jake the money." He signed the note and gave it to Jake, who smiled and gave it to Hutch.

"What the hell is goin' on here?" Clara interrupted angrily.

"We had a bet, honey. Ole Jake just won a thousand bucks." Then he handed the note to Hutch and said, "Go over to the bank up the block and get the money from Duffy—he's holding a grand from both of us. You add it to this here money on my desk, and you hightail it back to Ardmore and give it to Dings to deposit in my account."

"Jake, explain yourself. We just went through hell to get here for you—and all because of some asinine bet? What were you thinking? You two been drinkin'?"

"Just a little Red Bud, darlin', no harm in a few drinks with an old friend." Jake then turned to Hollingsworth and said, "Old Hoss, the next time you think something can't be done, I'll loan you my Six-Shooter Man here—and I'll take more of your bankroll." Jake then laughed almost uncontrollably.

"Why the $30,000?"

"Simple, Hoss here told me it couldn't be done when I told him I could have $30,000 cold, hard cash on my desk by three o'clock today. I had to prove the old bastard wrong," he said, as he and Hollingsworth roared with even more laughter.

Hollingsworth then said, "It's like he said. I said that he might have that much in the bank, but no bank in Ardmore could put that much cash together in such short order. But he said that his honey and Six-Shooter could do the deed."

Clara and Hutch seldom agreed on much of anything, but they were on the same page as the Hudson made its way back toward Ardmore, this time a much slower journey. They were both angry.

Maybe that's when the problems really started.

SEVEN

"...SIGNS OF IMPENDING DISASTER..."

Hutchins had been noticing changes in Clara's behavior and demeanor for many months. She had never been much of a drinker—leaving that vice for Jake—but lately, he had smelled alcohol on her breath on more than one occasion.

One day while Clara was out shopping—something she seemed to be doing more and more—he entered her room at the Randol. He'd been entrusted with keys to rooms twenty-eight and twenty-nine. He didn't have to hunt hard to find several empty Old Tom Gin bottles.

He was reminded of a trip to San Francisco a few months earlier and their stay at the Occidental Hotel. One night Jake and Clara spent several hours knocking back drinks. Jake was drinking his usual Red Bud Rye, and Clara was introduced that night to a new cocktail—new to her at least.

Hutch had planted himself that night at the opposite end of the bar, just close enough to keep an eye on things. He drank root beer. Once, when the bartender came his way, he asked, "That lady over there—what's she drinking?"

"Oh, I brought that concoction with me from the old Occidental Hotel after it was destroyed in the earthquake back in '06. Called it a Martinez back then—Old Tom gin and a spritz of vermouth. These days folks have taken to calling it a martini. Seems to be pretty popular. I hear a couple of the big hotels in New York now serve 'em. Wanna try one?"

"Oh no, not now. I work for the man next to her, and I was just curious—on duty right now."

"Private Dick? Pinkerton, like that?"

"No, not Pinkerton, just a private security guy."

Now back in Ardmore in Clara's room, the empty bottles told him that Jake's lady had developed a real taste for the stuff. It made him a little sad. Not that he liked Clara, mind you, but he still didn't want to see the girl spiral downward. He'd seen it too often in his life. He knew the signs. She was sad. Sometimes she was angry. She lashed out at Jake more than ever before, and she was suspicious that he had other women in his life. The classic warning signs of impending disaster.

Hutch knew about the other women, but he never told Clara. And he decided not to tell Jake about Clara's drinking. In fact, he was beginning to think it might be time to consider moving on.

A few years earlier, in the days when Jake's business was beginning to boom and his love for Clara was in full bloom, she was fun to watch. Smart and inquisitive, even charming. Hutch never fully understood Jake's relationship with her, nor did he approve. But he never let Jake or Clara even suspect his true reservations. But back in the day, it was easier. Clara had a certain innocence about her, in spite of her living arrangement with a married man.

But not anymore. Clara had grown into a more cynical and selfish person—at least that's how Hutch saw it. She began to disengage from the business side, showing up to work sporadically. No doubt the late-night drinking while alone in her room was a factor.

She was spending money—Jake's money—with reckless abandon. And this was what brought push to shove, literally, for loyal Bob Hutchins. Some of the local store owners—those specializing in women's clothing—fed Clara's all-consuming desire for finer things. They wined and dined her and treated her like a queen. Hutch suspected that some of the shop owners were spiking her wine, because there were many days when she'd show up at the office just after lunch three sheets to the wind.

One such day turned out to be when Six-Shooter Man's job with Jake ended. Hamon was in Chicago visiting his real wife and their kids. Hutch was once again sitting at Jake's desk smoking a cigar when Clara staggered in and approached a company bookkeeper, a man named John Spencer.

"Mr. Spencer," Clara said, the words slightly slurred, "write me a check for four hundred and ninety-nine dollars. Write it now."

"Now, Clara, you know I need more information than that. What is it for?"

"Oh, they're holding a beautiful dress for me up the street. It was once worn by a queen in Europe. It's divine."

"I don't see how that's a business expense. I could lose my job."

"Oh hell, John, don't be such a scaredy cat, just do it. I'll square it with Jake," Clara barked.

"Can't do it. I don't have that authority."

"Listen, you son of a bitch, I'll be back in ten minutes. If you don't have the check ready, I'll have you fired."

Hutch was watching and listening from Jake's office. After Clara stormed out, the bookkeeper went into Jake's office to talk with Hutchins. "You heard that, right?"

"I did."

"What should I do?"

Hutch sighed and rubbed his eyes. "Your call, my friend. You could be fired whichever way you go. If Clara doesn't get the check, she could put the squeeze on Jake to dismiss you. If you write the check, Jake'll probably fire you for that."

Spencer sat in a chair and began to weep. "But Hutch, we have a son just a couple of months old. I need this job. Took me forever to find it."

Right then, Clara came back. She found the two men in Jake's office and shouted at John Spencer, "Hand over the check, or your time is up when Jake returns. You might as well clean out your desk and hit the road."

That was when Hutch decided he'd had enough—enough of all of it. Something snapped in him. He leaped out of Jake's chair and went over to Clara and grabbed her and threw her out of the office. She fell and cried. "Bob Hutchins, you just wait. Jake'll be back tonight, and tomorrow, he's gonna fire your ass—along with that bastard Spencer."

Jake did indeed return to Ardmore from Chicago that night. But when he showed up at the office the next morning, John Spencer and Bob Hutchins were nowhere to be found. They'd saved Jake the trouble of firing them face-to-face.

That same morning, Bob Hutchins was walking down Main Street pondering his next move. A friend who worked in the insurance business said hello, and they talked for a bit. It seemed that the man was looking for a good bookkeeper, and he asked Hutch for any recommendations he might have.

"I've got just the guy for you. He's efficient, honorable, and trustworthy. You'll never find a better man for the job."

As for Hutchins, he traveled to El Paso and took a job as a deputy sheriff. But his dealings with Jake Hamon were not quite finished.

He'd be back.

Shortly thereafter, Jake decided to tighten things up in the office. With his Six-Shooter Man out of the picture, he needed someone he could completely trust managing his affairs—and helping him manage Clara. He turned to a local businessman named Frank Ketch and made him an offer he could not refuse.

"Frank, you come to work for me, and I'll guarantee you $1,000 a week in salary, plus a bonus."

"I'm your man," Ketch replied with a smile that accented a gold tooth. And he was in Jake's office the next morning reporting for duty. He was a tall man, always impeccably dressed, with every strand of his slightly graying brown hair always in place. He had chased success all his life, and now he had hit the mother lode.

Clara was not happy. She had been glad to see Hutchins go and thought she was in a much stronger position with Jake. When Frank Ketch was hired, Clara disliked him from the moment they met.

EIGHT

"I COULD BE YOUR FIRST LADY."

In July 1919, Jake took Clara on a trip to the American Midwest. She was just excited to be on the road with Jake. They traveled by train to Detroit, Michigan, where Jake had managed to get a meeting with Henry Ford. Ford, a man with his own long-time mistress, assumed Clara was Jake's wife and kept addressing her respectfully as Mrs. Hamon. She didn't mind one bit.

They stayed at the new Statler Hotel on Washington Boulevard in a room on the fifteenth floor with a view of the booming city and area. Then, to celebrate America's 143rd birthday on the Fourth of July, they borrowed a car from one of Mr. Ford's friends and drove south to Toledo for the day.

Jake had two tickets to see the long-awaited heavyweight championship boxing match between the champion Jess Willard and his challenger, a fellow named Jack Dempsey. Willard was bigger at six feet, seven inches. He also had a sixty-pound weight advantage over Dempsey. The champ was also a fellow-Kansan, and he and Jake were mild acquaintances. So Jake, ever the gambling man, placed a sizable wager on Willard. After all, the champ had been the "great white hope," the man who ended Jack Johnson's reign over the sport.

On the drive down from Detroit, Clara read to Jake from the Detroit Times about the fight, or better, the controversy.

"Says here that several cities turned the fight down."

"What for?"

"Oh, it's the same people, those crusaders who want to tell everyone how to live, the ones who are pushing that law to ban liquor."

"Oh yeah, Prohibition, they call it. I can't believe somethin' like that could happen; this is s'posed to be a free country. So what's the beef with the fight?"

"Here's something someone from the Women's Christian Temperance Union said, 'The boxing match will bring thousands of criminals, prostitutes, and gamblers whose presence in any city is demoralizing, and whose influence on the youth of the community is a pollution. No single thing could injure the good name of a city more than to be known as a place where a national prize fight was pulled off.'"

"Does the paper say the fight is still on? Are they gonna stop it? No need to go to Toledo if there's no fight—it's gonna be hotter than hell today," Jake grumbled.

"No. Says here that the Governor of Ohio—name is, let's see, oh, James M. Cox was asked to cancel it, but he has refused. Good for him!"

"That man's runnin' for president, darlin'."

"How do you know that, Jake?"

"Oh, I have my ways. The boys over at the Republican Club think he's the likely nominee for the Democrats next year. No way Wilson's gonna run again; no one wants him and he's very ill."

"Hmmm … you friends with those Republican fellas, Jake? I thought you washed your hands of 'em when they treated you so bad back in Lawton."

"Aw, darlin', can't hold a grudge like that forever. Besides, it's just good business. We need to elect someone who understands our business. Oil is the future, and Wilson and the Democrats are willing to let Great Britain run the show on that. We need to remind them that we saved their asses in the war. Somebody needs to put America first again."

"Why, Mr. Hamon, sounds like you're makin' a speech. Maybe you should be president, and I could be your first lady," Clara said as she slid over close to him and laid her head on his shoulder.

He just smiled and then got lost in thought for the rest of the way to Toledo.

The big fight took place in Bay View Park. An arena had been built on a Lake Erie inlet called Maumee Bay, a few miles north of town. Jake and Clara joined 45,000 others in the 110-degree heat. Of course, they handled it better than the locals—such weather was an everyday thing back home. Jake left Clara for a few minutes. She wasn't sure where he went. He came back with two cold drinks—soft drinks. He pulled out a flask and poured some rye whiskey in his. He offered it to her, but she said no. The she pulled out her own flask.

"I prefer my gin," she said as she poured and smiled. "What took you so long?"

"Oh, I was just puttin' some money down on my boy, Jess. He'll finish this fight right quick."

"How much did you bet?"

"I gave the man a picture of old Ben Franklin."

It was one hundred dollars Jake would never see again. Jake and Clara watched the preliminaries impatiently. There was a patriotic display—some marines from Philadelphia, led by a Major Drexel Biddle, demonstrated bayonet thrusts and jabs. But the crowd grew increasingly restless in the hot sun. Finally, the two boxers entered the ring.

"Oh my, that Mr. Willard is a giant of a man," Clara nearly shouted to be heard above the crowd. "Will he hurt the smaller man?"

"Maybe—but Jess is a sportsman, so he'll do just what he needs to, not any more."

"Good. I'm afraid for Mr. Dempsey."

Following some time in the center of the ring with the referee, the fighters retreated to their corners.

"Isn't there supposed to be a bell?"

"Usually."

Just then, they saw the referee throw his whistle over to the man who was supposed to ring the bell, a bell that apparently didn't work. The whistle blew, and the boxers approached each other.

"This is so exciting!" Clara shouted to Jake.

But her mood changed quickly. Willard chased Dempsey away with a jab or two, then, all of a sudden, Dempsey hit the champ with a hard blow to the midsection. Jake and Clara heard Willard groan. Then Dempsey unleashed a vicious left hook, one aimed at the champ's chin, but that landed on his jaw instead. It opened a large gash on Willard's face and sent him to the canvas in the first minute of the bout. Dempsey hovered over Willard, and when the champ got up, he hit him even harder. In fact, Willard went down seven times that round.

Dempsey left the ring thinking Willard had been knocked out. He had not heard the whistle. No one had. But he was hustled back into the ring by his corner man, where he continued to torment big Jess Willard for two more rounds. Before the whistle for a fourth round, someone in Willard's corner threw a towel into the ring, signifying surrender.

Jack Dempsey was the new champ as the nation and the world prepared to move into a new decade. He would become a household name.

Little did he—or anyone else, for that matter—know that sitting in the crowd watching him destroy Jess Willard that day, were two people whose celebrity would soon rival Dempsey's.

At least for a while.

Jake and Clara drove back to Detroit that night, returning the car to Mr. Ford's friend. The next day, they went to Belle Isle in the Detroit River. They had a picnic lunch and visited the greenhouse and botanical garden. Clara was deliriously happy.

They traveled back to Oklahoma and went back to work.

A few weeks later, she came to the office a little late, and a little more hungover, just as three men were leaving.

"What was that about, Jake? Who were those fellas?" Clara asked, after the well-dressed men left his office. His door had been closed when she arrived for work.

"Ah, just a couple of the boys from over at the Republican office. They're tryin' to talk me into runnin' for the chairmanship of the state party."

"Chairmanship?"

"Yeah, I'd be the top man in the state for the Republicans. How'd you like that? I guess my name and money has made 'em forget how they kicked me out back in Lawton. But I sure haven't forgotten. It would be nice to be in a position to settle some old scores."

"Oh, Jake, it's just like you used to talk about when you'd drop in at the store. I'd be so proud of you!" She ran around the desk and kissed him passionately.

"Well, darlin', I didn't give 'em an answer yet, but I think you just made the decision for me."

Jake had, of course, been bitten by the political bug years earlier. And though he moved away from politics to pursue business success, the idea of eventually leveraging his wealth into political power was never far from his mind. He just needed a pathway. Now opportunity was knocking at his door.

The local and state conventions were still several months away, scheduled for the month of February in the new year to come, 1920. If he was victorious, it would put Jake smack dab in the middle of what was looking to be a year for a Republican sweep. His imagination raced. And his conversations on the subject with Clara reminded her more and more of how it had been when Hamon's dreams had swept her off her feet.

Now Clara found herself dreaming. A few years earlier, when President Wilson was courting and then married Edith Galt, she read everything she could about the story. She envisioned a fairy tale of her own—one that put her in the White House with Jake Hamon, as man and wife. His megalomania had rubbed off on her. He believed anything was possible.

Now, she did too.

NINE

"A DECENT CITIZEN OF ARDMORE..."

Clara understood Jake's regular trips to Chicago to see Georgia, Jake Jr., and Olive Belle. He loved his kids, even though he didn't spend nearly enough time with them to be a good father, in the traditional sense. He lavished gifts on them—and Georgia, as well—the latter more out of guilt than anything else. But the trips always made Clara feel jealous and insecure.

Not that there was any pretense of Jake and Georgia being together as man and wife, even when alone. Their distance from each other when he happened to be in the Windy City remained as vast as the mileage from Oklahoma to Illinois. It had long been a marriage of convenience. Georgia enjoyed the financial security Jake faithfully provided for her and the children. He was a generous guy—she had to give him that.

Of course, she knew there had to be other women. Jake was a man's man. She never asked, though—and he, of course, never told. They lived separate lives and moved in separate worlds.

Once, a few years earlier, someone had sent her an anonymous letter about Jake carrying on with a young lady from Lawton, but she ignored it. She received a similar one in 1915 and another in 1917. Whether it was true or not, she knew she was in no position to do much about it. At any rate, her life in Chicago was a happy one, and she really didn't want to be all that close to Jake and his world.

In September 1919, Jake Jr. began studies at the University of Chicago. He wanted to be a lawyer. His younger sister, Olive Belle, though just ten years old, was already beginning to be noticed as a promising violinist. She sometimes performed at clubs and parties, making her mother very proud. It was just the kind of sophistication she wanted in their lives: class and civility, not oil fields and railroad ruckus.

One day that same September, two letters arrived addressed to "Mrs. Jake Hamon," and they were part of the kind of synchronicity that suggests the hand of fate. The first was yet another anonymous letter about Jake's philandering, and it came bearing an Ardmore postmark.

This one had a few more details:

"Dear Mrs. Hamon:

Do you know that there is a lady living in our town and who lives with your husband at the Randol Hotel in rooms twenty-eight and twenty-nine? She even has the Hamon last name. Her name is Clara and she works in his office. Some people in town treat her like the Queen of Sheba, but she is more like Queen Jezebel, if you ask me.

Mr. Hamon is starting to get into politics, and this is the kind of scandal decent people do not need. Why don't you come to Ardmore to confront Mr. Hamon and the whore he is passing off as his wife?

Has he no shame? Have you no honor?

Sincerely,
A Decent Citizen of Ardmore"

As for the synchronicity part, the other letter in that day's mail was from a group called The Oklahoma Federation of Women's Clubs. The group was planning its annual meeting to be held at Ardmore's Convention Hall in early November. The Hamon name was well known, if not the unique domestic arrangement. Somehow word had reached Oklahoma from Chicago about the musical talent of young Olive Belle Hamon, and she was being invited to play her violin at the Ardmore meeting.

Georgia didn't hesitate. She called Western Union and sent a telegram accepting the invitation on behalf of her daughter. But she didn't breathe a word of it to Jake. She was pondering a plan. It involved confronting both Jake and that Clara tramp.

TEN

"SHE'S HERE, JAKE. SHE'S IN TOWN."

Olive Belle knew her music by heart, but she still practiced it every day. She had chosen for her solo at the Ardmore a piece called Concerto No. 2 in G Major by Joseph Haydn. Her mother took her shopping for a new dress at Marshall Fields, followed by a lunch at the brand new Drake Hotel.

"Will we see Daddy when we're in Oklahoma?" Olive asked her mother.

"Oh my, yes, dear, of course. He's looking forward to seeing you, baby."

"Will he come to hear me play?"

"Certainly, dear."

"I wish Jake Jr. could come."

"Me too, dear, me too."

A few days later they went to the Dearborn Street Station and boarded an Atchison, Topeka, and Santa Fe train called the Antelope for the long trip to Oklahoma City, where they caught another train for the short trip to Ardmore. Georgia had booked a room at the brand new Hotel Ardmore. She used her maiden name—Georgia Perkins—to avoid any chance that Jake would get wind of her visit.

They checked in, had a nice dinner—just the two of them—then went to bed early.

The next morning, Georgia and Olive Belle made their way over to the convention hall, where they met the organizers of the event. Olive was introduced to a young man named Henry, who had been assigned to accompany her. He was seventeen and shy. They never learned the lad's last name.

Georgia left Olive at the convention hall to practice.

"I'll be back in a while, dear. I'm gonna go see your father."

Olive smiled and climbed onto the stage as Henry began playing the introduction to her piece.

Georgia walked over to the Randol Hotel. She walked into the lobby and went quickly to the stairs. No one noticed. She was taking a chance. She didn't know if Clara was even in her room, or if Jake was around. No matter, though. She was determined.

She found room number twenty-eight and paused for a moment, gathering her thoughts and emotions. Then she knocked, firmly. She was surprised, happy, and a little scared when she heard a voice—a lady's voice.

"Come in; it's open!"

Georgia turned the knob and opened the door tentatively. She saw her husband's mistress across the room. Clara was standing in front of a mirror, brushing her hair.

Clara saw Georgia's reflection in the mirror, and she was stunned. The woman looked quite different from what she remembered. Her memories of Mrs. Hamon were from back in Lawton—even before she met Jake. Georgia had gone around town in gingham dresses, usually with a baby on her knee. That's the mental image of her lover's wife she had carried in her head for nearly ten years.

But the lady who was now in her room—who stood staring at her—was far more impressive, almost regal looking. She was beautiful. A real lady.

"Mrs. Hamon, what're you doing here?"

"I came to see for myself, honey. Came to see what I've been hearing about for so long. Came to see the woman who has no morals and who thinks she can steal my husband."

Clara was terrified. She thought about what to say, but no words came to mind. She just started to cry. Then she ran out the door adjoining the next room, then out into the hall and down the stairs. She almost got run over by a car as she streaked across the street toward Jake's office.

Georgia remained in Clara's room for a few minutes, sizing the place up. She saw a dressing table and noted some dainty toilet articles. There was perfume from Paris—the same brand Jake brought to Chicago for her a year earlier. There were a couple of framed photographs of her husband. And there was a gun—a small revolver. She took the photographs and the revolver and put them in her purse. Then she left and made her way back to the convention hall, where Olive was finishing her rehearsal for that evening's show.

Clara, meanwhile, sat sobbing in Jake's office after bursting through the door and interrupting a business meeting.

"She's here, Jake. She's in town. She just tried to have it out with me across the street. She's here—do you hear me?"

"What the hell you talkin' about, honey? Who's here?"

"Your wife—that's who!"

Jake turned instantly ashen, and, one by one, the men who had been meeting with Jake sheepishly left the office, closing the door behind them.

"Okay, Clara, calm down. Tell me what happened."

"I was standing at my mirror and brushing my hair. There was a knock at the door, and I told them to come in. I thought it was the coffee service I'd ordered. But it wasn't. It was her," she said. "She walked in and said ugly things to me, Jake. I was humiliated and ran out of the room like a little schoolgirl. Why is she here? What does she want?"

"Honey, I had no idea she was coming to town. No idea. But I'll get to the bottom of it."

Just then, there was a knock at Jake's door. "Not now, I'm busy!" he yelled. But there was another knock. "What? What!"

The door opened, and man named Harvey Wiggs came in and said, "Boss, you may wanna see this. Someone dropped it off the other day. They were looking for a donation. Some women's group. They left a program for a big deal going on this week at the convention hall."

"What the hell does that have to do with anything, Wiggs?" Jake asked.

"Well, sir—says here that there's a concert tonight, and one of the musicians is named Olive Belle Hamon."

"Gimme that." Jake read the program and said, "Thanks, Harvey—good catch. Now listen to me. You call the hotels in town and see where a lady named Georgia Hamon from Chicago is registered. Can you do that for me?" He then looked over at Clara, sheepishly.

"Right away, sir," Wiggs said, as he raced out the door.

Clara was still crying. Jake was really at a loss for words, but made his best effort. "Honey, I'm sorry. Georgia can be mean and vindictive. I'm sorry she done that to you. Guess she came to town because my daughter is playing her violin in this here program, or something. I'll find out what's going on, I promise you."

Clara had calmed some and responded with measured reason. "Oh, Jake, it's your little girl. I understand that. You need to go and hear her play. You must be proud. I'll go back to the room and keep out of sight. Just see to it that Mrs. Hamon doesn't stay any longer than she needs to, okay?" She smiled.

"You're quite a gal, Clara. You got it," he replied, returning a smile.

"I'd sure like to meet your daughter one day."

"I know, Clara, I know. You will, all in good time."

Just then, Harvey Wiggs knocked at the door.

"Yes?"

"Sir, there is no one named Georgia Hamon at any hotel in town. But there is a Georgia Perkins from Chicago staying over at the new Hotel Ardmore."

Jake laughed. "Well, that's her. Perkins is her maiden name."

Clara had stopped smiling.

When Georgia and Olive walked back into the lobby of their hotel, someone at the front desk saw her and shouted, "Mrs. Hamon, could I see you for a moment?" She had registered under the name "Perkins" and wondered how anyone knew her real name.

"Olive, dear, you sit over here and wait. Mother will be right back," she said before walking to the front desk.

"Yes?"

"I'm sorry, ma'am, but Mr. Hamon's been calling for you for the past quarter hour. He left word that he'll be in the lobby shortly," the man said, with no mention of the last name issue. Georgia knew very well that Jake was influential and well known in Ardmore—all of Oklahoma, for that matter.

"Thank you, sir," Georgia replied.

By the time she'd made it back to where Olive was seated, Jake walked into the lobby larger than life, swagger and all.

"Daddy!" Olive screamed as she ran to him and jumped into his arms.

Jake looked at his wife and said, "Georgia, if I'd known you were comin', I'd have baked a cake." He tried to smile, but couldn't.

"Jake, it's about time we had a good talk, don't you think?" Georgia barked in return.

After visiting in the hotel lobby for a few minutes, most of it involving hugs, Georgia sent Olive Belle up to their room. "You go up and practice some more, okay, dear?"

Jake directed Georgia to a coffee shop just off the lobby.

"Hello, Mr. Hamon," said an attractive young waitress who met them. "Coffee?"

"Yes, two please."

Jake began, "I don't know what to say, Georgia. I had no idea you were coming to town. Why didn't you tell me about Olive's concert? I can't wait to hear her play."

"Don't try to sweet-talk me, Jake. You're a dirty old rascal, and you know it. I saw that woman today. She's young enough to be your daughter."

Jake didn't respond to that comment, but said, "Let's not kid ourselves, Georgia. We haven't lived as man and wife for years. Most people like us would've been divorced long before now. But you won't have any of that. I just don't understand you. I'd make sure you had plenty of money for the rest of your life."

"Don't believe in divorce, it's as simple as that, Jake. You know my views on the subject."

"Oh, most certainly, I know all your views," he said sarcastically.

"Don't use that tone with me, Mr. Hamon. I'm the mother of your children."

"I know that—and I love 'em."

"Don't you love me, your wife?"

Jake paused and then changed the subject. "What time's the concert tonight? Save me a seat."

Georgia saw that the conversation was at an impasse, as was their relationship. "Sure, Jake. Be there at 7:30. I'll save you a seat. One seat," she said, holding up one finger.

Georgia left the table just as the pretty waitress brought the coffee.

Jake arrived at the convention hall a few minutes early, with time to find his way backstage to give his little girl a good luck kiss.

"Oh, Daddy, I'm so glad you're here. But you make me more nervous than anyone else. Hope I don't make mistakes."

"You'll be perfect, Olive—you'll be a big hit."

He kissed her and left to find Georgia. She was seated near the front and had indeed saved a seat for him. There were whispers as he made his way toward her and sat down. The whispers continued, accompanied by pointing and stares.

Jake and Georgia exchanged not a word the whole time they were seated next to each other. Olive Belle's solo was midway through the program. She was introduced as, "the very talented daughter of a prominent local citizen, who is here with us tonight. Please welcome Mr. and Mrs. Jake Hamon." There was mild applause, and Jake simply raised and waved his right hand.

Then there were even more whispers.

Olive performed her piece flawlessly. Following the show, Jake walked Olive and Georgia back to their hotel.

"We're leaving on the early train tomorrow. Have to get back to Chicago," Georgia volunteered.

Jake asked, "Can I meet you for breakfast before you leave?"

"Can he, Mommy, please?" Olive added.

"Now, dear, you know how early we have to get up. We'll get something to eat in Oklahoma City. We have almost two hours between trains."

Jake got the message, but he was relieved that Georgia was leaving town before she could cause Clara any more pain. Olive pouted for the rest of the night. As they parted, Jake pulled out a roll of hundred dollar bills—had to be about thirty of them—and handed it to Georgia.

"Thanks, Jake. And thanks for coming tonight. Goodbye."

A few minutes later, he entered his room at the Randol. Clara had been drinking while she waited for him. She kissed him passionately.

Clara was relieved to hear that Georgia and Olive Belle were catching an early morning train out of Ardmore. But she was also somewhat curious. She didn't tell Jake until much later that his wife had taken the photographs and revolver from her room. She slept fitfully that night and woke up well before dawn.

She dressed quietly in room twenty-nine after slipping out of Jake's bed in room twenty-eight. Jake was still sound asleep when she left the Randol and went over to the train station. She got there early—well before Georgia's train to Oklahoma City was scheduled to depart. She positioned herself on a bench near where she assumed Jake's wife would check in for her train.

About twenty-five minutes later, she saw the woman who had surprised her less than twenty-four hours earlier. Clara was once again impressed with how she was dressed—a beautiful fur coat and all. Clara smiled when she saw young Olive Belle and noted that she looked a lot like Jake. The smile was chased away by a tinge of guilt, then a dose of fear.

After Mrs. Hamon had taken care of business at the ticket window, she led her daughter over to some seats in the waiting area. That's when she saw Clara. She was startled at first. Then she sent Olive over to the newsstand.

"Go get us some chewing gum, dear—and get Mommy a newspaper. Would you do that, sweetheart?" she asked her daughter while handing her a dollar bill.

"Can I get a Hershey Bar, Mommy? I'm hungry."

"Of course, dear," Mrs. Hamon said as she stroked Olive's long brown hair. At that, the little girl half-skipped away, oblivious to the presence of her daddy's mistress and any tension in the air in that section of the train station.

Georgia Hamon sat in a seat directly across from Clara, but where she could keep an eye on her daughter across the way.

"Surprised to see you here, young lady."

Clara paused and nervously replied, "I just thought I should say something to you, since all I did yesterday was run away like a schoolgirl."

"Well, you ain't much older than one, that's for sure."

Clara was taken aback by Georgia's use of the word "ain't." It didn't seem to fit the image the lady seemed to be cultivating. It also had a surprising effect—it disarmed Clara a little, as if to indicate that the lady across from her was trying hard to be something she wasn't.

"Mrs. Hamon, I just felt I needed to tell you that it was never my intention to hurt you or your children. Your daughter is quite beautiful, like you. And I can see that she has her father's eyes."

But Georgia wasn't moved by the faint flattery and attempt to play nice. "Well, you're a homewrecker, so your opinions aren't worth a bucket of warm dung."

Clara chose to ignore the dig. She expected as much, but was determined to have her say.

"Jake and I are in love, Mrs. Hamon—have been for years. It's simple as that. He wants to spend the rest of his life with me."

"Girl, you're dumber than a sack of rocks. Do you really think Jake is all that committed to you? The man doesn't know the meaning of the word. No doubt that old hound dog has girls all over the place—some of them even prettier than you. Probably younger, too. No, young lady, you're in for it. You hitched your horse to the wrong wagon."

Clara did wonder about other women. After all, Jake had demonstrated how easy it was for him to disregard his marriage vows when it came to her. But she put that thought aside for the moment and continued to address her lover's lawful wife, "Then why don't you divorce him? You don't live together as man and wife—he lives that way with me."

"Honey, I don't believe in divorce. Besides, I'd never give that rascal the satisfaction. No, you're never gonna be Jake's real wife. That title's been taken."

About that time, Olive made her way back over, candy and newspaper in hand. Both women knew that it brought their conversation to an end. The girl had seen the two women talking. So when she came over, she said to Clara, "Hi, my name's Olive, Olive Belle, what's yours?"

Clara looked over at Georgia, who nodded slightly, indicating her approval for a reply.

"Well, hello, Miss Olive Belle, I'm Clara—Clara Ha—er ... Clara Smith. I work for your father."

Georgia grabbed Olive's hand and said, "Dear, we need to make our way to the train."

"But the board says it's not here yet, Mommy."

"It'll be along in a minute or so," she said. Then she looked at Clara and said, "Goodbye, Miss Smith."

"Goodbye, Mrs. Hamon. Please think about what I said. And goodbye to you, Miss Olive Belle. Did anyone ever tell you that you have your daddy's eyes?"

The little girl smiled as she was whisked away by her mother. She turned back and smiled again at Clara. They waved at each other.

ELEVEN

"...A DANGEROUS GAME."

As Jake and Clara celebrated the annual calendar page turn on December 31, 1919, like most Americans, they had no idea what the future held. Certainly, there were no hints that the decade before them would be one of the most memorable of the century. Nothing roared that night. The mood was somber.

Prohibition was imminent, scheduled to be the law of the land on January 16. Hardly a family had not been touched in some way by the ravages of the Spanish Influenza that killed millions worldwide in the wake of The Great War. The year 1919 had been filled with labor unrest and marked by an economic downturn en route to a depression. Americans had been shaken by a "red scare" that took hold and by the strong-arm tactics of United States Attorney General A. Mitchell Palmer. They were called "Palmer Raids," and on New Year's Day 1920, thousands were arrested on suspicion of Bolshevik leanings and activity. One man making a name for himself in the process was a young G-Man named J. Edgar Hoover.

But the nation was on the verge of a dynamic process— the result of growing tension between two polar forces. On the one hand, there was the emerging trend of wanting to break free from the restraints of norms and values, in the pursuit of pleasure and prosperity. This would be countered by an equally powerful pull back from change to a sedate and conservative way of life—not to mention the whole idea of engaging the rest of the world. The same decade that would give us jazz, bootlegging, flappers, and speakeasies would also see the rise of fundamentalism and the Ku Klux Klan.

As for Jake Hamon, he saw the new year as one of great opportunity. He hit the ground running as part of a plan to chart a course that would make him one of the most powerful men in America. It was heady stuff, but all very possible as far as Jake was concerned.

And his master plan would begin with a takeover of the Oklahoma Republican Party.

Jake had been working the edges of Republican politics in Oklahoma for several months by the time the new year dawned. The man to beat for the post of state party chairman was J. J. McGraw, President of The Exchange National Bank in Tulsa. When McGraw heard that some had reached out to Jake as a potential party leader, he went to work to make sure the "right" people knew about Hamon's darker side.

Jake heard about McGraw's efforts and confronted him one day in an Oklahoma City restaurant. "You're fightin' a losin' battle, Mac. I'll get the votes and beat your ass."

"Ah hell, Jake, no one's gonna vote for an old alley cat like you. You need to remember, women got the vote now. No way they'll support an adulterer. Simply no way."

Jake replied sarcastically, "You're wrong, you jackass, women love me."

Shortly after the beginning of the year, a group of women took out an advertisement in the Oklahoma City Times. It was an endorsement of McGraw, but clearly aimed at Hamon and those who were backing his candidacy.

"TO THE REPUBLICANS OF OKLAHOMA: When there is a crisis at hand, wherein is involved the character of a man who is asking the support and endorsement of the voters of the state, there can be no better judges of his character than the women of his home city...The women of Oklahoma are now in politics. Much depends upon us. We cannot afford to support for any office, any man whose life has not been clean and who cannot secure the approval of the good women of his home community..."

Jake had no way of knowing how powerful the women would prove to be when it came to actual votes, but he knew that McGraw had a point. Hamon had earmarked $100,000 for the campaign, most of it designed to pay for favors and votes. But he knew that he needed to counter the moral issue.

So he traveled to Chicago.

He wasn't in a great negotiating position, but he knew that he had one card to play—an appeal to Georgia's vanity. What people thought was very important to her. This was one of the reasons she enjoyed Chicago so much, being away from what she considered the sordid aspects of Jake's world.

Jake made the best case he could. "Now, honey, I know I've got no right askin' anything of you, but this is a great opportunity for both of us. If we played our cards right, we could move the whole family to Washington to live together. I really think I can win, with your help."

Georgia looked Jake square in the eye. She was always wary of Jake and his way with words. He could pour it on thick. She didn't know if she should believe him or not.

Frankly, Jake wasn't sure if he believed himself. Was he just playing Georgia to gain a quick victory, only to discard her in the long run? He knew he was playing a dangerous game with her. Of course, he was also playing a dangerous game with Clara. But that was far from his mind as he tried to sweet-talk his real wife.

"Jake, if I do agree to do this, to help you, I don't want the kids involved at all."

"I understand, and that's fine by me."

"And another thing, I'll appear with you a few places, but not in Ardmore. I'll not be in the same town as your whore."

Jake knew he had to ignore the comment, but he chose to respond with something that surprised Georgia. "Ah hell, honey, me and Clara ain't what we used to be. She's a drunk and lettin' herself go. I feel sorry for her," he said. He didn't really feel this way, and he felt bad speaking bad about Clara, but he knew he had to do what he had to do.

That evening, Jake took the whole family to dinner at the Blackstone Hotel. He didn't know it yet, but Jake would be back at the Blackstone, several floors up, in a few months. And the dinner that night with his family helped to seal one deal in advance of another one to come.

Georgia agreed to help Jake's efforts to become chairman of the Republican Party of Oklahoma. They planned to meet in Oklahoma City two weeks later. And Jake hoped her presence would neutralize the character issue.

Clara knew nothing of the real reason Jake traveled to Chicago. They never discussed his visits to see his wife and children. She assumed the most recent trip was more of the same. So she was stunned when Jake explained it all to her two nights after he returned. They were in his room.

"But Jake, why?"

"Because McGraw and his cronies are doing everything they can to smear me. Here—look at this," he replied, while opening the newspaper he'd brought with him. It had a full page advertisement, with the words "JAKE HAMON SHOULD BE REBUKED" in large, bold letters. The ad called Jake "a traducer of women." It also suggested that Jake really lived in Chicago.

"I don't care what the papers say. You shouldn't either. And you certainly don't need Mrs. Hamon's help," Clara said as she started to cry.

"Honey, please, you have to trust me on this. I know what I'm doing. Once I get the job, back to Chicago she goes. Easy as that. You have my word."

Clara stormed into her room and slammed the door. Jake then heard it lock. He resisted the urge to knock and try to continue the argument. He just hoped she'd come around.

The next morning, Clara came into his office across the street from the hotel. She looked awful, he thought. Her eyes were swollen and bloodshot. But her demeanor was calm.

"Jake," she said, "I don't think I'll ever figure you out. But I love you, and I need to trust you. If you say this is just temporary, I believe you."

"It is, darlin', I swear."

"Then fine. I don't like it. But, fine. I'll have to live with it," she said with a pout.

"That's my girl, Clara."

"Am I? Am I, really?"

"Come here, darlin'…"

The next week, Jake met Georgia's train in Oklahoma City, and they spent the better part of four days driving from town to town, meeting with delegates and influential Republicans. She was polite and smiled a lot. Jake was at his arm-twisting and back-slapping best as he worked room after room. Of course, it helped that he was a generous man, promising the moon to would-be supporters.

Georgia was glad when the ordeal was over. "Jake, I hope you win, but I'll never do such a thing again. Put me on a train home," she said.

When the various caucuses and then the convention met, it was clear that Hamon's efforts—with his wife's help—had not only calmed concerns about his character, but had brought him to victory.

Jake Hamon was the new leader of Oklahoma Republicans. He was also, by virtue of this, a member of the Republican National Committee, as well as the head of the state delegation slated to attend the national convention that July in Chicago.

He was now in position to exert his influence on national politics, and he planned to make his mark.

While in Tulsa during the campaign for the party chairmanship, Jake saw Bob Hutchins in a hotel lobby, and decided on the spot to fix things with him.

"Hutch, how the hell are ya?" Jake said as he approached him, extending a hand as if nothing had happened between them.

"Doing fine, Mr. Hamon, just fine."

"Now you listen to old Jake," Hamon said as he leaned in close, "I was wrong back then—what happened to you and all—and that bookkeeper. I should've never let that happen." About that time, Georgia walked over to the men.

"Morning, Mrs. Hamon," Hutch said.

"Bob is it? Haven't seen you in a while."

Jake interrupted, "Yeah, well, Bob's been down in Texas helping a marshal, but I've just about got him talked into coming back to work for me. How 'bout it, Hutch? If I win this thing—and that's sure as hell gonna happen—I'll need you by my side from here to Washington."

Truth be told, Hutch missed his job with Hamon. It didn't take him but a few seconds to reply, "Okay, okay, you got me. How 'bout I see you Monday in Ardmore and get back on board?"

"Fine, Hutch—just fine. I appreciate it, old boy!"

A week later, Hamon was the new party chairman, Georgia was back in Chicago—out of sight, out of mind—and Bob Hutchins was back at work for the boss. Clara was surprised when she saw him, but she decided to make the best of it.

"Welcome back, Hutch," she said as she gave the man a rare hug. "It's like you're family and this is where you belong."

Hutch found Clara's reception puzzling, but then, very little in Clara's world made sense to him.

It was around this time that a famous actress named Lillie Langtry had been contracted by a couple of theatrical producers—the Dubinsky brothers—for an engagement at the Ardmore Opera House. The producers and the actress had a falling out, one that threatened the show. The actress threatened one of the Dubinsky brothers—said she was going shoot him.

Langtry had been a stunning beauty in her day—though she was now in her late sixties. She once had a lengthy affair with the Prince of Wales (who later became Edward VII). The prince had even presented her to his mother, Queen Victoria. But that was then. Now she was a nearly-forgotten actress who still insisted on being treated as if she were a star.

Dubinsky knew Bob Hutchins and decided to ask him to help. "Hutch, the lady is mad—completely mad. She carries around a little pearl-handled .25-caliber Colt pistol. Hides in between her breasts! I think she's just crazy enough to use it."

"Where is she now?"

"Over at Ramsey's Drug Store."

"Okay, I'll check it out."

Bob Hutchins walked over to the drugstore located at the corner of Washington and Main. Entering the store, he saw the actress and began a casual conversation with her. She didn't know him from Adam. After a few minutes of polite conversation, and while no one was looking, Hutch reached into the top of her dress and into her bosom and pulled out the pistol.

"Why, you filthy man. Unhand me!"

Hutch countered, "You don't wanna go killin' anyone. Now, let me give you some advice. There's a train leaving in less than an hour. You go gather your things at your hotel and get on that train."

Lillie Langtry was flustered and speechless. They talked a bit more. Then she calmed down and started to cry. She even thanked him for saving her. She did as she was told and caught the next train to Oklahoma City and points east.

The big show would never go on.

Later that day, Hutch rehearsed the story for Jake and showed him the pistol. Jake took a look at it and then put it in his pocket. "You misplaced that gun somewhere. Just forget about it."

A few days later, his curiosity got the best of him. "Boss, what'd you do with that pistol?"

"Gave it to Clara. She loves it."

"Not sure you should've done that, Boss. You know how Clara can get sometimes."

"Aw, hell, Hutch, you worry too much. Clara's never gonna hurt old Jake."

TWELVE

"SENATOR HARDING, MEET JAKE HAMON."

The circus came to town in New York City every spring, and 1920 was no exception. The venue was always Madison Square Garden, which had occupied the space between 5th and Madison, and 26th and 27th Streets since 1890. John Ringling didn't always travel with the show, but he seldom missed the opportunity for a trip to New York.

And while acrobats, clowns, and elephants amused capacity crowds at the Garden, Ringling found time to rub shoulders with other bigwigs, from business, to entertainment, to politics. Staying in the Waldorf Astoria, about three floors down from him, was a man from Ohio some were starting to talk about—Senator Warren Gamaliel Harding. The two men had met many years earlier, when Ringling's big road show made its way to the state capital, Columbus, about fifty miles from Harding's Marion, Ohio home. Warren wasn't a politician at the time. He was a newspaper man—owner, actually, and publisher, and editor of the Marion Daily Star. The circus ran a lot of ads in the paper, and Harding always got an ample amount of free circus tickets to give away.

Ringling had followed Harding's career, and they dined together often whenever the showman happened to be in Washington. So hearing that Harding was in the hotel, Ringling arranged a little party one evening in his suite. He invited about twenty-five men and their wives.

Jake Hamon was in town, too. He had spent a couple of days working on a series of loans—enough to give him a war chest of well over $1,000,000, money he planned to spread around at the Republican convention in Chicago.

Whenever he and Ringling were proximate, they'd meet and talk business. Their railroad was booming, and good news always made for a good time. Ringling invited Jake to the party and told him about Harding, who was being mentioned in some circles as a potential candidate for vice president, or even president.

Ringling didn't know it—largely because he didn't pay a whole lot of attention to Jake's enterprises other than the one they were in together—but Hamon very much wanted to meet Harding, and all the other would-be candidates for high office, for that matter. He had become politically active, not out of any sense of civic responsibility, but because he had learned the hard way that government could be either helpful to business or it could stand in the way. And it'd been doing mostly the latter, lately.

Ringling also didn't know much about Hamon's political coup in Oklahoma—his takeover of the state Republican Party. And the impresario had no clue that his business partner was now a bona fide member of the Republican National Committee.

But soon he would learn all about it.

Jake entered Ringling's suite as one of the last guests to arrive. He was alone. Clara was back in Ardmore, and Georgia, well, she was in Chicago and far from Jake's thoughts. But not for long.

Senator Harding was at the center of the room, and of everyone's attention. He was a big hit. Handshakes, back slaps, smiles, laughs, whispers, jokes, and serious conversation was the simultaneous activity going on. After a few minutes and several handshakes, Jake heard Ringling shout, "Jake, Jake Hamon, over here!"

Ringling was standing with Warren Harding and a well-dressed woman. The circus man said, "Senator Harding, meet Jake Hamon. He's my business partner back in Oklahoma."

Hamon took Harding's extended hand and said, "Pleasure to meet you, Senator. I've heard a lot about you."

Harding tilted his head back as he laughed, "Well, old boy, I hope it was all good."

"It was indeed, Senator."

"Mr. Hamon, this is my wife, Florence."

"Charmed, ma'am—as they say, behind every successful man is a good woman."

"You have no idea, Mr. Hamon." The men laughed, but Florence kept a straight face. "Mr. Hamon, did you know that we are related?" At this mention, the men grew quiet.

"Ma'am?" was all Jake could muster in meek reply.

"Well, your wife is my cousin. Actually, a second cousin, but we spent time together when we were young in Ohio. Surely, she's told you."

"Oh, well, uh, I'm sure she did at some point. I just forgot, I guess," Jake said, trying to recover. Actually, he had no idea that his estranged—though legal—wife was related to the lady some called "The Duchess," a woman reputed to be domineering and difficult.

"Why, yes, we are. Haven't seen her in years—how is she these days?"

"Oh, she is doing quite well. Jake Jr. has started college in Chicago, and Olive Belle is doing well in music there, so Georgia is spending a lot of time in the Windy City," he replied, hoping the woman wasn't noticing the sweat breaking out on his upper lip and brow.

"Well, you boys go ahead and talk politics or whatever it is you want to talk about. I'm going over there to see Mildred," Florence said as she moved away from her husband, John Ringling, and a still-stunned Jake Hamon.

Ringling was the first to speak after the Duchess left. "Now, that was a bit of news. How 'bout that, Jake?"

"News—yes, news, right," he said, giving Ringling a look.

"Am I missin' something, boys?" Harding asked.

Jake had now caught his breath and thoughts and replied, "No, Senator, not at all—just that I need to call my wife tonight and give her hell for not preparing me for this meeting." They laughed.

But in reality, Jake Hamon was more than surprised by the revelation, he was floored by it, and wondered what it all meant to his big plans.

After a while, Harding invited Hamon into a side room. Jake had mentioned that he was now part of the Republican National Committee, and the Senator instantly realized that he needed to seize the moment. Jake didn't mind a bit.

"Jake, now, you're an Oklahoma oil man, so I imagine you take an occasional drink—legal or not—am I right?"

Jake smiled. "You're right, Senator. I'll have what you're having."

"Bourbon and water coming up."

The men soon sipped their drinks and sat down in chairs opposite each other. The senator said, "As you know, Mr. Hamon, I'm letting some of my friends mention my name here and there as a possible candidate for president."

"I'd heard the vice presidency mentioned."

"Nah, not for me. I'd stay in the Senate representing Ohio before I'd ever do that. No, it's the presidency or nothing—I told Harry Daugherty that just this morning. You know Harry?"

"Don't know him, but I know who he is—worked for McKinley, didn't he?"

"Indeed he did. He'll tell you that he made McKinley president and wants to do the same for me. He's a pretty persuasive fellow. He's been in my corner since I first started to get interested in politics some years back. So tell me, Jake—how are the boys out in Oklahoma? They lining up behind anyone yet?"

"Oh, some of them like Wood, but I pretty much call the shots out there. I plan to deliver our delegates to the man who can best represent our interests."

"I'm assuming you mean oil?"

"Yessir! And the current administration seems to be much more interested in helpin' Europe, while Britain helps itself to the world's oil supply. That's why we need an administration that'll understand what we have here in this country. We have all the oil we'll ever need. We just need the green light to go after it in places where drilling ain't allowed right now."

"You're talking about public lands?"

"Right, that's a big part of it. We can't let the world pass us by. The world runs on oil now."

"I sympathize with you, Mr. Hamon. How can I help?"

"Well, Senator, can I speak frankly?"

"Certainly."

"I'm prepared to give a great amount of cash to the candidate who sees things my way—and the way the other oil boys back home see it. We want the next Secretary of the Interior to be in agreement with us."

"Is that a job you'd be interested in, Mr. Hamon?"

Jake smiled and then took a long drink from his glass.

After several minutes, Hamon and Harding made their way back out to the party. Jake was now sure that the senator was open to his ideas and influence. He just wasn't sure how good the man's chances were. Harding, for his part, felt confident that he had a good shot at some significant oil money flowing into his campaign coffers in the future.

A couple of hours later, after most of the guests had gone home, Ringling talked with Hamon about Harding. "I'm glad you were in town for this, Jake. I wanted you to meet the senator. I think he may go all the way. Any idea on whether or not you'd be willing to support him?"

"Had a good talk with him, John. Seems like a great guy. But it's early. I'm not going all-in for anyone just yet. I can tell you this, though, he impressed me. I think he'd be good for our business."

"Glad to hear that, Jake. You plan to be in Washington any time soon?"

"Actually, I've got to be there in about two weeks, why?"

"Well, how's 'bout I set up a meeting for you with a friend of mine, name's Harry Daugherty?"

Jake didn't let on that Harding had already brought the political fixer's name up in conversation. "Daugherty, Daugherty ... oh yeah, he's that political guy who worked for McKinley."

"He's in Warren's corner now. You two should definitely meet and talk."

"Sure, sure—whatever you say, John. You set it up. I'll be there. I usually stay at the Willard. I'll be there a week from Monday."

Thirteen

"...A REAL MAN'S BREAKFAST..."

Jake took a walk before breakfast. He left the Willard Hotel just as the sun was rising and walked several blocks. It was a brisk April morning, but the cherry blossoms didn't seem to mind—they were in full bloom. He loved the city. New York was grand, but the combination of Southern charm and the history of Washington, DC, always moved him. He walked near the Washington Monument and paused and looked back at the White House. He smiled. It was almost as if an audible voice was telling him that if he played his cards right, he could live there one day. It was a dream that was becoming a little more believable every day.

As he continued his focus on 1600 Pennsylvania Avenue in the distance, he thought about the current occupant. President Wilson hadn't been seen in public for quite some time, and the city—hell, the country—was rife with rumors. Most of the scuttlebutt had to do with Wilson's wife—the second one, the one he married just a few years ago, after the tragic death of

Ellen. Edith was no Ellen, however much the president loved her. And then there were those other rumors, the ones about how Wilson had been unfaithful to Ellen, not with Edith mind you, but with a gal named Mary Hulbert. There were hundreds of love letters, so the rumors said.

But poor Woodrow wasn't in much of a mood for love, or much of anything else lately. Truth be told, Jake and many others—probably half the country—were convinced that he was completely incapacitated and that Edith was running the show.

After a few minutes, Hamon snapped out of his almost trance-like focus on the famous house. He looked at his watch and noted the time. He didn't want to be late for his important breakfast meeting. It was with one of most powerful Republican political brokers in the country, the man who had helped make William McKinley president twenty-five years earlier. Now he had a new potential political champion in training, though the man was still a long shot.

But ever the gambling man, Jake loved to bet against the odds.

Harry Daugherty was already at a table when Jake entered the restaurant at the Willard. Jake loved the hotel, and it was his base whenever he ventured to Washington. Just two blocks from the White House, it was a great place for the kind of politics Jake was used to—arm-twisting, deals, and the like. And he liked the fact that important people regularly walked through the lobby and ate in its eateries. This day, for example, Jake noticed none other than Thomas Marshall, the Vice President of the United States. The oil man had half a mind to drop by Marshall's table and ask the guy what was really going on down the street. But he quickly dismissed the notion. Marshall was engrossed in that morning's edition of the Washington Post, and probably didn't know all that much, anyway.

It was pretty well known that the man hated his job and couldn't wait for his term to be over. He was a risk-averse politician. When Wilson went abroad to the peace conference in Paris more than a year earlier, Marshall was put in charge of Cabinet meetings. He told his boss that he wouldn't be responsible for anything that happened. And more recently, he yielded the floor—all of them at the White House, actually—to Wilson's wife.

Passing Marshall's table, Hamon made his way toward Daugherty. Harry stood up. He was an imposing man with a receding hairline, meticulously attired in his trademark three-piece suit, and sporting his usual pearl pin in his colorful tie. Hamon took note that most eyes in the room were on Daugherty, and now him, as he approached the man.

"Good morning, Jake!" Daugherty said while extending his hand. Hamon gripped it and tried to squeeze a bit.

"Great to meet ya, Mr. Daugherty."

"It's Harry, boy, Harry."

"Well, Harry, our mutual friend John Ringling wanted this meeting to happen, so here I am. They have a great breakfast here—and I'm starved."

"Fine, let's order and then get down to business."

A waiter came over and poured coffee and orange juice. Before the server even asked, Jake blurted out his order, "I'm gonna have three eggs sunny-side up, and give me a big piece of ham—not that sweet stuff, give me the salty ham. Oh, and potatoes, and toast. And slice a tomato up and add it to my order. Got it?"

"Yes, sir," the waiter replied.

Harry seemed a little stunned. His usual breakfast choice might be oatmeal, or some dry toast and tea, but he chimed in, "Give me the same."

Jake looked Harry in the eye for a moment and then said, "Well, Harry, you may live among the tenderfeet, but you sure know how to order a real man's breakfast." Both men laughed a little, and Harry felt at his jacket pocket to make sure he had brought his stomach medicine with him.

"So, Jake, Senator Harding tells me you two met in New York a couple of weeks ago," Daugherty begins.

"Sure did. I was very impressed with the man—sure looks like a president. Talks like one, too."

Hamon's mind flashed on his earlier meeting, but not on Warren Harding. No, rather, the man's wife, The Duchess, and the surprising revelation that the woman who could be the next first lady was related to his own estranged wife. Jake chased the thought from his mind and listened to Harry make his best pitch for the man from Ohio. He had no intention of letting anyone in the Harding circle know about his domestic "challenges."

"I read the papers, Harry, and I know that your man is a ways back in the pack. What, there are about a dozen men who want the nomination, right?"

"Closer to twenty, my friend. But that may work to our favor."

"How so?"

"Well, there's going to be a deadlock in Chicago, that's clear. The thing could go on for days. I predict at least ten ballots. And in a situation like that, anything can happen. The real decisions then will be made, not on the convention floor, but in the back rooms. And that, Mr. Hamon, is where I do my best work."

"So I hear. What's your attraction to Harding?"

"Well, like the late great William McKinley, he's from Ohio—my home state, so there's a regional affinity. But more than that, I've been grooming the man for higher office for some time. I saw his potential long before he did. Hell, when I met him, he was like a turtle sitting on a log. All it took was for someone to push him in the water. That someone was me."

"So, you really think he has a chance?"

"Most certainly. But there are some, shall we say, challenges."

"Like what?"

"Money. Simply put, we need cold, hard cash. We don't have much of a war chest, and we're gonna need some money to throw around. Hell, I'm trying to find a hotel, one that will extend us credit for the rooms and services we need."

"Well, I might be able to help with that."

Daugherty smiled and fiddled with his pearl tiepin. "Indeed, and I'm sure that's why the circus man wanted us to meet today. We're gonna need, as far as I can see, about $25,000 for convention expenses, and—"

"Whoa, horse, slow down a bit ... we ain't there yet; you need to hear me out."

Daugherty was a little taken aback by Hamon's tone, but he decided to let the man make his case. "Of course, certainly. I'm all ears. What's on your mind?"

"Good. Well, all I want to do is make money, and I don't care much how I make it. I like this politics stuff mostly because I see it as a way to get ahead, if I may be so blunt."

Harry nodded. "Go on ..."

"I came to this same city 'bout a year ago. Stayed right here in this fine hotel. Ate the same breakfast we just ordered. Then

I walked over to one of the big buildings not far from here and met with Frank Lane—you know the man?"

"I don't know him personally, but I know who he is, the Secretary of the Interior."

"Right, 'course you do. Well, I set up an appointment to see him about drilling on some lands out west. There's an Indian reservation in my state—Osage—and there is a shit-load of oil in that land. Same with other areas out where I live controlled by the government, some even in Old Mexico that we control. The oil is just sittin' there, waiting to be tapped."

"What was Lane's response?"

"The man acted like a stuck up son of a bitch. Didn't give me or my idea the time of day. Frankly, I wanted to kick him in the balls and punch him in the nose, but I'm more civilized these days," Jake said, as they both chuckled like mischievous schoolboys.

"So how does this relate to our meeting today, as if I didn't know?"

"You're a smart man, Mr. Daugherty. You see, I got to thinkin' after I left that big fancy building and walked back over to this beautiful hotel. The bar had just opened, and I sat down to enjoy a drink. 'Course, that was before they made it a crime."

"Of course," Daugherty replied with a smile.

"This fine hotel used to keep a bottle or two of my favorite refreshment, good ole Redbud Rye Whiskey from Oklahoma. So I had a few glasses of that, and then it hit me. You want a job done right, do it yourself!" Jake slammed his palm on the table, and his voice was a bit loud as he said this. He caught himself immediately and looked around at some people staring at him and said, "Sorry, folks!"

"So you had a great idea while you were drunk, huh?"

"Nah, wasn't drunk, just feeling good about my future, my friend. So it hit me, there's an election coming up; why not spend some of your hard-earned money to make a lot more money?"

"Right! By getting someone elected who'll be more open to new ideas. Well, I can tell you that ..."

"Now, Harry, you let me finish my piece, okay?"

"Sorry—as you were saying?" Daugherty said, making a sweeping motion toward Hamon.

"Gettin' a better man elected is not enough. I think we need to ensure that the government gets out of the way of business progress. So it's not just about getting someone to replace Wilson; that's gonna happen no matter what. What I'm interested in—and I might add, I'm not alone. There are powerful men who agree with me on this—is to see the right person sitting in that jackass Frank Lane's chair a year from now."

"And, Mr. Hamon, do you have any ideas about who that right man might be?"

"Sure do. Yours truly. And I'm prepared to make sure you have very few financial worries as you go forward, starting with a check today for $25,000 for the Chicago expenses."

There was a pause in the conversation as the waiter came by with coffee. Jake took another cup, while Harry covered his with his hand and waved the man off.

Daugherty broke the silence. "I see. Well, you're nothing if not forthright, Mr. Hamon. But you must know, I'm not in a position to promise you anything."

"Sure you are, Harry. You just wait for the right time—let's say, after your man's nomination—and you get in that there water with your turtle and make him think it's his idea, the best one he ever had," Jake replied, while leaning toward Daugherty and speaking deliberately in a more hushed tone.

Daugherty looked into Hamon's eyes for a moment as if sizing the man up. Then he fiddled with his tiepin again and broke into a broad smile and said, "Well, how 'bout that check for Chicago?"

FOURTEEN

"...DOMINATED BY SINISTER FORCES..."

J ake and his war chest rolled into Chicago in early June
before the start of the Republican Convention. He
checked into the La Salle Hotel and made his suite on the
twelfth floor his headquarters. He was also footing the bill for
the Harding forces staying at the La Salle. Clara, however, was
back in Ardmore minding the office. She wanted to be there
with Jake, and had even bought several outfits to wear. But Jake
was insistent—Clara was to stay in Ardmore. He didn't want his
worlds to collide.

On the surface, it didn't look as if the senator from
Marion, Ohio, had much of a chance. As delegates began
making their way to Chicago's Coliseum, four candidates stood
out. General Leonard Wood, who had been the Army Chief of
Staff, as well as governor of both Cuba and the Philippines,
was ahead in the delegate count. As things stood, there were
only thirty-nine votes Harding could count on. To win, he'd
need more than 450 more.

But crafty old Harry Daugherty had a plan. For it to work, he needed Jake's help. So he made his way to Hamon's suite the day before the Republicans convened.

"Been wonderin' when you'd get up here," Jake said with a laugh as he invited Daugherty in. "How're things with your man?"

"Well, Jake, I'm hoping to make him the man. But to do so, I need him to be your man."

Hamon just nodded and did not reply. He offered Daugherty a drink, but was waved off.

"And I have a plan—a way to get this nomination for the best candidate, Mr. Harding."

"I'm sure you're here to tell me, Harry, so give."

"I want you to throw your support, for now, behind Lowden, the Governor of Illinois."

"Well, some of the gang in the Oklahoma delegation like the governor, but why?"

"As a way to stop the frontrunner, General Wood. See, if we can get his support to erode, it'll go to several of the others, Johnson, and maybe even Hoover, or Coolidge."

"Coolidge?"

"Governor of Massachusetts, the guy who put down that police strike in Boston last year. He's not a flashy guy, but has a good head on his shoulders. I think he'd make a good vice president under Harding."

"My, oh my, Mr. Harry—you sure think of everything," Jake said. He was clearly impressed with Daugherty's political sense. It reminded him of how he thought through business issues.

"Well, things are going to start slow this week. Then they're gonna pick up speed and move along pretty fast. It'll all be about timing. And I tell you, it'll all be decided in a room like this," Daugherty mused as he looked over Hamon's suite.

"Okay, Harry—I'm in. I'll start working on my people for that poor sap, Lowden. When do you want me to get 'em to switch to Harding?"

"Just hang on until you hear from me. I'll let you know."

Neither man saw much of Warren Harding that weekend. He was occupied with things of a more, shall we say, personal nature. Mrs. Harding was not scheduled to arrive until Monday around noon. So Warren had several days to catch up with an old friend. Actually, she wasn't old at all, quite young, in fact. And she was much more than a friend.

Her name was Nan, Nan Britton. Her daddy was a doctor back home in Marion. She had developed a crush on the much older Warren back when she was just a schoolgirl. She would cover her bedroom walls with pictures of the big man in town, and she would find ways to see him around town. When her dream man became a politician, well, her head really turned.

Not long after she graduated from high school in 1914, somehow, someway, the young girl and the much older man began a love affair. Warren was nearly fifty years old at the time. A few years later, Nan gave birth to a daughter—Harding's daughter—Elizabeth Ann.

Now she was in Chicago with the would-be presidential nominee, hidden away in a suite at the La Salle. But she had to be out before Florence Harding checked in.

Nan and little Elizabeth Ann took up residence two floors below.

Harry Daugherty had put together quite a team for Chicago. He brought a staff of 500, and recruited three times as many volunteers to work the convention floor, corridors, not to mention hotel lobbies and suites. One special touch was the presence of a Glee Club from Columbus. They could be found just about everywhere there were delegates, singing songs like, "A Great Big Man from a Great Big State" and "We'll Nominate Harding in the Morning."

And Hamon wasn't the only oil tycoon in town with money and ideas. Harry Sinclair was there, as well. In fact, a whole slew of wealthy men were in the wings—all wanting to see a friendly face in the White House. They were weary of reform and progressivism and longed for the relaxation of government involvement in their affairs.

This fact was ignored by some journalists, but not all of them. William Allen White, known as the "Sage of Emporia," was a nationally known and widely read and respected writer with a progressive bent. He came to Chicago hoping to see Herbert Hoover—the great and wealthy engineer who had orchestrated relief efforts for a European continent overwhelmed by starvation and disease during and after The Great War—somehow get on the ticket. In fact, just a week earlier, White had written an article for The Saturday Evening Post pushing for Hoover and a progressive platform in the vein of the late Theodore Roosevelt.

But White was disillusioned.

"Mr. White," a younger journalist asked, "what is your opinion, sir, of what you see here in Chicago?"

The writer paused and replied sadly, "I've never seen a political party so dominated by sinister forces as this one is." At that, White walked away shaking his head.

White's opinion was justified. The convention marked the end—at least for a generation—of any significant progressive leanings for the GOP. Speech after speech, including those nominating candidates—and there were many, many of those—stressed the need to get back to normal.

And that was just the way Warren Harding saw it, and he decided to base his campaign on it. He even invented a word—normalcy.

"Well, Harry, things have played out just 'bout the way you said," Hamon said to Daugherty as they shared an elevator at the La Salle.

"Yes, sir, and now it's time for you to deliver your votes to our boy."

After an endless stream of speeches, and ballot upon ballot, there was no clear front runner. The convention temporarily adjourned Friday afternoon, and that night a group of powerful men met in suite 404-406 of the Blackstone Hotel. Booze flowed freely, and the smoke from dozens of fine Cuban cigars clouded the air.

In this famous, some would say infamous, smoke-filled room, deals were struck, delegates traded, and arms were twisted. And somewhere around 1:30 AM on Saturday, June 13, Harry Daugherty's plan—and Jake Hamon's money—made Warren Harding's nomination inevitable. The good old boys at the Blackstone also decided to ignore the other major candidates and tap the lesser known Calvin Coolidge to run with Harding as their vice presidential candidate.

Hours later, when the next roll call was done, Harding had captured 675 votes—nearly 200 more than he needed to win. Florence watched from the balcony.

So did young Nan Britton.

"Jake, I'm taking the senator over to my cabin in Ohio for a few days, and I want you to join us. Jess Smith's gonna be there, too. So just the four of us. There's lots to talk about, and we'll get some work done. And before you answer, I had one of my boys get some of that RedBud Rye whiskey you're always going on about. We'll drink some and toast the next President of the United States. How's that sound?"

"Sounds like a great idea, count me in! Where's it at?" Jake asked enthusiastically.

"'Bout halfway between Cincinnati and Columbus, near my hometown, a place called Washington Court House. Take the train to Columbus, and I'll have someone there to pick you up and drive you out. See you day after tomorrow, okay?"

"Lookin' forward to it, Harry. Do you imagine I'll have a chance to talk more about that Interior job?"

"Count on it, Jake. You've been a good friend to this campaign. And we are determined to be good to our friends!"

Jake placed a call to Clara back in Ardmore.

"Hello, darlin'."

"Jake! So good to hear your voice. When are you coming home? Your name's been in the newspaper all week. It's so exciting. You are a friend of the man who'll be the next president," Clara almost shouted in a giddy sort of tone.

112

"It's been quite a week, Clara. Amazing. Now listen, honey, I'm gonna be stuck here for a few days. Harding and the boys want to talk business with me."

"Aw, Jake ..." Clara said, her tone and mood quickly changing. "You promised you'd be back by Monday. I miss you."

"Miss you too, darlin'. I'll be home before you know it, and we'll celebrate real good."

Daugherty's cabin was far off the beaten path. It was stocked with steaks, liquor, fine cigars, and a beautiful view of nearby Deer Creek. As the four men began their three-day stag party, they were basking in the glow of victory. They saw themselves as on the verge of being the most powerful men on the planet.

And the more they drank, the more they dreamed.

"Hamon," Harding said, with a bit of a slur in his speech, "this rye stuff ain't bad. Not Kentucky Bourbon, mind you, but not bad at all."

"Glad you like it. You need to come out to Oklahoma during the fall campaign. We'll fix you up with some private stock for the White House."

"That'd be great, Jake, but not sure we're gonna get out that way. Old Harry here thinks we ought to do things like Mr. McKinley did back in '96 against that Bryan. He just stayed home and ran for office from his front porch. I gotta tell you, that sounds a lot better than train after train and driving on bumpy and dusty roads," Harding said.

Jake was taken aback, but had the presence of mind not to argue with the man who held much of his future in his hands. But it troubled him. He had viewed Harry Daugherty as a political genius—something confirmed at the recent convention. Now, however, for the first time, he wondered if the veteran political operative knew what he was doing.

"Yes, I think that's the way to win. Looks like the Democrats are gonna put Governor Cox against us, so it'll be two Ohio boys going at it. He'll probably tap some young fella like that Roosevelt kid from New York to run with him. And remember, that front porch strategy not only worked for McKinley, but also for another man from Ohio who used it with success—President Garfield."

"Yeah, well, that didn't work out all that good for Garfield, Harry," Jess Smith said with a smile. The men laughed.

"You boys leave the details to me—I'm an old hand at this. Hey, let's get a fire started for the T-bones, whadaya say?"

By the third and final day of the party at the cabin in the woods, Jake was frustrated that neither Harding nor Daugherty had talked to him about becoming Secretary of the Interior should they be victorious in November. He hesitated to push the matter, and he really did enjoy the company of Harding and his men. He longed to become a permanent crony.

Finally, he found himself taking a walk with Harding, just the two of them.

"Damn, it's beautiful out here. You got places like this in Oklahoma, Jake?"

"Well, we have beauty all our own, but it's different. One thing, you can't beat the clear Oklahoma sky at night."

"Sounds wonderful. I want to thank you again for all your help. And I want you to know that my door is always open to you, Jake."

"Thank you, Senator," he replied. Then he decided to speak up. "I was thinkin' a bit ago about the first time we met, back at the Waldorf in New York."

"Yes, yes, John Ringling's party. Nice evening."

"Yes, it was, and we had a nice talk. We talked about a possible role for me in a Harding White House."

Harding didn't reply.

"You remember, it was about me becoming your Secretary of Interior."

"Of course I remember, Jake. And I've given it a lot of thought."

Jake didn't like where this seemed to be going, but he listened without comment.

"I think you'd make a superb Cabinet secretary, and I'm prepared to give that post to you, but there could be a problem."

"Problem?" Jake asked. He was stunned.

"Yes. It has to do with the missus, my wife."

"I don't follow."

"Well, a few weeks ago, she came into the room when Harry and I were talking about you and the Interior Department. And she gave us both a piece of her mind. I can tell you from experience, the woman can be more difficult than an old Missouri mule."

"Why would she have any problem with me?"

"It's about your wife, Jake. And it's also about some woman named Clara."

"How the hell do you know about Clara?"

"My wife and your wife are related, remember? Florence has talked with her several times since we met back in New York."

Jake was shaken by this news. Georgia had never given him any hint that she had been communicating with Harding's wife.

Harding continued, "Now, here's the thing, Jake. My wife tells me that there is no way she'll stand for scandal in my administration. She plans to keep a sharp eye on everything. And I can tell you from experience, the woman doesn't miss much."

"Senator, I don't know what to say. Sure, Clara, is one of my gals, but you know how it is. You're a red-blooded man. You know what I'm up against."

"Sure do, Jake. So I wanna give you some advice. You go make things right with your wife. And then you work something out with this Clara girl."

"Work something out?"

"Sure. Easy. I have some experience in this. The important thing is to be wise about it. Just like having a drink or two—it's not legal, but if no one knows, what's the harm? You get your ducks in a row on this and I'll put you in my Cabinet guaranteed."

"I'll work on it, Senator. I give you my word."

"Jake, old boy, you're a man of means. Hell, you can afford a wife and a boatload of mistresses. If you just have this Clara gal in your life, just set her up some place in Washington. I've done it for years," Harding said, then he paused and smiled while looking right, then left. "But, of course, you didn't hear that from me. After all, I'm gonna be living in that big white fish bowl up on Pennsylvania Avenue," Harding said, as he laughed and slapped Hamon's back.

It took all of about five minutes for Jake to size up his situation following his walk in the woods with Warren G. Harding. He was nothing if not decisive.

As he stared at Deer Creek and listened to the sounds of nature, it was clear what he had to do. He had to patch things up with Georgia—after all, she had helped him in the race to become state party chairman.

And he needed to start thinking about breaking things off with Clara. He'd make it worth her while—she'd be set for life. He knew that no amount of money would make a scorned Clara happy. But he had time—a few months at least. Harding had to win first. No sense stirring a hornet's nest before that.

Now it was time to start planning the biggest political event Oklahoma had ever seen.

FIFTEEN

"SO I GUESS THE JOKE'S ON YOU."

Thanks, honey, this here letter is so private that I don't want anyone else around here to know anything about it. That's why I wanna dictate it to you, darlin'—it ain't a demotion. I promise," Jake said to Clara as he flashed a smile.

In fact, the letter he was preparing to dictate to Clara was the most important he would ever write. It was risky, too. If it failed to accomplish its purpose, or was in any way less than well received, all his plans and vision for grand things as part of Warren Harding's Cabinet could come to nought.

It wasn't a long letter, but it was blunt. The key point was in the words, "Frankly, Senator, I am of the opinion that if the plan of campaign that is now being pursued is continued up to the election, you will be defeated." The letter was sent, and Jake Hamon waited for a reply.

Four days later, Clara came into Jake's office and said, "Jake, a Mr. Harry Daugherty is on the line." Jake was hesitant to pick up the phone. After all, his advice in his letter directly contradicted the famous politico's strategy.

"Harry, great to hear from you! How are things in Ohio?"

"Fine, Jake. Just wanted to let you know that the boss got your letter, and he agrees with you. We're gonna get out on the road next month. We'll leave Marion, head to Chicago, then Des Moines, and several small towns on the route. He'll say a few words from the back of the train. We've got the boys working on things all along the way already."

"You comin' to our neck of the woods?" Jake asked.

"Oh, hell yes. The boss wants to come to Oklahoma City in October and wants you to be his host. We're looking at the idea of a big rally in Oklahoma City on Saturday the ninth. How's that work for you?"

"Harry, we'll put on the biggest political rally your eyes have ever seen. Leave it with old Jake! Brass bands, big parade, fireworks, it'll be like the Fourth of July, Christmas, and Armistice Day all rolled into one."

"Great—knew we could count on you. Now, you get yourself to Wichita the day before and you can ride with us in the Senator's Pullman car, okay? Now, The Duchess is coming along on the trip. She asked about Mrs. Hamon—they're related, I guess?"

"Yes, cousins."

"Well, if she could get on board with you in Kansas, that'd be great."

Trying very hard to sound happy and sure of himself, he replied, "Oh, er, sure, Harry. Not a problem at all."

Clara had been listening to Jake's side of the conversation, and she ran around the desk after the call was over. She climbed into Jake's lap. "Oh, Jake, I can't believe that I'm gonna get to meet the next President of the United States!"

Jake hugged her, but uttered not a word. He was lost in thought about how complicated things were becoming. One thing he knew for sure, he needed to make another special trip to the Windy City.

The Blackstone Hotel had become Jake's favorite spot in Chicago. Just being back in the place late that August rekindled the memories and heady feelings of June, with its already famous smoke-filled room. He knew that if he played his cards right, he would soon become one of the most powerful men in the country. But as with poker, he knew that a good deal depended on his capacity to bluff.

He enjoyed a couple of days with his children and tolerated the time with his wife. He even tried to sweet-talk her a bit, but she was, as usual, cold, aloof, and wary. Nevertheless, he pulled out all the stops his last night in town with a lavish—even romantic—dinner for two in the hotel restaurant. No children.

Just an agenda.

"Jake, you obviously have something on your mind. I know you too well. You could've saved your time and money by just spitting it out."

"Well, can't blame a fella for tryin', honey."

"Honey? It's honey now, is it? Now I'm sure you're up to something." Just then the waiter brought their entrees—a big steak for him, and pork chops for her.

"Should never try to put anything over on you, Georgia. Should've learned that lesson years ago."

"Well, Mr. Hamon, you treat me nice when you need something. So what is it?"

"I was thinking 'bout how good we were together back when I was runnin' for the Republican job. It was fun, too."

"Tolerable, I guess. I'm glad you won, and it looks like you are moving in some pretty big circles with Senator Harding."

Jake looked across at her and stared for moment. Then he blurted out what had been on his mind, or at least part of it. "Georgia dear, were you ever gonna tell me that you're related to Senator Harding's wife?"

Georgia smiled. Then she laughed. She loved the idea of having something about her that Jake needed. "How long have you known?"

"I met her last spring in New York. Ringling introduced us. She told me."

"I'll bet you about shit your pants," Georgia said with a chuckle. She was enjoying the moment.

"Not quite, but I was stunned, to say the least. Do you two ever talk?"

"Hadn't for years. But lately, we've swapped letters and a couple of phone calls. She's been asking a lot of questions about you and us."

"What have you told her?"

"The truth—or at least some of it. She knows that we are married in name only these days."

Jake paused, then asked, "Did you tell her about...?"

"Clara? You want to know if I told her about your mistress, Jake? No, I didn't. But I have the feeling she knows, or at least suspects. From what I've been hearing in certain circles, it's a subject my famous cousin knows all too well."

Jake ignored the dig at Harding. He knew for a fact that the rumors were true. But he was a faithful member of the good old boy network. He forged ahead: "The Senator and Mrs. Harding are coming to Oklahoma City in October. They are putting together a campaign swing through the Midwest. Plan to stop here in Chicago first."

"How nice."

"Thing is, they've asked me to join them for part of the way—meet 'em in Wichita. And she asked specifically about you joining us for the ride."

There, he said it. Then he waited.

Georgia looked at him and smiled. "Well, Jake, you may be gettin' on that train in Wichita, but they're picking me up at the station here in Chicago. She wants to catch up and talk about plans for our future in Washington. She says you're gonna be in her husband's Cabinet and that she is looking forward to spending a lot of time with her long-lost cousin. So I guess the joke's on you."

Joke indeed. Jake was speechless.

"What's the matter, Mr. Hamon, cat got your tongue? Why, you look flushed; need a glass of water or something?"

Finally, Jake replied, "Looks like you two Ohio girls have got Jake by the balls ..."

"Language, Jake, watch your tongue. You're talking to the mother of your children and wife of a future Presidential Cabinet member," she said with a wink and a mischievous smile. "I think things are starting to turn around for us. I hear Washington is a great place to live."

Jake sat there for a moment, then he sighed. "I guess. Yes, a great place to live."

He finished his steak. She ordered dessert. He didn't. An hour or so later, dinner being finished and a fragile peace to rival the recent Treaty of Versailles having been negotiated, they parted company.

Jake went to his suite. He was supposed to call Clara that night, but he just couldn't. He was a man being torn apart by ambition and divided loyalties.

Back in Oklahoma, Jake immersed himself in the dream and details of the big day coming up in October. He was determined that Harding, Daugherty, and company would be impressed—with the event itself, and with Jake's managerial skills. He considered Harding's visit to be the final part of his several-months long interview for the job of Secretary of the Interior.

He commuted several times a week between Ardmore and Oklahoma City. And Clara sensed that his preoccupation was not just about the logistics of a presidential campaign rally, but something else. But she couldn't figure out what that something else was.

Then, about a week before Harding was scheduled to come to the state, Jake and Clara were spending a night at the Lee Huckins Hotel in Oklahoma City. It was one of their favorite places—and it would be where a big banquet for the Harding forces would be held. Jake chose the venue and the moment to have the talk with Clara he had been dreading for several weeks.

"Remember when I was in New York earlier this year— when Ringling introduced me to Senator Harding?"

"Sure I remember. I remember that you were in New York without me," she said.

"Yes, well, I met Mrs. Harding that night, too."

"You did? You never mentioned it. What's she like? I've been reading 'bout her in my magazines. They say some call her 'The Duchess.' She must be fascinating."

"She's nice enough, I guess. Strong lady. Speaks her mind. Anyway, when I met her, she shared some news—something I didn't know."

"News, with you?"

"Yes, Clara. And it's big news. You see, it turns out that Mrs. Harding is, well, related to Mrs. Hamon."

"Your wife?"

"That would be her, darlin'. They're cousins of some sort. Spent a lot of time together in Ohio when they were young."

"Are they still close?"

"They hadn't talked in years, but lately they have been, and that's what I need to talk to you about."

"I don't like where this conversation is going, Jake. I was a good sport when you had her help you campaigning, but you said that was that."

"And I meant it, honey, but that was before I met Mrs. Harding and learned about her connection to Georgia."

"All right, so they're cousins. What does that have to do with us here in Oklahoma?"

"That's what I need to tell you. Now, don't get upset, because old Jake is going to fix things just fine—I promise …"

"Yeah well, I've heard your promises before, Mister."

"The thing is that when the Harding people start the campaign swing out this way—they're gonna make several stops for speeches and the like—well, they're gonna pick up Georgia in Chicago. She's gonna come out here with 'em in Harding's private Pullman car."

Clara covered her mouth and started to cry. In the space of a moment, she felt any sense of having the upper hand as Jake's mistress start to change. All Jake's protests and promises notwithstanding, she now had serious concerns as to her future with the man she'd loved for more than a decade—the only man she'd ever loved.

Sixteen

"And what's your name, young lady?"

The first week of October 1920, Warren Harding left his front porch in Marion, Ohio, and boarded a train for points west. He traveled in a specially and lavishly equipped Pullman car he dubbed the Superb. The first stop along the way was Chicago, where the candidate met with local citizens, and at least one passenger joined their delegation: Mrs. Jake Hamon.

"Now you sit yourself down right here, Georgia Mae," Florence Harding said. "We have a lot to catch up on, and much more to plan. It's going to be a fabulous trip."

"Why, thank you so much, Flo, for the invitation."

At that moment, the senator made an appearance. "This must be Mrs. Hamon. Warren Harding, ma'am. Your husband has sure helped us a lot. He tells my man Daugherty that there's gonna be a rally to end all rallies out in Oklahoma. Glad to have you aboard with us."

"An honor to meet you, sir."

"None of that sir business, Mrs. Hamon—I'm just plain old Warren, who married this fine lady from your wonderful family."

"Well, Warren—er, that'll take some gettin' used to, but I'll try," Georgia replied.

"Okay, well, you girls have a good ride over to Des Moines. I have a speech to work on," he said.

Jake and Clara had one of the worst fights of their sometimes-stormy affair on Friday, October 8. She had done everything in her power to get Jake to take her to meet Harding, but he wouldn't budge.

"Just can't do it, darlin'—too risky."

"Jake, I won't make a scene. I promise. You just can't leave me here in this room. Please, please, take me with you—or at least let me go to Oklahoma City to be in the rally."

"Now, Clara, I promise, honey, you're gonna be able to meet all the great people in good time. But Harding has to win first, and then he's gotta offer me the job."

"You've always talked like it was all set."

"It is, well, almost. I think his wife has some kind of say, or veto, and that's why we have to be careful."

Jake felt bad. He knew he was lying to her. But he kept telling himself that there was no reason for drastic action with Clara unless and until the senator from Ohio was, in fact, elected. For now, he just planned to play it safe, even if that meant stringing poor Clara along.

But it was clear that Clara was very unhappy and would not be handling things well. She slammed the door connecting their rooms at the Randol and proceeded to drink half a quart of gin. She banged on Jake's door an hour later. He let her in, and she proceeded to curse him with vile language. He just took it.

What else could he do?

The crowds at every stop along the route were large and enthusiastic. Hamon's advice was vindicated. The tour was a smashing success. And as the Superb moved from town to town, Flo and Georgia Mae talked, bonded, and plotted. So by the time they reached Wichita, Kansas, and were joined by Jake early Saturday morning October 9, their social calendar for just about the next year was all planned.

Jake heard all about it over breakfast, followed by several cups of coffee as the train made its way toward Oklahoma City. The way the cousins from Ohio talked, Jake realized that he was in even deeper water than he had previously thought.

At one point, he and Harding had the chance for a private conversation. The senator began, "Jake, it appears that our wives have become best friends like when they were little girls. Don't know what that means for you, but for me, it'll be great to have someone in Washington to occupy Florence's time. That way she won't be on my back—or trail—as much, if you know what I mean." He winked at Jake.

"I hear ya, Senator, but I'm not sure it's quite as big a help to me."

"You mean with your gal ... what's her name?"

"Clara. We've been together for more than ten years."

"I know what that means," Harding said. But he didn't elaborate. He had been muzzled by Harry Daugherty—forbidden to talk about Nan Britton, or any other woman, for that matter.

"I'm trying to figure out what to do. It may be time to end things with the girl. I really want a future in Washington—and I really feel I can help you, Senator."

"And you can help yourself and your friends in the oil business. The way I see it, if it's good for business, it's good for America."

"You see, we agree on that. And that has to take precedence right now."

"Well, Jake, I'm sure you'll figure it out. Pay the girl off—you have the money. Maybe that's the best thing. But just keep it all away from 'The Duchess,' ya hear?"

"Yessir!"

As the train pulling Harding's Pullman car approached Oklahoma City, Jake Hamon was mildly nervous. He had done his best to chase his domestic challenges from his mind. Now he was wondering if all the detailed planning he had overseen for the past several weeks would translate into a successful event for Harding, Oklahoma, and, of course, Jake himself.

The weather was beautiful, and Jake was thrilled to see a large throng of people when he got off the train. A band started to play when Warren and Florence Harding appeared. It was clear to nearly everyone that the senator certainly looked like a president. And seeing as this was the first presidential election in American history where women were allowed to vote, the presence of The Duchess, was highly effective, not to mention deliberate.

A motorcade of ten automobiles took the delegation to the Lee Huckins Hotel. The ride was slow and deliberate, with the candidate and his wife in the last car, waving and smiling. When the party pulled up to the hotel, Harding went over to an assembled group of sightseers and shook hands for several minutes. He even kissed a baby.

One particularly attractive lady extended her hand, and he grasped it with both of his. "And what's your name, young lady?"

The lady leaned in toward Harding and nearly whispered in his ear, "Mr. Harding, so pleased to meet you. I'm Jake's girl, Clara."

Harding reacted, but he didn't overreact—he was surprised. "Well, mighty fine to meet you, Clara." And with that, he broke from the group and headed toward the doors into the hotel, where a press conference had been planned.

"Ladies and Gentlemen," Harding began as he faced a group of about twenty-five reporters, as well as dozens of other observers. "First, I want to tell you how delighted Mrs. Harding and I are to be in your wonderful state and city. And I owe a special thanks to my good friend, Jake Hamon, who organized things."

"Senator, what is your position on the League of Nations?" one journalist asked.

"What you need to know about Mr. Wilson's League of Nations is that Mr. Cox is for getting in, and I am for staying out. Simple as that. We've done our part to, as Mr. Wilson used to say, 'make the world safe for democracy.' Now it's time to take care of our problems at home. We need to get America moving again."

Harding pointed at a man in the back of the room. "You have a question?"

"Yes, Senator, thank you ... do you support the effort in Ireland to get independence from Great Britain?"

Harding gave a measured reply: "When I am elected president, I'll first join the friends of Irish freedom and make sure that no League of Nations blocks the way to the fulfillment of Ireland's righteous aspirations ..."

One reporter scribbled the word "bloviation" and showed it to the man standing next to him. Both men smiled and nodded.

Harding continued, "...but I don't mean to say that I will tell Great Britain what to do in her own affairs, because, as an American citizen, I wouldn't permit Great Britain to tell us what to do in our own affairs."

He was asked about something near and dear to many Oklahomans—oil. "England has been busy since the Great War, bottling up resources for herself—including oil. I am for putting America and her interests first. And that means we need to do everything we can to utilize the great resources the good Lord put here in this here land."

Following the press conference, Harding made his way up to the presidential suite and entered quietly.

The Duchess was taking a nap.

Jake and Georgia were in another suite at the Lee Huckins Hotel—this one a floor below Harding. They had a civil conversation that, on occasion, moved toward the warmer, friendlier side. But it never stayed there very long.

Clara had booked a room—under the name Clara Smith—three floors down. She was equally determined to see Jake as she was to not be seen by Mrs. Hamon. Jake had not seen Clara, but after the press conference, he and Harding had shared an elevator—just the two of them. The senator told him about his encounter with Clara.

"Pretty girl, Jake. That's for sure."

"Yes, sir. Pretty, but she can also be downright mean."

"Can't they all?"

"I s'pose."

"Whatever you do is your business, Jake—just keep that pretty young thing away from our wives."

"I know, I know. I will. Count on it."

Shortly before six o'clock that evening, Senator and Mrs. Harding made a grand entrance to the hotel's ballroom. Following closely were Jake and Georgia Hamon. They joined other luminaries at the head table on the dais. Dinner was served to about 200 people—most of whom had paid handsomely for the privilege of proximity to Harding.

Several state and local politicians made very short speeches, but not Harding. He was saving his remarks for a big rally out under the pavilion at the Fair Grounds. But before that, he'd be honored with a torchlight parade. Senator and Mrs. Harding were led to a special elevated booth to watch things. There were more than a dozen marching bands, cowgirls and cowboys, bronco busters, a group performing a silent drama spoofing the League of Nations, and even a couple of elephants and other animals from the city zoo. Oklahomans lined each side of the street.

Finally, around 7:45 PM, the candidate and his wife got into a car and rode the length of the parade route—now illuminated by torches. As they arrived at the Fair Grounds, a fireworks display greeted them.

More than 10,000 were gathered to hear a major address by Senator Harding. No other speeches were scheduled. And it fell to Jake Hamon to introduce his friend to the crowd. As he stepped to the podium, he saw Clara sitting about five rows back—dead center.

Jake Hamon's introduction of Harding that night at the rally on the Oklahoma State Fair Grounds was stirring. He described the senator as a leader's leader, as well as a man's man. He also hinted that Harding was a friend of interests near and dear to the hearts of many Oklahomans. The crowd welcomed Harding with a prolonged standing ovation.

His speech was a combination of set pieces he had used effectively across the country since even before his nomination:

"America's present need is not heroics, but healing; not nostrums, but normalcy; not revolution, but restoration; not agitation, but adjustment; not surgery, but serenity; not the dramatic, but the dispassionate; not experiment, but equipoise; not submergence in internationality, but sustainment in triumphant nationality. It is one thing to battle successfully against world domination by military autocracy, because the infinite God never intended such a program, but it is quite another thing to revise human nature and suspend the fundamental laws of life and all of life's acquirements...

"My best judgment of America's needs is to steady down, to get squarely on our feet, to make sure of the right path. Let's get out of the fevered delirium of war, with the hallucination that all the money in the world is to be made in the madness of war and the wildness of its aftermath. Let us stop to consider that tranquility at home is more precious than peace abroad, and that both our good fortune and our eminence are dependent on the normal forward stride of all the American people...

"We have protected our home market with war's barrage. But the barrage has lifted with the passing of the war. The American people will not heed today, because world competition is not yet restored, but the morrow will soon come when the world will seek our markets and our trade balances, and we must think of America first or surrender our eminence."

But the Harding line that became a headline across the American Southwest was, "United States supremacy has been lost by idealism. It's time to put American business first!"

Jake Hamon was at Warren G. Harding's side as he worked the crowd shaking hand after hand. He shook a few himself, in fact. His attachment to the man who everyone assumed would be the next President of the United States raised his profile significantly in the eyes of his fellow Oklahomans.

The two men talked briefly back in the Superb Pullman car around 11:00 PM, just before the train pulled away for the long trip back to Harding's front porch in Ohio.

"Jake, you did great with this rally. First rate, my friend. Best crowds we've seen in the whole campaign. You get things done!"

"Thank you, Senator, and I look forward to calling you Mr. President real soon."

"And I'll likely be calling you Mr. Secretary, Jake. Just get that personal situation under control, okay?"

"I will. I promise."

Georgia Hamon caught the first train to Chicago the next morning. Her work in Oklahoma was done—for now.

It wasn't necessarily a landslide, but as the Ardmore newspaper put it on the day after Americans went to the polls in 1920, it was "an earthquake." In bold letters, readers were told, "Harding and Coolidge Sweep the Country." In fact, it was the most decisive win for a presidential ticket in American history up to that time.

The president-elect planned a vacation after the election. He wanted to go duck hunting, then to make a trip to Panama to see the canal. He also planned a stop in Ardmore to see and confer with Jake Hamon. The job of Secretary of the Interior was his. Harding just wanted to make sure that pesky problem had been taken care of.

Harding did indeed take the vacation, including a trip to the Panama Canal, but he never made it to Ardmore. By that time, circumstances had changed significantly.

A few days later, about a hundred Republican Party members hosted a banquet in Jake Hamon's honor. Georgia was back in Chicago, and Clara wanted to attend, but Jake told her no. It was yet another reminder to Clara that Jake had changed, as had their relationship. It was held in the ballroom of the Hotel Ardmore. He was given a gold and silver cup by the group. They knew he was going places.

Hamon's banker, P. C. Dings, the man who had put together that fast $30,000 one day a few years earlier when Clara and Bob Hutchins needed it for Jake, was one of the speakers. He talked about Jake's ability as an organizer—and of his future. "I think most of us know that Jake Hamon is not long for Ardmore, or Oklahoma for that matter. We just want him to know that we love him and appreciate all he has done for this community and state. And we look forward to the next big thing in this great man's life!"

Indeed.

SEVENTEEN

"WHAT AM I SUPPOSED TO DO?"

C lara Hamon's descent into depression was hastened in the aftermath of the presidential election. All the talk of Jake's pending appointment to Harding's Cabinet just drove her deeper into despair—and her bottles of gin. She felt lousy, physically and emotionally.

Jake was on the road a lot and not around much to watch her fall apart. He was moving on. He knew it. And she knew it. But she couldn't accept it. When Jake was in town, they argued. Sometimes heatedly.

Harding wasn't necessarily in a hurry to put his Cabinet together. His inauguration wouldn't take place for several months, until March 4, 1921. So there was nothing official yet about the Secretary of Interior post. Jake had heard the occasional rumor about Albert Fall, a United States Senator from New Mexico, supposedly lobbying Harding for the post, but Harry Daugherty assured Hamon that he was sure to get the job.

That was all Jake needed to finally prod him to action on the Clara matter. So he planned to talk to Clara on Thursday, November 18, just before leaving for business in Oklahoma City. He would break the news. Break up with her—then hightail it out of town.

It seemed like the best way.

Clara's parents, James and Sally, along with her younger brother, Jimmie, had moved from Lawton, Oklahoma to El Paso, Texas, a few years earlier. This made trips to see them less frequent for Clara. But now she really wanted to spend time with them and to talk frankly with them about her life with Jake, her mistakes, and her future. She telephoned them, and they told her to come home. Start over. Advice like that.

It had a certain appeal to Clara, and she was sorely tempted, but she felt compelled to talk through things with Jake and try to persuade him that her loyalty to him through the years ought to be worth a measure of reciprocation, if not love.

She traveled to El Paso for a few days. She slept late, ate home cooking, and took a break from the gin. After a few days, she started feeling much better.

When she returned to Ardmore, she started going to the office early and busying herself with Jake's business in a way she hadn't done for a long time. One of Jake's assistants got word to the boss on the road that Clara was back at work—just like old times. Hamon wondered what it meant, though he assumed it likely made what he had to do much harder. But he took it as further confirmation that he needed to part ways with the girl he had swept off her feet and into his life so many years earlier in Lawton.

So when Thursday the eighteenth arrived, a few days before yet another big political dinner was scheduled, presumably to celebrate his appointment as the next Secretary of the Interior, Jake was ready to have the big talk with Clara.

It was late afternoon, and Jake had a ticket on the 6:00 PM train to Oklahoma City. He and Clara were up in rooms twenty-eight and twenty-nine at the Randol Hotel, where they had lived for so long. She had been sipping gin for the better part of an hour when Jake came to her.

"Honey, we need to talk. I've got something I need to tell you, and it's the hardest thing I've ever had to talk about."

Clara just looked at him, as if sensing what was coming.

"I'm gonna be moving to Washington soon. Just a matter of time. And Georgia and Olive Belle are moving there with me. It's the way it has to be for me to take the job the new president wants me to have. It's a big job, and there's a lot riding on it. I stand to make a lot of money. But it's about more than money, honey. It's about my dreams."

Jake waited for her response and was mildly surprised that she hadn't thrown anything yet.

Finally, she spoke. "You know, Jake. I was thinking recently—when I went home to see my folks—about when we met. I was thinking about how you came into Miller's Store every day and just talked to me. You talked about your dreams. Big dreams. And soon you invited me into them. I jumped in, all the way into the deep water for you, Jake. I really believed up until now that I was still always gonna be part of those dreams. I believed 'em, Jake. I believed you." She started to weep.

Jake was paralyzed. Her words had moved him. There was a part of him that still cared for her. There was still a connection. But they had grown apart. They had changed. He knew what he needed now, what he wanted.

"Aw, darlin', please don't cry. I'll always love you."

"Sure you will, Jake. Sure you will. Okay, tell me what you want me to do. Just give it to me straight without your usual bullshit." She said this in an almost businesslike manner.

"Well, I need to leave for Panama on Monday—meetin' President-elect and Mrs. Harding there. After that, my Cabinet appointment will be announced. And he's gonna ask me about you. I don't want to lie to the man."

"Sure, Jake—lie to me for years, but by all means, tell that asshole who's moving to the White House the truth! I s'pose Mrs. Hamon is going too."

"Now, Clara, don't talk like that. Harding's a great man and gonna make a great president. And, no, Georgia is not going. She's staying put in Chicago until—" Hamon caught himself.

"Well, I voted for Cox and Roosevelt," Clara said sarcastically.

"Sorry to hear that, darlin'."

"Okay, Jake, so you need to be gone on Monday. What am I supposed to do?"

"Well, I think the best thing for both of us is to cut and cut clean. Let's both leave town on Monday. Let's move out of this hotel. You go your way; I'll go mine."

"So I've got the weekend to plan the rest of my life? Mighty generous of you, you son of a bitch!" Her anger was growing. Then she caught herself. "All right, if that's what you want, I'll go. But I won't go empty-handed, Jake. You owe me something for all the years of devotion and loyalty. You need to do right by me, or I could still be trouble for you."

"I'm well aware of that, Clara. And I'm making provision for you. Frank Ketch is setting some things up for you financially. You're gonna be a rich gal. I'm gonna see to it that you want for nothing for the rest of your life. I promise you."

"You promise me? That's funny. I think I now know what your promises are worth."

"Well, these promises will be in writing—papers drawn up by a lawyer. You'll have them Monday. You'll have your car and anything else you need. Will you go back to Lawton for now?"

"Hadn't thought about it, but maybe."

"Now, Clara, I gotta be in Oklahoma City tonight. I'll be back Sunday afternoon. And we'll talk more. This'll give the both of us a few days to think and plan. There's a big dinner Sunday night downstairs here at the hotel. Hutch and the boys are gonna go out and shoot some ducks. Some of the political big boys are gonna be here—including one of Harding's gang. So I need to be back for that."

Clara never bothered to ask if she was going to be invited. She already knew the answer.

Eighteen

Mr. W. F. Gilmer, the manager of the Randol Hotel, was a nervous wreck as he started his workday early that Sunday morning. It was well before dawn, but he couldn't sleep. For several days he had known about the big dinner scheduled for that night in the dining room. They were expecting at least fifty of the most influential citizens in Oklahoma.

Several of them had checked into rooms the night before. They were all coming to the Randol to honor its most famous resident—Jake Hamon, the man who made Warren G. Harding the next President of the United States. It had been rumored that Harding was going to be at the dinner, but the papers said that he was vacationing on some boat headed for South America, or some such thing.

Gilmer had hoped to serve the guests an early Thanksgiving dinner, turkey and all the trimmings. But Jake didn't want that. He wanted duck. So, duck it would be. But as yet, there wasn't a single bird in his kitchen. A few days earlier,

Bob Hutchins, Jake's bodyguard, had promised several mallards—some of the boys were going hunting. But time was running out.

The hotel manager watched the clock, knowing it was too early to call Hamon's room, even though the man was an early riser. Clara wasn't, and there was always trouble when she was awakened too soon, or so said Jake. Henry looked over at his twelve-year-old daughter, Ella, sitting nearby in a pretty blue dress. He pondered the idea of sending her up, thinking Clara might treat a young girl better than anyone else.

As he wrestled with what to do, a door opened and a half-dozen men walked in. He knew the men—all local fellows. The last one in the door was Bob Hutchins.

"Gilmer, old boy, betcha were thinkin' we wouldn't deliver the ducks, but ain't these birds things of beauty?"

"Mr. Hutchins, I can honestly say that they are just about the most beautiful creatures I ever saw. Thank you!" he said. A broad smile appeared on his face for the first time in several days. He directed the men into the kitchen, where several workers got busy pulling feathers and otherwise preparing the birds for the feast that evening.

Jake was not upstairs that morning. He'd left a few days earlier with some friends to look at some oil leases near Oklahoma City and still hadn't returned. The hotel man knew that things were not right between Jake and Clara. They had been fighting. Some on the staff had heard raised voices in the vicinity of rooms twenty-eight and twenty-nine, but there was little discussion about it. Certainly, no one in the hotel had any idea what Jake and Clara were arguing about.

Clara woke up late that Sunday and called down for some coffee, eggs, and toast to be sent up. A few minutes later a steward knocked at her door. When she opened it, the server was briefly taken aback by her appearance. Clara was uncharacteristically unkempt, almost disheveled. She had clearly been crying, and she smelled of alcohol. The latter was further confirmed when the breakfast tray was brought into the room. There was a near-empty bottle of gin on the table next to the bed. There were also several pieces of luggage that looked partially packed.

"Just put it down over there," Clara barked at the girl, who followed the instruction and quickly moved to leave. Whenever Jake was away, the likelihood of any tip diminished significantly. But Clara surprised the server. "Thanks, so much. I must look a sight, sorry—had a bad night. This breakfast, and particularly that coffee, will do me a world of good. Here, this is for you," she said as she handed the server a crisp twenty-dollar bill.

"Well, thank you, ma'am, thank you very much!"

Meanwhile, Jake Hamon awakened early that morning in a room at the Lee Huckins Hotel in Oklahoma City. He was hungover, but recovered quickly, as was his habit. A big glass of tomato juice, a cup of coffee, and about a half-shot of rye whiskey—hair of the dog—usually did the trick. He read the Sunday edition of the Daily Oklahoman while waiting for the cure to take hold.

As was his habit, he looked for anything about him in the paper, and he wasn't disappointed. There was yet another article about his role in the recent presidential campaign and more speculation about Hamon's political reward—a job in Harding's Cabinet. Not just any job, mind you, but the job Jake had asked for months earlier in that breakfast meeting with Harry Daugherty. He was going to be the next United States Secretary of the Interior. He also read about Harding's visit to Panama, where Jake planned to join the president-elect in about thirty-six hours.

Jake smiled as he read the paper, but then felt sad. Telling Clara that she couldn't go to Washington with him upset her so much. He had underestimated that, thinking that more money and expensive gifts would ease her pain. He was sad that she was drinking so much. He had hoped Hutchins would be able to keep an eye on her while he was away on business, but Bob was still on that hunting trip. He wondered why he had made such a fuss about Ducks.

A knock at the door chased that rare self-loathing thought from his mind. He went to the door and opened it. Frank Ketch, his business manager, came in. "Jake, looks like we'll be leaving on the ten o'clock train back to Ardmore. Should be back there early afternoon," he said.

"Yeah, fine. All the boys going?"

"Sure thing, Jake. Wouldn't miss the big party tonight for all the tea in China. Love roast duck!"

"When does Jess Smith get in?"

"Actually, he'll be on our train. He is changing trains here in town and will be waiting for us at the station."

"Great. This should finalize everything, and after I get down to Panama there should be an official announcement. Jess and I are traveling there together Monday morning."

As soon as Hamon and company walked into the lobby area of the train station, he saw Jess Smith and made his way toward him.

"Jess, how the hell are ya?"

"Mighty fine, Jake. Been thinking about that duck feast you promised—mouth's been watering all day."

"Well, I imagine you have something with you to quench your thirst," Jake said. Both men laughed as they shook hands.

"How's the President-elect? He relaxin' in the sun?"

"I talked to Harry this morning, and he told me they're having a marvelous time."

"I'm sure lookin' forward to headin' that way."

Jess just nodded his head up and down as they made their way toward the track for the train to Ardmore.

Of all the members of what was already being referred to as "The Ohio Gang," Jess Smith was by far the favorite of Florence Harding. He looked out for her interests when he could, and she loved the gossip he dished up when they talked. In many ways, Jess and Florence were allies.

What Mrs. Harding did not know was that one of Smith's regular assignments was to watch for and quiet any potential problems with women—women who became, for whatever length of time, the object of Warren's attentions and affections. For example, he had been managing Harding's Nan Britton problem for years.

The irony was that the main purpose of Smith's trip to Ardmore was not necessarily to work on the president-elect's behalf. He had been tasked by Florence to make one final—and very thorough—examination of Jake Hamon. Jess was to report directly to The Duchess on Monday in Panama about the real state of things between Jake and his young mistress, Clara. Jake did not know it, but Smith's visit could make or break his chances for the big job in Washington.

Jess did not plan to bring the subject up in an overt way. He merely planned to watch, even snoop a bit. He had a trained eye, and a highly-developed sense of smell when it came to sniffing out illicit romance. Not that he had any real experience with women.

Jess preferred men—but none of Harding's family or gang knew that. To them, he was just one of the boys. He was fixer, a gopher, and sometimes a court jester.

Jake walked into his office that afternoon after getting off the train from Oklahoma City. As he walked toward his office, he glanced at Clara's desk and noted that it had been cleared off and presumably cleaned out. The visual was just one more reminder of his breakup with the woman with whom he had long ago promised to share his dreams. He was only there for a few minutes—it was a delaying strategy. But he knew he couldn't put off seeing Clara at the Randol any longer.

When he entered room twenty-eight of the hotel, he saw that the adjoining door to room twenty-nine was opened. He looked into Clara's room and saw her on the bed, asleep. It was obvious from the state of the room that she had been packing her things. He saw a bottle of gin on the table next to her bed. It was about two-thirds empty. He didn't disturb her, but walked back into his side of the suite.

Clara must have heard him, because after a moment, she entered his room and just stared.

"Hi, honey. I saw you were sleepin'; didn't want to wake you," he said. He wondered how drunk she was.

She surprised him—she was completely sober. The bottle of gin was from the night before. She had been crying on the bed.

"Aw, Jake, I'm just sad. So sad. My heart is breaking. I gave my life to you, and now you're just throwing me away like garbage."

"Don't say that, darlin'; it's not like that. You know that. I've always loved ya, still do, it's just that this is the way things have to be."

"I'm trying to understand and accept things, but I can't. Can I come with you to the dinner tonight? It's all the folks in the hotel have been talking about. They say the ducks that Hutch got are perfect."

"Clara, I'd love to be able to have you with me, but Jess Smith is here."

"Who the hell is Jess Smith?"

"He's one of Harding's men. I've told you about him before."

"I think I'd remember a name like Smith, Jake—it's mine, remember? Oh yes, that's right, you forced me to take your name—only not really your name," she said. Clara started to cry.

Jake moved toward her. As he did, she slapped him on the face and said, "That's what I think of you and your Mr. Smith from Washington. You can have each other—you deserve each other."

Jake backed away and rubbed his cheek. He decided to let her simmer down and left.

Clara went back to her bed and poured herself a drink. Then another, and yet another.

Jake went back across Main Street to his office. A short while later, several of the men who would be at the dinner that evening showed up, including Jess Smith. It didn't take long for some bottles to emerge from hiding. Being unlawful had made booze more attractive—and, ironically, almost more available.

The men swapped stories and drank RedBud Rye whiskey for the next couple of hours. Shortly before six o'clock, they made their way as a group across to the hotel. Their boisterous entrance into the dining room signaled the beginning of a great evening of celebration.

The booze continued to flow, though now it was found in china cups trying to disguise itself as strong tea or weak coffee. The main dining room was closed to other business until eight o'clock because of Hamon's private party. The highlight of the dinner was the moment the hotel wait staff brought out the ducks. They were golden brown and cooked to perfection. The men applauded and prepared to dig in.

Clara had spent the afternoon packing. She had a little more gin, but she was by no means drunk. However, she was angry. And when she looked at the clock and saw that it was approaching seven, she decided to join the party in the restaurant, whether Jake wanted her there or not.

She fixed her hair and makeup and put on one of the few dresses she had not yet packed. She took one more swallow of gin and then headed for the restaurant.

Jake's back was to the door—something rare for him— when Clara appeared. But he noticed Bob Hutchins and Frank Ketch look beyond and behind him—they seemed startled. Jake turned around to see Clara and decided to be friendly.

"Well, hello, Clara—pull up a chair. We'll get you a plate. This is one fine meal."

"Not interested, Jake. Which one is your friend Smith from Washington?"

Several men looked over at Jess.

"Hello, Mr. Smith, that's my name, too. Smith. Clara Smith. Pleasure to meet you. I hear you have big plans for our Jake Hamon."

Jess stood and said, "Pleasure to meet you, ma'am."

"I'm not sure Jake told you that he had promised to take me to Washington with him, but now—"

"Clara!" Jake said. "Enough. Either sit down and eat with us or go back upstairs. If you make a scene, I'll call the sheriff."

"Well, that duck sure looks tempting," Clara said. Then she went toward the table and picked up a full platter of dark meat and threw it in Jake's lap. "Have some more duck, Jake. And while you're at it, go to hell!"

Hutch leaped from his seat and grabbed Clara and forcibly dragged her out of the room and up the stairs to her room. Several hotel employees hurriedly tried to remove the food from Jake. But he waved them off and worked on the mess himself.

"Sorry about that, boys," he said. He looked over at Jess Smith, who was shaking his head in disapproval. Jake knew at that moment that his chances for a Cabinet post were slipping away. He picked up his coffee cup and drained its contents in one swallow. "I've been mean to her. I told her the other day that we were through. I was going to Washington with Georgia and the children. She's upset, that's all. I'm sorry you had to see that, Jess."

Jess Smith replied, "Jake, that's all right. It's the old wisdom about a woman scorned and all that. We've all seen it before." It was a gracious remark, and as Jake heard it, he wondered if maybe his situation was salvageable, after all.

Then he said, "Excuse me, Gentlemen. You all finish this fine meal. I'm sorry for what just happened, but I need to go upstairs and take care of this."

Hutch said, "Jake, don't go up there. Not now. Let her cool off—sleep it off. You can say your words in the morning before you leave town with Jess."

But Jake insisted on going up. And within fifteen minutes, the big dinner was over and the tables were being cleared. The local men went home, and the out-of-town guests went to their rooms. They had all been drinking whiskey for hours. Sleep awaited them.

The restaurant was then opened for business, and a local physician, Dr. A. J. Cowles, and his wife sat down for a quiet meal. All evidence of the party, with its attendant drama, was gone.

Nineteen

"Clara Shot Me!"

Dr. Cowles was using the remnant of a buttered roll to soak up a few smears of gravy left behind from his roast beef dinner when he heard a loud pop echoing in the building. He looked at his wife (who had ordered the duck). She clearly heard it too, but then the waitress came by and offered coffee. They ordered pumpkin pie. The room was quiet, Jake Hamon's large party having ended shortly after Clara made her scene.

Just as Cowles was dabbing his mouth with his napkin and pronouncing the meal both wonderful and finished, he looked through the restaurant door and out into the lobby—toward the staircase to be exact. Someone was struggling, even stumbling apparently, down the stairs. The man was either drunk or in distress—or both.

After a brief moment, the doctor recognized the man—it was Jake Hamon. The doctor knew, as did most everyone in town, that Jake lived with his mistress, Clara, in suites twenty-eight and twenty-nine of the hotel.

Jake Hamon was indeed drunk, but that wasn't his big problem at the moment. That pop that Dr. Cowles and his wife had quietly noted was, in fact, gunfire. And as Jake Hamon careened through the hotel lobby and made eye contact with Cowles, the doctor noticed Hamon grabbing his side in pain. There was an ominous bright red stain spreading on his white shirt.

Jake had been shot.

The physician sprang into action, jumping up from the table and meeting the wounded man, stopping him in his tracks. They exchanged words, more like animated whispers, because, for all the apparent peril of the situation, Jake Hamon didn't really want people to know what had happened to him.

Within seconds, the two men, now linked arm in arm, made their way back through the hotel lobby toward the front door, leaving a trail of blood behind. Bob Hutchins had been over at the office and walked back into the Randol lobby just as the doctor and Jake were preparing to exit. The three of them staggered and stumbled down the poorly lit street, heading toward a place called the Hardy Sanitarium, located just up the street. It was about eight-thirty.

The small hospital was managed by its founder, Dr. Walter Hardy, a man well known around town as the hardworking physician who delivered all the babies, nursed all the wounds, and performed the occasional needed surgery. When not at work, he loved to spend time in his fruit orchard and vineyard. But that was a rare respite. He loved his work and took proprietary pride in it—as evidenced by the fact that the good doctor was on duty that night as the two men abruptly came through the door.

When Hamon saw Dr. Hardy, a longtime friend, he broke free from Cowles and rushed to him, blurting out some words. Cowles later asked Hardy what Jake had said to him.

"He said, 'Clara shot me!'"

While the two doctors talked about how to treat Jake Hamon, the oil man called Bob Hutchins over to his bedside. In a weak whisper, he said, "Hutch, Clara didn't mean to hurt me. I don't believe she would hurt me. It must've been an accident. Now you go to her and help her. These doctors are gonna work on me. You bring her here to me in the morning. Then I'm gonna need you to take her out of town, ya hear?"

"Yes, Jake. I'll take care of it. Now you just rest, and let the doctors do what they need to do."

"Oh, and make sure Frank knows what's going on. Tell him it was an accident, I was cleaning my gun, or something. Don't blame it on Clara. Please don't blame it on her, Hutch!" Jake sobbed.

"Okay, Boss. I understand," Hutch replied. He then left the room and headed back over to the Randol.

Cowles and Hardy agreed that they had to operate immediately. They moved Hamon to an operating table and administered an anesthetic. No one else was in the room.

The bullet was from a .25-caliber pistol. It had entered Jake's body on his right side, passing through the upper lobe of his liver. It then stopped in his back, near the spinal column.

They removed the bullet and then moved him to another room to recuperate.

He was still conscious when Frank Ketch came in. He motioned for his business manager to come close.

"Frank, Clara needs to get out of town. It's just a matter of time before Georgia hears about what's happened. I know that woman, she'll hightail it here. Last thing she needs to see is Clara. If that happens, Georgia might shoot me herself." He ventured a small smile after that remark.

"I'm gonna have Hutch bring Clara over to see me. Then I'm sendin' her to you. Give her money, whatever she needs. Start with five grand, and make any promise you need to make to get her to play ball. She just needs to go away."

Frank decided to ask. "Jake, did Clara shoot you?"

"She sure as hell did. On purpose, too. But don't tell anyone that. I'd rather it be spread around that it was an accident while I was cleaning my gun."

"No one's gonna buy that, Jake."

"Sure they will, because you're going to tell 'em I was drunk."

"Whatever you say, Jake. I'll be ready for Clara when she comes to the office in the morning."

Hutch met with Clara at the Randol. She was distraught and nearly hysterical when the bodyguard found her. He did his best to calm her down. He noted that several suitcases and trunks had been packed. Hutch told Clara to rearrange the items in the cases and trunks. He assumed that she needed to get out of town and that she was in big trouble, though that was far from Clara's—or Jake's—mind at the moment.

But Hutch was thinking clearly.

"Jake wants me to take you to see him tomorrow. Then we'll go see Frank and get you set to leave for a while."

"I was already planning to leave—but I can't leave Jake now. He needs me."

"What he needs is for you to listen to him, for once, Clara. This is serious. He's in bad shape. I've got a bad feeling about this. You need to lay low. I can help. But you gotta listen to me, too, okay?"

"I'm so tired," she said.

"I know you are, Clara, but you're not sleeping here. I'm gonna take you to the house of that friend of yours—Elizabeth Mayes. You'll stay there tonight, then drive over to Dallas tomorrow morning. You bring what you need for a few days. I'll take care of getting the rest of your luggage to you."

Clara nodded affirmatively. She was too exhausted to be anything but compliant.

The next morning, Hutch brought Clara to Jake's hospital room. Hamon was weak, but he was clearly glad to see her. She was afraid of the encounter at first, but when she saw his smile, she felt better. He repeated the instructions that Hutch had given her the night before.

"Clara, I'll beat this thing in no time. I promise, your name will be left out of it. You need to get away from here—don't talk to no one," Jake whispered.

"I'm leaving this morning."

"First, you go by Frank's office. He'll give you some money. I want you to have it."

"Okay, Jake, whatever you say. I just want you to get well," she said, as she wept and tried to hug him without hurting him.

"I will, darlin'. I promise."

She left with Hutch, and they went over to Frank Ketch's office. Ketch gave Clara an envelope containing $5,000 in cash.

Meanwhile, Hutch had a friend of his named John Gernand take several of Clara's trunks to the rail station and had them sent to Kansas City. That's not where Clara was headed, but he thought it'd be a welcome diversion for anyone trying to find her. John Gernand passed out five-dollar bills to several people in return for them "verifying" the story that Clara Hamon had gone to Kansas City.

It was a good idea, but for one factor. One of the trunks en route to Missouri contained something very personal, something Clara would never want to fall into the wrong hands.

As for Clara, she drove the Packard toward Texas, stopping for the night in Fort Worth. She checked in at the Westbrook Hotel. However, only Jake, Frank Ketch, and Bob Hutchins knew this. Other interested parties thought she was on her way to Kansas City, Missouri. The next morning, she drove over to Dallas, where she met her brother. She handed the keys to her car to him for safekeeping. He dropped her near a terminal where the Dallas Auto Company had cars and drivers for hire.

She approached a young man who was preoccupied with a scratch on his Oldsmobile. Everett W. Sallis was rather thin and had a pronounced nose. He didn't notice her at first, so she said, "Excuse me, sir? I need a ride to the aviation field. Can you get me there?"

"Love Field, sure no problem. Hop in."

Clara climbed in and they took off.

"You know why they call it Love Field?" the driver asked, trying to make conversation.

"I don't know, and I don't care," she replied.

"Named for a man named Moss Love, died in a plane crash in California several years ago, one of the first to die that way."

Clara looked away.

When they arrived at the airfield, Clara went looking for a pilot and plane to hire.

"No one here right now, Miss, but expect to have someone available in an hour or two," one worker said.

Clara went back over to the Oldsmobile.

"Okay, Mr. Sallis, I've got some traveling to do, and I was hoping to use an airplane. But there's no one here, and I need to get moving. What would you charge to drive me around for four or five days?"

Sallis sized her up and replied, "I could do it, but it'd cost you a hundred bucks, up front, plus gasoline. Repairs, too, if needed."

Clara smiled at the driver and pulled a roll of bills out of her purse. She peeled one off and handed the driver one of the few hundred-dollar bills he'd ever seen.

"Wow, great! Where to?"

"Just drive, and I'll tell you as we go," she said. He watched as she put the roll of bills back into her purse, which was opened just wide enough for Sallis to see her pistol.

"Head south," Clara said.

TWENTY

"...A TELEGRAM FOR MR. HARDING."

President-elect Warren G. Harding was enjoying his Monday morning without a care in the world. He had taken Florence on a long-promised vacation. Harry Daugherty traveled with them.

"What a beautiful morning, Harry. Wish they all could be like this."

"Well, Boss, enjoy it, because tomorrow Jess will be here with Jake Hamon, and then, watch out," he said with a laugh.

Harding joined in the laughter. "Yes, old Jake knows how to roll, that's for sure. He get that thing worked out back in Oklahoma?"

Daugherty knew exactly what he was talking about. He looked around before replying, making sure The Duchess wasn't nearby.

"No worries, Harry, she won't be back for a while. Jake get that resolved?"

"That's why Jess went over to Ardmore, to confirm everything for himself."

"Good," Harding replied. "I really want Hamon in my Cabinet. He can make things happen, and he sure helped us on the campaign."

"Indeed, he did. I can't imagine that we could've won nomination, forget about the election, without him."

"You know, Albert Fall is hot on my heels about the Interior position. But I think Jake is a better fit," Harding said.

"I agree. We should be able to work it out for a big announcement tomorrow, in time to make the morning papers."

"Speaking of papers," Harding said, "did we get one yet?"

"Should arrive anytime," Daugherty replied.

One of the wait staff at the resort approached Harding and Daugherty. He was briefly stopped by a security guard, but then let through.

"I have a telegram for Mr. Harding."

"Give it to me," Daugherty said. He pulled out a dollar bill and gave the young man a tip. Then he opened and read it. As he did, his eyes grew wide with a look of alarm. "Oh my God," he said.

"What? What is it? Who's it from?" Harding asked.

"It's from Jess in Oklahoma. It says that Jake Hamon has been shot and is in serious condition at a hospital in Ardmore."

"Shot? By whom?"

"Jess says that it appears that Jake's mistress, Clara, shot him last night."

Within a couple of hours, Daugherty was able to talk with Jess Smith by phone. Smith was monitoring the situation.

"Yes, it's pretty clear that Clara shot him. Now she's disappeared. I saw Jake this morning. He's in bad shape but in good spirits. Funny thing, though," Jess said.

"What?"

"Jake says that the girl shot him by accident."

"Is that what happened?"

"Not according to his doctor, a fellow named Hardy. He told me that Jake told him last night that Clara shot him after a fight about him not taking her to Washington."

"Oh my God! This is bad. The Boss just sent a cable to Hamon."

"What did it say?"

"It said: 'DON'T WORRY. YOU WILL GET WELL AND WILL BE SECRETARY OF THE INTERIOR IF YOU WANT IT.'"

"Now listen, Harry. You need to put a muzzle on Harding. He needs to put some daylight between him and Hamon. There's no way in hell that, even if Hamon does recover, he's ever gonna be part of Harding's Cabinet. Not after everything I've seen."

"What do you mean?"

"I saw the gal in action Sunday night about an hour or so before she took after Jake with her gun. She's not someone you want on the fringes. Trust me. I'll fill you all in when I get there. Gonna hang out another couple of days, then head your way. I'll be enjoying the sun with you by Friday, latest."

Carter County Attorney Russell Brown was suspicious. He was also determined. Having recently lost an election, and therefore a job he loved, to his Republican challenger, James Mathers, he wanted to leave office on a high note and quickly began to see the Hamon shooting as a story that didn't smell right. He had seen Clara at Jake's side for years. Now the lady was conspicuously absent.

Hamon had spent tens of thousands of dollars to help elect Republicans. He was on his way to Washington. That was the word on the street. And it seemed quite reliable. Of course, Brown reasoned, that would be motive for a cover-up of the real story. There had been whispers around town—almost from the moment Jake staggered into Dr. Hardy's hospital—that Clara and Jake had argued and that she had, in fact, fired the gun. To Brown, there was enough for an investigation.

Brown called his secretary in. "Mrs. Greer, I need to dictate a telegram to be sent to every county attorney in the state."

"Yes, sir."

"I also want them to advise people at train stations to be on the lookout for Clara Smith Hamon."

"I'm ready. How do you want it worded?"

"You organize it, but basically, I need it to say that she is about twenty-seven or twenty-eight years old, dark brown hair and eyes. She's about five feet seven inches tall. She may have a fur coat and several diamond rings."

"That ought to stand out, sir," Mrs. Greer remarked.

"Give my contact information here at the office," he said.

Arthur Brisbane, editor of the Chicago Herald-Examiner, chomped on the stub that remained from his cigar. Its fire was long dead. He was sitting at his rolltop desk. He opened a drawer and pulled out a bottle of scotch that was more than half empty and poured two fingers into a glass. He drank it in one swallow.

"Get me Sam Blair," Brisbane barked to no one in particular. But three young ladies within earshot sprang into action.

"The boss wants to see you," a near-breathless girl said to the young reporter. He grabbed his suit jacket and followed her back toward Brisbane's office.

"Any idea what he wants?"

"He didn't say. I'm sure you'll find out soon enough," the girl said to him with a wink and a smile.

Blair looked into the office. Brisbane was reading. Blair knocked on the side of the door. "You wanted to see me, sir?"

"Blair, yes, what the hell took you so long?"

"Well, I was—"

Brisbane interrupted and continued, "Got a story for you. I've been told that you are hungry for a big story."

"Yes, sir. What's it about?"

"Well, first question shouldn't be what, but rather, 'where.'"

"Where?"

"Oklahoma. Used to be Indian Territory. Place called Ardmore."

Sam looked at his boss with a face that suggested mild confusion.

"Don't look at me like that. I can smell a big story from a thousand or more miles away. Ever tell you about my first big scoop?"

"No, sir. Was it in New York?"

"No, but it was when I was working for Pulitzer, before Mr. Hearst made me an offer I couldn't refuse to come work for him. My first big scoop was when I was in London more than thirty years ago. I was just a cub reporter, but the biggest story of the century fell in my lap. I was one of the few Americans to send dispatches back to New York."

"Thirty years ago, that was about 1890?"

"Close. It was 1888. Ever hear of 'Jack the Ripper'?"

"Of course. The murders in London that have never been solved."

"Well, I was the man sending direct reports back to papers in America. That's how Mr. Pulitzer heard about me and led to my job with him in New York."

"Sounds like it was a big break."

"The biggest. Now, I have no way of knowing this, but what I'm about to send you to cover just may become a big story itself. You interested?"

"Absolutely, Mr. Brisbane. What's the story?"

"That's what you're going to find out. You recall when the Republicans were here in the summer for their convention and there were all sorts of rumors about secret deals and money being spread around pretty thick by some oil men?"

"Sure. There was a guy named Sinclair and his friend, Do-Do—"

"Edward Doheny. Ever hear the name Jake Hamon?"

"Sure, I recall that. He was one of the oil men who helped Harding."

"More like he bought and paid for him. Well, it seems that this Oklahoma oil man, who's been in line to be the next Secretary of Interior when Harding takes office, somehow shot himself the other night."

"Shot himself?"

"So they say. And he's in pretty bad shape."

"Sounds pretty straightforward."

Brisbane stared at Blair for a moment. Then he said, "Now listen, kid. One thing I learned back in White Chapel in '88 when that maniac was butchering whores, is that it takes three things to sell a lot of newspapers."

"Three things?"

"Yes, murder, mayhem, and mystery. And I think that this Jake Hamon story just may have some of those things somewhere. I mean, remember the last time we heard of a famous man 'accidentally' shooting himself while cleaning his gun?"

"Sorry, Mr. Brisbane, I don't."

"That's right, you were still a boy when it happened. It was Marshall Field Jr., heir to the store and fortune, back in '05. They said he shot himself the same way. But there was much more to the story."

"Oh, yeah, I heard about that. Nothing was ever proved, though."

"Well, that family paid a pretty sum to keep the real stuff from the papers. I wasn't in Chicago then, mind you."

"Real stuff?"

"Sure, the kid was probably shot in that famous brothel from back then—Everleigh's—you ever hear about that place?"

Blair blushed for a moment and replied, "Sure, Boss, everyone's heard of that. Was Hamon maybe in a whorehouse when he took the bullet?"

"No, he was at his hotel—where he lives—but here's the thing: there's a county attorney down there, guy named Brown, who is telling anyone who'll listen that good old Mr. Hamon, friend of Warren Gamaliel Harding himself, was shot by his mistress. Now that's your story."

"That'd be a big scoop, for sure."

"Well, it's all yours, my boy. I want you on a train in an hour. Pack your things. I'm authorizing some expense money for you. But you report directly to me, understand?"

"I do. And thank you, Mr. Brisbane. I won't let you down."

"See to it, then, kid."

Sam Blair was on a train that very afternoon.

Georgia Hamon and Olive Belle were on the same train, though several cars separated them from the reporter. A telegram had arrived at Georgia's home in Chicago, letting her know what had happened. Though the message insisted that Jake's wound was not serious—certainly not fatal—she was determined to be at his bedside.

When they arrived in Fort Worth the next morning to change trains, Georgia picked up a copy of the late edition of the Fort Worth Star-Telegram, which had the news of the shooting on the front page. But there were few details. The shooting was described as "accidental," and there was no mention of her husband's mistress. She made sure of that before passing the paper to her daughter, who was anxious to read about her father.

They arrived in Ardmore just after the dinner hour on Tuesday and went immediately to the Hardy Sanitarium to seek Jake.

"Oh my," Georgia said. She covered her mouth with her hand and was clearly shaken when she came near him. He was ashen and listless. But he managed to find the presence of mind to tell a story.

"Honey, I was cleaning my gun, and it went off. I guess I'd had too much to drink. I feel like a fool."

"You tellin' me the truth, Jake?"

"Scout's honor. That's exactly what happened. And if anyone says anything different, they're lying. That's all there is to it."

"And where is she?"

"Who, Clara? How the hell do I know? I broke that off a while ago. Sent her on her way with enough money to forget about me. I promise, Georgia, it's me and you, and we're going to Washington as soon as I get better. Look here, it's a telegram from the president-elect. See for yourself."

With a trembling hand, he gave Georgia the telegram. She read it and then wiped a tear from her eye.

"That's what I want, Jake. That's what I want. You're gonna get better. I'm here, and I will take care of you and we can start over."

Jake smiled weakly. Georgia then brought Olive Belle in to see her father. This brought a much bigger smile to the wounded man's face. But a few moments later, Jake drifted off to sleep, and a nurse told them it was time to go.

"You can come back in the morning," the young nurse assured them.

The travelers checked into the Hotel Ardmore. Sam Blair had checked in an hour earlier.

Meanwhile, Clara was in the wind.

TWENTY-ONE

"WE WERE GOING TO START OVER."

Clara and her driver stopped for lunch at a café in Waxahachie, about thirty miles south of Dallas.

"Wonder if the fried chicken is good here?" Sallis asked.

"How would I know? Never been here before."

"Well, I think I'll try it, with potatoes and gravy. 'Course I may need a nap after—where are we headin' next?"

"I'll let you know, Mr. Sallis," Clara said with an icy stare.

While they were working their way through a less-than-stellar fried chicken lunch, Sallis saw alarm in his rider's eyes and noticed that she had stiffened in the seat across from him. He turned to see what she was looking at and saw a sheriff sitting down for lunch.

Clara said, "Mr. Sallis, I'm full, and we really need to get back on the road. Please settle the bill. I'll meet you at the car." She pulled a five-dollar bill out and slid it across the table to the driver.

"Yes, ma'am. I've had better chicken, anyway."

When he got to the car, Clara told him to drive to Hillsboro. The driver saw that she had a pistol on her lap.

Sallis, who was now very curious about his mysterious passenger, tried a couple of times to initiate a conversation, but Clara didn't bite. He looked back at her a few times and thought she seemed fearful. He finally squeezed a reply out of her when he asked, "You running from somebody?"

"I didn't pay for conversation, Mr. Sallis, just for the ride," Clara replied, curtly.

"Yes, well, you have a gun back there, and you left the café in a hurry when that lawman walked in. I may just be a driver, but I'm not stupid, ma'am. I think I deserve some answers, or maybe I'll just stop and let you out here."

Clara started to cry.

Sallis instantly regretted his threat. "You need to stop? We'll make Hillsboro in about twenty minutes, or so."

"No, sorry, don't stop."

"Anything I can do to help?"

"No, Mr. Sallis, you can't help. I don't think anyone can," Clara said. "Haven't you been reading the newspapers?"

"Sure, I read the papers, why?"

"Well, you ought to know what's wrong, then," Clara said.

"Sorry, ma'am. I'm not sure what you're talking about," Sallis said. Then a light came on. "Was it a shooting scrape?"

Clara didn't answer directly, but replied, "Tell me something, what's the best kind of gun to shoot a man with— old or new?"

"I'd guess an old one, one that was rusty. If the bullet doesn't get him, blood poisoning will."

"Wish I'd known that. My gun was a new one."

"What?"

"I shot a man in Ardmore. I won't tell you who. You'll read his name in the papers."

"Mind me asking why you shot him?"

"He lied to me. Then he came in drunk and tried to make me do things a brute or worse wouldn't do."

"Do you think he will die?"

"I most certainly do. I hope so, anyway."

Soon they were in Hillsboro. "I need to get some gasoline," Sallis said. "So, we'll need to stop for a bit. Want something to drink?"

"Yes, thank you. I could use a cold drink."

Sallis pulled into a place called "Henry's Filling Station," and had his car filled. Clara stayed in the back seat, and he brought her a bottle of Dr. Pepper soda. She took a long swig and smiled at him.

"Thank you. It's great."

When he got back in the car, Clara said, "I want you to take me to Cisco. How long will that take?"

Sallis opened the case and the seat next to him and pulled out a map. "You sure are testing my navigatin' skills, ma'am."

"Sorry. I have my reasons."

"I'm sure you do," he said. It took him a minute, running his finger along the map. "I think it's about a hundred and forty miles, so it's gonna take a while, probably close to five hours. It'll be dark by then."

"That's fine. Let's head there. Make good time when you can. Take me to the train station in Cisco."

Sallis found himself a bit sad at the mention of the train station, sensing that his four-day fare was going to be much shorter. He looked at Clara, who had a flask in her hand. She was crying again.

"Hey, lady, listen, cheer up. Maybe it isn't as bad as you think?"

"Yes, but it is," she replied. "He's worth a lot of money, and some of the men he thought were his friends helped me

175

get away. I left my jewels there and my diamonds. They were worth thousands. Someone sent some of my things to Kansas City. I was gonna try to get to San Antonio. I know an aviator there. He used to be in the army. Was hoping to get him to fly me somewhere far away," she said.

Then she fell into silence, and a few moments later it appeared to Sallis that his passenger was sound asleep.

About an hour later, Sallis hit a large bump in the road, and Clara woke up. She rubbed her eyes and looked at her bejeweled watch. The time was a few minutes before seven o'clock.

"Now, Mr. Sallis, would you be interested in another hundred-dollar bill?" Clara asked.

"Sure, who do I have to kill?" he replied, immediately realizing how inappropriate that crack was.

She didn't laugh, but said, "When we get to the train station in Cisco, I'd like you to go in and purchase a ticket for the next train bound for El Paso. I'll give you money for the fare and the hundred for you. Will you do that for me?"

The driver looked at her for a moment and grew suspicious. "I guess so, but it seems kind of strange. Why didn't you just take the train from Dallas to El Paso? Why drive all around the state just to catch a train?"

"I just need a train ticket now, and you can drive back to Dallas with a pocketful of cash. In fact, let's make it a two hundred-dollar tip. How's that?"

"Okay, I'll do it. Just promise me that I won't get into any trouble."

Clara smiled at the driver, remembering her charms, and said, "You have my word, handsome."

They pulled up at the Cisco train station a little after eight o'clock that evening. Sallis went in and purchased her ticket. The next train to El Paso was leaving in twenty minutes.

Clara thanked E. W. Sallis (for a brief moment he thought she was going to kiss him, but she didn't even shake his hand). She disappeared into the train station. The driver scratched his head and wondered just what he had gotten himself into.

He decided to keep an eye on the newspapers, though he wasn't much of reader. In fact, he'd soon be seeing his own name in the papers.

Frank Ketch met with reporters in his office that afternoon. He made a statement about Jake's condition. Then the reporters took off on him. The pool of journalists had swelled significantly, with several large metropolitan newspapers sending people to cover the story. Sam Blair was in the group.

Blair spoke up. "What do you have to say about the persistent rumor that Mr. Hamon was shot in a lover's quarrel with a woman not his wife?"

Ketch looked at the unfamiliar face and replied, "That's not only untrue, it's ridiculous. It happened the just way I told you. He was cleaning his .25-caliber gun and it went off. He told me that right as he was slipping the magazine in place it discharged."

"Have you talked with Clara Smith?" Blair asked.

"I have not."

"Where is she now?" Blair pressed.

"How would I know?"

"Word has it that she has fled before being arrested."

Frank replied, "I have no knowledge of that. You'd have to check with the sheriff. But frankly, I'd be shocked if they are giving any serious attention to such salacious gossip. That's all, gentlemen. I have work to do."

One of the men who had spent much of Sunday with Jake was Kellie Roach, an Ardmore insurance man. He wanted to help his friend, so he dropped by the offices of the Daily Ardmoreite newspaper with a letter to the editor. In the letter, he talked about his good friend Jake and alleged that any attempts to somehow suggest that the shooting was anything other than an accident was "politically motivated" by one of Jake's enemies. He called the ugly rumors surrounding the case "cruel and inhuman" and told the readers that Hamon was a devoted husband and father.

Jake smiled when Frank Ketch showed him his friend's letter in the paper. Then he winked at Frank, giving the business manager a moment of hope. He was catching a glimpse of the real Jake.

"Hey, Frank, do me a favor?"

"Of course, Jake. Name it."

"Bring me some cash, just small bills."

"Glad to, but why?"

"These nurses are like angels around here. A couple of 'em ain't all that hard on the eyes, either," Jake replied with a smile and another wink. "I want to tip 'em."

"This is not a restaurant or hotel, Jake. I don't think you tip your nurses."

"Jake Hamon does. Now you get me that money, okay?"

Thursday was Thanksgiving, and Georgia and Olive Belle were invited to dinner at the home of friends Ernie and Sally Dunlap.

"My, what a beautiful table, Sally," Georgia told her friend.

"Why thank you, Georgia. We're so delighted to have you as our guests today. Now, you both make yourself at home. How's your husband doing?"

"He's doing much better. I think he's out of the woods and will make a full recovery in good time."

"Well, you know a lot of people are praying for him—and you."

"I know. People have been so kind and supportive. Jake has a lot of friends in Ardmore."

"Well, he has done a lot for this town. We'd sure hate to lose him," she replied. Then she said, "Sorry, that didn't come out right."

"Oh, no bother, Sally. I know what you're saying. Now, is there anything I can do to help? That turkey smells wonderful."

"No, you just sit down and relax."

They had a delightful Thanksgiving Dinner, after which Georgia asked her hosts, "Could Olive Belle stay here a bit longer, while I go back to the hospital?"

"Why sure, that'd be our privilege to have her grace us for a bit longer. She can help me with the dishes."

Olive was not at all happy to be left behind, and even more unhappy about the dishes.

Dr. Hardy met Georgia just outside Jake's room.

"Surprised to see you here at this hour on Thanksgiving, Doctor Hardy."

"Well, Mrs. Hamon, we need to talk. Let's sit down."

"What—what? Has something happened?"

"No, Jake is still fighting, but I need to prepare you that he may lose this fight."

"But I thought he was improving?"

"Only a little here and there. Now he has a fever and has gone into a coma. I'm not sure Jake is going to make it through the night."

Georgia cried and said, "Well, I'm staying right by his side."

"That's fine, of course, Mrs. Hamon. And you let my staff know if you need anything."

Frank Ketch was at the hospital early on Friday. Jake was unconscious, and Hardy told the business manager that it was just a matter of time. He tried to talk with Georgia, but she was unusually quiet. Then she wept and said to no one in particular, "We were going to start over. We were going to start over."

Shortly after eight o'clock the next morning, Friday, November 26, Jake awakened briefly. He saw Georgia sitting in a chair next to his bed.

"How long you been here?" he asked.

"Jake, I've been here all night."

Jake smiled and said, "I'm thirsty. Could you get me a glass of water?"

"Sure thing."

"Thank you," Jake whispered.

Georgia left the room to get the water. When she returned a few moments later, Jake Hamon's eyes were open. But he was gone.

"Oh, Jake, poor Jake," Georgia said as she wept.

A short while later, Ketch summoned reporters to the hospital.

"I have the sad duty to announce that Jake Hamon died a few minutes ago of wounds resulting from the accidental discharge of a firearm. Our thoughts and prayers are with Georgia, Jake Jr., and Olive Belle."

There were no questions.

Within a few hours, Georgia had composed herself and began to plan Jake's funeral. She was determined that it would be a fitting farewell to the "Oil King of Oklahoma."

TWENTY-TWO

"…A LAW-ENFORCEMENT ODD COUPLE."

Now, Russell, are you sure about this? Why not let the dust settle for a few days? Let's get Old Jake in the ground, and maybe then we can—"

But Sheriff Buck Garrett was interrupted, as he had been several times during the phone call that Friday morning from County Attorney Russell Brown. Always impeccably dressed, from his signature cowboy hat to his boots, Garrett was a lawman's lawman.

"You listen to me, Buck. I'm issuing the warrant for Clara's arrest, and it's your sworn duty to act on it. Get that crazy deputy of yours and do what you need to do to find the woman. I've already sent telegrams to every county attorney in Oklahoma. We have people watching for her at train stations everywhere. It's just a matter of time before the real story comes out."

"I know my duty, Russell. That's why the people of Carter County reelected me a few weeks ago," Buck said. He knew the words would sting. Brown had lost his race to Jimmie Mathers, who was swept into office on Harding's coattails, helped, of course, by Hamon's efforts and millions.

Buck continued, "I hope you're not letting your personal feelings about the Republicans get in the way of your better judgement, Russell."

"Go to hell, Buck. That warrant will be on your desk in twenty minutes, and I expect you to get busy," Brown said. Then he hung up before Garrett could reply.

Garrett prided himself on his self-control. Never fired his gun. Loved to ride his white horse down Main Street. Sometimes he'd stop and get the horse an ice-cream cone. He was a beloved figure, due in no small part to his level-headed and even-tempered approach to law enforcement in a county that still had a lot of old Wild West in its blood.

He called out, "Bud, get in here!"

Now David "Bud" Ballew, well, he was another kind of lawman. They were an odd couple. Ballew was "bad cop" to Garrett's "good cop." He was erratic, where Garrett was steady. He was a hard drinker in contrast to Garrett's temperance. He was flashy compared to Garrett's more conservative nature. But they made a great team. And they were soon to become celebrities.

Bud Ballew came into Buck Garrett's office. "What's up?"

"You heard that Hamon went to the happy huntin' ground a bit ago, right?"

"Yep, it's all over town," Ballew replied.

"I just had a call from Russell Brown."

"What'd that horse's ass want?"

"He's issuing a warrant for Clara's arrest."

"The hell you say. What does he think she did?"

"He's convinced Clara shot Jake in a lover's quarrel and is determined to find her and bring her back to Ardmore for a trial. I'm pretty sure he sees it as a last hurrah."

"Has he talked to Jimmie Mathers?"

"Doubtful. Their race was pretty heated, and Brown seems to be bitter. But I think I'll give Mathers a call and get his take. He takes over as county attorney in January. He needs to know what he might be inheriting."

President-elect Harding cried when he heard the news that Jake Hamon had died. He was having brunch with Harry Daugherty, and Jess Smith, who had arrived the night before. Smith briefed the boss about Clara and all the rumors.

As they sat at breakfast, Harding was emotional and remarked, "What a wonderful fellow he was. Too bad he had to be taken out. Too bad he had that one fault—that admiration for women."

Jess and Harry looked at each other and smiled.

For her part, when a reporter told Florence Harding about Hamon's death, she asked pointedly, "Was there a woman involved?"

That evening, reporters, their number increasing with every train coming to town, were hanging out in the Hotel Ardmore lobby, which became their "headquarters" of sort. Someone read a statement signed by Hamon's doctors:

"We, the undersigned physicians and surgeons, are of the opinion that Mr. Jake L. Hamon died as a result of a gunshot wound which penetrated the abdomen, entering at the ninth intercostal space, midway between the axillary and mammary lines, penetrating the right lobe of the liver, passing downward, outward and backward, the missile lodging beneath the skin, one inch to the right of the spinal column on a level with the crest of the ilium. The injury was followed by acute dilation of the stomach, resulting in acute dilation of the heart about twelve hours later. No autopsy was made. — Signed: W. Hardy, M.D.; A.C. Scott, M.D.; Horace Reed, M.D.; L.J. Moorman, M.D; A.C. Cowles, M.D."

Jimmie Mathers was finishing his fifth cup of black coffee when the black candlestick telephone on the desk in his office at the firm of Mathers and Coakley rang. He grabbed the earphone and leaned in to speak into the mouthpiece.

"Hello? This is Mathers."

"Buck Garrett here."

The sheriff and the lawyer had been friends for many years.

"What can I do for you, Buck?"

"Well, not sure you know this, but the man you beat in the election is swearing out a warrant for Clara's arrest."

"He's crazy!"

"I agree, but he's doing it, and I'm duty bound to track her down."

Mathers said, "If she were to ever go to trial, no jury would convict her. I'll tell you this, if that happens, I'll defend her for free."

"Well, in January it'll be your office prosecuting her."

After the call, Mathers pondered the situation, then he decided to call Russell Brown. He regretted that decision the minute he heard Brown's voice. But after several heated exchanges, Mathers seemed to momentarily locate a rare sensible groove in Brown's brain.

"Now, Russell, whatever you do, don't you think it'd be better for Hamon's wife and kids if you let the woman bury her husband before you start your war machine on Clara? I imagine folks in town will see it as persecution and sour grapes. Please put everything off until at least the day of the funeral."

Brown was silent for a moment, then he surprised the man who was scheduled to succeed him in office. "Okay, we'll shut it down until next week. Until after the funeral. But, Jimmie boy, we're going after her and the truth in this matter. It all stinks to high heaven."

Mathers ignored the last part and just replied, "Thank you, Russell. I appreciate it."

"Hey, Sam, some of us are getting together in Herb's room for some refreshment. Care to join us?" a reporter named Bill Foreman from Dallas asked.

"Thanks, Bill, but no. I'm kind of tired and gonna hit the sack. I think our work here is done for the day," Sam Blair replied with a smile. He watched a dozen or so of his competition walk away.

Blair walked to his room, where he grabbed his satchel. He had other plans for the evening. A worker at the train station had given him a tip that some of Clara's things had gone to Kansas City. He was going to be on the next train there, then back on Monday for the big funeral with time to spare.

When he arrived at the train station, he went to the Western Union window.

"I need to send a telegram to Chicago. The Herald-Examiner, attention Arthur Brisbane," Blair told the operator.

"All right, sir. What would you like it to say?"

Blair dictated the message slowly: "HEADING TO KC. STOP. PLEASE FIND TRUSTWORTHY OPERATIVE TO MEET ME THERE IN MORNING EIGHT A.M. STOP. WILL CALL FROM MUEHLEBACH HOTEL K.C. STOP. BLAIR."

"Okay, Mr. Blair, I'll send this right away."

Sam Blair smiled and handed the telegraph man a dollar bill.

TWENTY-THREE

"I'VE LIVED IN HELL TEN YEARS."

Frank Ketch knocked on the door of Georgia Hamon's suite at the Hotel Ardmore. Olive Belle answered it.

"Why, Olive Belle, how are you, young lady? We're all so sad for you and your mother. Your daddy was my best friend."

"Thank you, sir. My mother says for you to have a seat and she'll be in shortly," the girl replied.

Frank sat down and waited. But he didn't have to wait long.

"Mr. Ketch, thank you so much for coming by. I would like to go over my thoughts for my husband's funeral. I expect that you'll want to see things done in accordance with my wishes."

"Of course, Mrs. Hamon. Wouldn't have it any other way."

"Fine then. On Sunday, we'll have Jake removed from Harvey Brothers and taken over to convention hall for people to pay their respects. He'll remain there throughout the day and until about two o'clock on Monday afternoon. He'll then be taken by procession to the First Presbyterian Church for the funeral service, which will start promptly at three o'clock. Then we'll go out to Rose Hill Cemetery, where he'll be buried. Any questions?"

"None, ma'am. Whatever you need, I'm here to help. I was Jake's right hand, now I want to be yours."

Georgia didn't know whether to trust Ketch or not, but she was stuck with the man for the moment and knew to try to make the best of it. "Oh, there is one other thing, Mr. Ketch. One primary job."

"Name it."

"Make sure that a certain name is never uttered in my presence, or anywhere near me. Is that clear?"

"Perfectly. I'm at your service, Mrs. Hamon."

"Great. My brother is coming in from Wichita in a bit, and I need to get over to the train with Olive Belle."

"Would you like me to fetch him for you?"

"Oh my, no. He's family."

"I could go along. There are reporters everywhere, and I'd hate for you to have to deal with them."

"I can handle the press, Frank. You just handle your job."

Georgia stood up, and Frank took that as his cue to make a quick and quiet exit.

Clara was in El Paso. Her parents, though both in very poor health, were relieved when she made her way to their door that Thursday evening. She found out about Jake's death when she called Bob Hutchins at his office.

"Hutch, I want you to know that I'm very sorry this happened. I know none of you understand, but I am sorry."

"I know you are, Clara. But I think it's best we not talk for a while. Pressure's growing in these parts to find you and bring

190

you back on charges. County Attorney Brown is on the warpath."

"Well, I'm safe with my folks now in El Paso."

"That'll be one of the first places they'll look. I've made arrangements for you."

"Don't worry, I'll be okay here," Clara said, firmly.

"Clara, please, for once in your life take some good advice. You're not safe there. The wolves are coming to your door. You need to listen to me and do what I say, do you understand me?"

Clara paused for a moment, then she replied, "Sure, Hutch, whatever you say. I'm listening."

"Great, now you know I worked there in El Paso before I came back to work for Jake, right?"

"Yes, I remember."

"I spent some time south of the border and have some friends there who have agreed to look after you. A nice family. I'm wiring them some money, and they'll take great care of you. You can trust them."

"Who are these people?"

"Very nice people, that's who they are. Now, in a couple of hours, a man named Miguel will come to the door. He has a car, and he'll get you across the border safely."

"Okay, fine. But Hutch, I want to you to know again how sorry I am for all of this."

"I know, I know, Clara. Now, you give Miguel a thousand dollars from the money you have."

"A thousand bucks?"

"Don't worry. I'll drive down next week and give your father some more money for you, okay? You need to leave most of the money you have with him. Don't take a large amount to Mexico with you. Keep a few hundred maybe for yourself, and give the rest to your old man for safekeeping for a while. I'll be sending more to him, so you'll have a nice amount when you're able to come home."

"How long will I be down there—where am I going?"

"You are heading to Chihuahua City. This family has a big spread—a hacienda—down there. You'll have privacy. Probably have to stay there a couple of months until things settle down."

"Months?" Clara said as she started to cry.

"Get a hold of yourself. Be strong, Clara. You're gonna come out of this fine. You just need to do this right now."

"I always hated Mexico, Hutch. You know that. I don't like the people down there. I don't trust them at all. Jake liked them well enough, but I never wanted to go with him when he had business there. I can't imagine that I'll feel safe there."

"Now, Clara, this is no time for pettiness. You're gonna have to make this work. The Cabrera family, they're nice people. You won't have a care in the world. We need for all the talk about bringing you back on charges to die down. Jake, God rest his soul, wouldn't want you to be made into a public spectacle. You know that."

"Well, I don't care what Jake would want. That ship has sailed, Hutch. What am I supposed to do down there? I don't speak the language."

"I'll have Miguel take you to buy as many magazines and books as you want. You can catch up on your reading," Hutch said, rolling his eyes.

"Fine, Hutch. You just make sure I'm not stuck in that God-forsaken place for long. Please?"

Clara packed, and then she waited for Miguel with her father.

"I'll tell you one thing," her father said. "If you'd told me the truth about that rascal you worked for, I'd a killed 'im myself long ago and saved you the trouble!"

192

Clara smiled. "I know, Daddy. I'm so sorry for all of this. I didn't know what to do, so I came here."

"Sounds like you'll be with good people in Mexico. For that kind of money, you should live like a queen in no time."

"Daddy, I've lived the queen life. Don't want that anymore, I just want to be Clara Smith, again," she said as the tears really began to flow.

Mr. Smith hugged his daughter. "It's gonna be all right, honey. I promise." Her teenage brother, Jimmie, also hugged her, as did her mother. It was a tearful moment.

A few hours later, Miguel pulled up to the Smith house in El Paso in a Model T that had seen many better days. But Clara saw it as a golden chariot as she got in, and they headed for the border.

Sam Blair's train arrived at Union Station in Kansas City at 7:42 AM Saturday morning. As soon as he stepped off the train onto the platform and began walking, a man fell into step with him.

"You Blair?"

Sam looked at the man and replied, "Sure am, and your name is?"

"I'm Norris. I was told to meet you here."

"Great, Mr. Norris, you got a first name?"

"That is my first name, Mr. Blair. I'm Norris Gibson. I run a detective agency here in town. What can I do for you?"

"Well, I'll tell ya, Mr. Gibson, I'm hunting some luggage that would be waiting somewhere in this station. It was sent from Oklahoma a few days ago."

"Your luggage?"

"See, that's just the problem. It's not mine. Name on it is Clara Smith, or it may say Clara Hamon. How would one go about getting hold of it?"

"Follow me," Gibson said. He led Blair toward an office area. One door read: 'Lost Luggage.' "Wait here," he said. Sam picked up a newspaper at a nearby stand and waited as the detective disappeared into the office.

The front page of the Kansas City Star carried the story of Jake Hamon's death, including the fact that authorities were looking for a woman (unnamed in the article) in connection with the shooting. Blair was just turning to page thirteen to finish reading the piece when Gibson called over to him.

"This what you're lookin' for?" The detective was in possession of a large suitcase as well as a larger trunk.

"How the hell'd you get them so fast?"

"I got my ways, Mr. Blair. Anything else I can do for you?"

"Not at all, can I buy you breakfast?"

"No time. Gotta get to the office. Thanks. Some of the fastest money I ever made," Gibson said. Then he smiled, and they shook hands before he disappeared into the crowd in the terminal.

The reporter tipped a porter to grab the luggage and help him find a ride to the Muehlebach Hotel.

A short while later, after Blair checked into the hotel, a bellhop arrived at his eighth-floor room with the luggage. He tipped the young man and then began to sort through the contents of the suitcase and trunk. He immediately knew that he'd hit the mother lode. He arranged the most important items on the bed.

The telephone rang. Blair picked up the earphone and listened. "Yes, yes, Operator, I'll take the call." A moment later, he said, "Yes, Mr. Brisbane, the man you had meet me was very helpful."

"You get that gal's luggage?"

"Got it right here, sir. I've been looking through the material."

"Anything worth shootin'?"

"Oh my, yes, sir. It's full of surprises."

"Such as?"

"Well, first off, there are some receipts for life insurance and some calling cards with the name, 'Mrs. F. L. Hamon.'"

"F.L.? Did that Jake fellow have a different name?"

"No, sir. It appears that those initials are for a fellow named Frank Hamon. Lives in Texas."

"What the hell?"

"Well, makes sense. Folks in Oklahoma have been referring to Clara as 'Mrs. Hamon' for as long as anyone can remember. Turns out she was married, not to Jake, but to this Frank fellow."

"Ah, clever rascal."

"Yeah, well, there are also divorce papers. I haven't read through 'em yet. Sure there's a story there, though."

"Well, you read it all, and make notes. I can get you a photographer to take photos of it all. I'm sure people will be looking for all of it before long. Get it all down, you hear me, Blair?"

"Yes, sir. Loud and clear."

"This may be the biggest story of your career; don't let me down."

"You can count on me, Mr. Brisbane."

After the call, Sam went back over to the bed and picked up what appeared to be a scrapbook. It was filled with pictures and news clippings about Jake. In the back of the scrapbook, he found several typewritten pages. It was something written by Clara. Looked like an article of some kind. He read it through, and his eyes fastened on one portion of the document:

"Through no fault of my own, I've lived in hell ten years—the best years of my life. I've slaved and I've suffered, and the loneliness and the tragedy and the hopelessness of it kept tearing at my heart and nerves. They tortured me to madness."

Blair put the pages back in place and sat down. Then he noticed a book of some kind underneath some other papers. He reached for it and instantly realized that he was in possession of the kind of things most reporters only dream about. He had the personal diary of Clara Smith Hamon.

He grabbed his handkerchief and mopped his sweaty brow, as his hands trembled.

It didn't take Clara but a few hours to realize that she was in a safe place, once she arrived in Chihuahua City. The Cabrera family—a father, mother, and four young children—smiled at her and helped her carry her luggage into the house.

No one in the family spoke a single word of English, and Clara's Spanish was limited to less than a dozen phrases. But they quickly fell into a kind of sign language for communication and kept their distance.

She settled in and was surprised at how soon she felt at home. For the first few days, Clara took her meals in her large and comfortable room. She also got the rest she needed. Soon, however, she was sitting at the family table three times a day.

There was a telephone in the house, but it seldom rang. The spacious house sat on several acres on the outskirts of the city. It was a beautiful spot. There were flowers, fruit trees, and a view of mountains in the distance. From the first night, she was captivated by the brightness of the stars in the sky, far brighter, she thought, than anything she'd seen in Oklahoma. Or maybe it was that she had just stopped noticing such things.

All that weekend, every inbound train brought more visitors to Ardmore. A vast number of reporters, politicians, business leaders, and assorted curiosity-seekers quickly filled every available hotel room. Some local citizens positioned family members at the train station to invite travelers to stay with them—for a price, of course. And that price would always include the most delicious home-cooked meals, or so the pitch went.

Sam Blair was back on a train early on Sunday and made it to Ardmore late that night. He had spent the trip making notes about the materials. Particularly, the diary. He was glad to have kept his room at the Hotel Ardmore.

There was a telegram from Brisbane waiting for him when he went to the front desk to get his key. It said that a photographer was on the way from Chicago, but he wouldn't arrive until the morning. That was the good news. The bad news was that because there were no rooms available, Blair would have a bunkmate for the next couple of days.

Sam shrugged and yawned. He was too tired to be upset by anything. In fact, he was sound asleep thirty seconds after his head hit the pillow.

Clara's luggage was right next to the bed.

Georgia was insistent about using the convention hall for the viewing and visitation because she had good memories about the place from the night Olive Belle had played her violin there earlier in the year. But it turned out to be a very practical decision. More than 25,000 people filed through on Sunday. She had her husband dressed in a new dark blue vested suit. Several remarked to her how handsome he looked in it.

"Jake bought this suit special for Mr. Harding's inauguration next March," she told several of the people who filed by. She always added, "Of course, by then, we would have moved to Washington so Jake could help the new president as part of the Cabinet."

When asked if the president-elect was coming to town for the funeral, she pulled out a telegram—well worn by Monday afternoon—from Harding. "He's on the S. S. Pastores on his way to Jamaica, but he sent his regrets and that beautiful flower arrangement over yonder," she said, pointing to a massive display about five feet from Jake's casket.

Then, on Monday afternoon, precisely as Georgia had planned, there was a procession over to the First Presbyterian Church. Every seat was filled but for 200 reserved for the family, by the time Jake's body arrived. As the casket was brought in, the church organist played Beethoven's Funeral March. The choir then sang "Home of the Soul," a song chosen by Mrs. Hamon.

Dr. J. T. Irwin and Dr. J. E. LaGrone, both from Lawton, helped Dr. Charles C. Weith, pastor of First Presbyterian Church of Ardmore, with the service. There was much talk about Hamon's generosity.

During the funeral sermon, Pastor Weith began, "My friends, we are today face-to-face with mystery. What is this great change we call death?" His twenty-minute message answered that question from the Bible.

When the service at the church was finished, a smaller procession, just family and very close friends, journeyed with the casket out to the cemetery on the south edge of town, where Jake was buried as the sun set in the Oklahoma sky.

TWENTY-FOUR

"...WHAT HAPPENED TO THAT GUN?"

Outgoing County Attorney Russell Brown, true to his word, wasted no time the day after Jake's funeral. He issued a warrant for the arrest of Clara on the charge of murder. He also charged her with violation of the Mann Act, even though such a charge was usually made against a man for taking a woman across state lines "for immoral purposes."

"Boys, this case is getting hot. But I've got no more news for you at the moment," Brown said to the handful of reporters, including Sam Blair, he had invited into his office that morning.

"Is Sheriff Garrett on Clara's trail?" Blair asked.

"You'll have to get information about that from Buck."

"Yes, well, the sheriff doesn't seem to be anywhere around town. His deputy is missing, too," another reporter remarked.

Brown smiled and shrugged. "Well, I can't help you on that one."

"Mr. Brown, there are some round these parts who suggest you have a political reason for turning Hamon's death into a salacious murder story. After all, Jake Hamon's influence and money were certainly part of the big Republican sweep a few weeks ago," Blair continued.

Brown looked at the reporter. "If you want to talk about politics, I think you fellas need to take a good long look at the fact that the young lady who was at Hamon's side for the past several years is not among the mourners here in town. I think you'll find, if you're willin' to dig for it, that the real political story is how the friends and cronies of Mr. Hamon have hidden her away somewhere, while spreading that ridiculous story about him shooting himself. This whole thing stinks like a pile of steaming shit! Now, I'll let you know when I have something else to say. So let me get back to work. Last one out, close my door, please," he said, adding a dismissive wave of his right hand.

The reporters filed out. When the door was closed, Brown nearly shouted into the mouthpiece of his telephone, "Get me Frank Ketch." In a moment, Ketch was on the line.

"Mr. Ketch? This is County Attorney Brown. Now, I'm counting on your cooperation during this investigation."

"How does 'go to hell' sound? That cooperation enough?"

"Sorry you feel that way, Frank. We can do this the easy way or the hard way, that's up to you. I need you to deliver the gun that shot Hamon, along with his clothing from that night, to my office immediately."

"I don't have either, so tough luck, you horse's ass."

"Who would have these things?"

"Your guess is good as mine. Good day," Ketch said as he hung up on him.

202

Brown fumed for a moment. Then he shouted for his assistant, a young man named Will. The assistant came into the office.

"Head over to Dr. Hardy's hospital and find out what happened to Jake Hamon's clothes the night he staggered into the place. If they're there, bring them back here. Be quick about it, kid," he barked.

For his part, Frank Ketch scratched his head and mumbled, "I wonder what happened to that gun?"

Georgia woke up early the morning after the funeral. She ordered a light breakfast to be sent up for her and Olive Belle, along with the morning newspaper. The food and news arrived about twenty minutes later.

Mrs. Hamon buttered her toast and took a bite, washing it down with a gulp of black coffee. She then picked up the newspaper and read the coverage of Jake's funeral. She made her way to page four and saw an editorial titled, "Not a Revolt—'Tis a Revolution." The column was about the vacancy left behind because of Jake's demise.

Georgia smiled as she read the piece, because she had some thoughts of her own. In fact, even before Jake's body was in the ground, she had swapped several telegrams with Florence Harding. Along with condolences and apologies coming from her cousin for not attending the funeral, they also discussed Jake's empty seat on the Republican National Committee.

Georgia expected a new telegram from Mrs. Harding that very morning, one that would have great bearing on the subject of the editorial in the newspaper. The assumption of the article was that the post would go to one of Jake's former political opponents.

That's why Georgia laughed out loud when she read, "...political patronage will now go to the men who fought Jake Hamon and not to the men who supported him. Down Eros— up Mars. The revolution is complete."

Then she smiled and whispered, "Jake's job is not even going to go to a man."

Shortly after ten o'clock, Olive Belle finally came into her room in their suite.

"Mommy, that man is here again."

"What man, dear?" Georgia asked while she yawned and stretched and tried to gather her wits.

"The one who worked for Daddy, the man who was here the other day."

"Oh, you mean Mr. Ketch."

"Yes, that's the man."

"Okay now, dear, you go back and tell him to wait a spell. I'll be out shortly."

"Yes, ma'am," the girl said.

Georgia, adorned in an ornate dressing gown, entered the sitting room a few minutes later.

"Mornin', ma'am," Ketch said, as he tipped and then removed his cowboy hat.

Mrs. Hamon nodded at him and said simply, "Mr. Ketch."

"I thought I'd go over a few things with you now that the funeral is past. If this is a bad time, I can come back," Ketch began.

"Not at all. I'm quite interested in whatever you have to say."

Frank cleared his throat, then said, "Well, um, I've been pretty much running the business side of things for a spell now.

Ever since Jake got involved with politics. I was hoping you'd let me look after things for you, now."

"Well, Mr. Ketch …"

"I wouldn't mind if you called me Frank, Mrs. Hamon."

"Fine, Frank, well, as I see it, you know Jake's dealings better than anyone, and folks round here tell me you're a fair and honest man. So I'm fine with this. But I intend to ask a lot of questions, and I expect a lot of answers. Do you have a copy of Jake's will?"

"Sorry, ma'am. To the best of my knowledge, he didn't have one."

Buck Garrett and Bud Ballew arrived at the Texas and Pacific rail station in Fort Worth around noon. Operating on a hunch, helped by the odd rumor or two, they visited the downtown hotels asking if a lady matching Clara's description had been around. The fourth establishment they visited was the Westbrook.

"Yes, that's her," the desk clerk said when shown Clara's photograph. "She was here, oh let's see, must've been a week ago. Just one night, I think."

"She make any calls?" Garrett asked.

The clerk peeked through a door near the front desk and said, "Mrs. Greer, can you come out here for a moment?" Fannie Greer was a telephone operator.

"These men are here looking for a lady who stayed here about a week ago. She was by herself." They showed the operator her picture.

"Oh, yes, I remember."

"Did she make any telephone calls that you recall?" Garrett asked.

"Yes, I think I remember her wanting to reach the aviation field in Dallas," Mrs. Greer replied.

It was a solid lead, and the duo made their way to Dallas.

"Now, Frank, before you go, I want you to know something I'm planning to do," Georgia said as their conversation that morning drew to an end.

Frank Ketch took a last sip of coffee and placed the cup and saucer on the table. "And what would that be, ma'am?"

"Well, as all those people filed by to see Jake, so many powerful people, I realized how important a man he had come to be. Not just round these parts, but to the country."

"He was indeed," Ketch said.

"I think the best way to honor my late husband's memory would be for me to take his place as the chairman of Oklahoma Republicans and on the National Committee. I already sent a telegram to my cousin, Florence Harding. I'm expecting a wire from her this morning containing the endorsement of the President-elect."

Frank Ketch was at a loss for words. This was beyond unexpected. It was incredible. And he immediately thought that it was a very bad idea. Ketch instinctively knew that the best way to protect Jake Hamon's memory was to let things die down. He knew that there were many skeletons in his former boss's closet.

"That's quite an idea, Mrs. Hamon," was all he could manage to say. He cleared his throat.

"Yes, it is, Frank, and I expect that as you take care of my late husband's affairs, you'll help me honor his name in this way."

"Of course, Mrs. Hamon. Of course." Frank wondered if she had noticed the blood draining from his face.

"Now, I want you to gather some of the reporters who are still around town. I know they haven't all gone home yet. Get them together in a room somewhere downstairs in this here hotel. I will announce this to them, myself, today."

Ketch thought fast. Then he said, "I don't see that there's a big hurry about this, ma'am. Why not wait to hear back from Mrs. Harding? I think it'd be bigger news if you had that endorsement to share."

"I suppose," she said. "But I want to reach the reporters who may be leaving town."

"Let me check and see who's around and who's staying, okay?"

"Fine, but I want to make this announcement soon, before others start to line up for the job."

"I imagine there were men lining up to step in for Jake before he breathed his last, ma'am. That's the nature of politics. It's Tuesday now. What's say we plan for your big announcement on Thursday, just before noon. How's that sound?"

"That'd be wonderful, Frank. And I want you right there with me, too."

He agreed and picked up his hat as he prepared to leave the room. He put the hat on then tipped it her way and said, "Ma'am."

Sam Blair spent most of the morning that Tuesday writing an article about Clara's diary. It was filled with tidbits and teasers and sure to create a stir. The photographer Brisbane had sent, an older man named Marvin Tucker, had painstakingly captured every page, from every angle, on film. And Blair had been making copious notes.

"This is the story that's gonna make us famous, Mr. Tucker," he boasted. "When Old Man Hearst sees what we have here, he'll have the thing on the front page of every one of his papers for a week!"

He wired the piece—nearly 2,000 words—back to Brisbane in Chicago by noon. Brisbane wired back that his byline would indeed be in all the Hearst papers that next morning.

President-elect Warren Harding found it hard to disagree with his wife. "Of course, dear," he said to Florence. "I'll send it off. You write it, and Jess will take it down to the radio room."

"Thank you, Warren. Georgia, that poor dear, has been through hell, and this will bring a smile to her face. If we couldn't be at the funeral, this will be some consolation. And she'll make a good member of the Republican National Committee. My cousin will be loyal as a puppy dog."

A few minutes later, the telegraph operator was transmitting a communication to Mrs. Jake Hamon in Ardmore, Oklahoma. It said, in part: "YOU HAVE MY STRONGEST RECOMMENDATION TO SUCCEED YOUR HUSBAND AS A MEMBER OF THE REPUBLICAN NATIONAL COMMITTEE. SIGNED, WARREN G. HARDING, PRESIDENT-ELECT OF THE UNITED STATES."

TWENTY-FIVE

"CLARA'S DIARY"

Russell Brown felt conspicuous and uncomfortable when he walked into an Ardmore beauty parlor that morning. The smell of cigarette smoke, combined with various cosmetic fragrances, just about knocked him over as he took off his hat and said, "Mornin', ladies," to several women.

"I'm looking for Miss Bertha Lipscomb," he said.

The women looked at each other and then over to one young beautician. It was Bertha, of course. "I'm Bertha. You lookin' for a shampoo or just a shave?" she asked mockingly. Everybody laughed, including the attorney.

"There some place we can talk, young lady?"

"Sure, mister, follow me." They walked through a curtain covering a doorway and into a small room.

"I'm Russell Brown, the Carter County Attorney."

"I know who you are. I saw your picture in the newspaper. I even voted for you a few weeks ago. Guess I should have voted a few more times," Bertha said as she smiled. She was chewing a piece of gum with a vengeance.

"Well, word has it that a gal named Clara is one of your customers."

"I know several ladies by that name, mister. You gotta be a little more pacific," she said.

"I think you mean, 'specific,' Miss Lipscomb."

"Bertha's my name, Mr. Brown. Thanks for the English lesson," she said scornfully.

"Well, um, I'm referring to Clara Smith, you may know her as Clara Hamon."

"Indeed I do, 'cause that's her name."

"Have you seen this Clara lately?"

"Can't say as I have. Probably been a couple of weeks. I imagine that with all that's gone on, she flew the coop," Bertha said as she cracked her gum and smiled coyly.

"Then you know why I'm here. I'm trying to get to the truth. There are many people who think Clara shot Mr. Hamon. They don't believe that the man shot himself in the way that's been reported."

Bertha Lipscomb looked over at the attorney as if trying to decide whether or not to talk honestly with him. Finally, she said, "Well, I can tell you this. If she did shoot the bastard, he had it comin'!"

"What do you mean?"

"The man treated her like a slave. She devoted her life to him, and then, just when he makes it to the big time, he tells her that it's over and throws her aside like yesterday's garbage. That's what I mean."

"I understand. Did Clara ever talk about hurting the man?"

"Mister, this is a beauty parlor. Women talk about all sorts of things in here. We're like priests," she said with a smile, "and we take confessions."

"How about Clara? She ever confess?"

"All I will say is this, mister. She was in here one day a while back, and her purse was open next to her. I saw a gun, and she saw that I saw, ya know?"

"Go on."

"So, I asks her, 'What's with the fancy pistol, Clara, gonna shoot someone?' You know, I said it kinda funny like," Bertha said. "But thing is, she didn't laugh. And she always laughs at my funny things. I think that's why she keeps coming back."

"She say anything after that?"

"Just that one day she was going to show Jake Hamon what she would do."

That afternoon, a hotel worker knocked on the door of Mrs. Hamon's hotel room. "Telegram," the man said. Georgia opened the door, took the telegram, and tipped the messenger with a quarter. She opened the envelope:

"FROM CHARLES WILLIS CHICAGO. STOP. ROBBERS BROKE IN AND SEIZED YOUR MAIL AND OTHER PAPERS. STOP. CALL ME IMMEDIATELY. STOP."

Mr. Willis was the landlord of the building where she and her children lived in a spacious and luxurious six-room apartment. The telegram shook her up, but a moment later, she called down to the operator and said she wanted to place a call to Chicago. "It's an emergency!" she added.

"There were four of them," she heard Mr. Willis say, though their connection was weak.

She shouted into the mouthpiece, "What were they looking for?"

"One of them said, 'We want Mrs. Hamon's letters and papers, where are they?' They had badges, but I'm sure they weren't with the police. I'd seen one of them around the neighborhood for a few days. I think he was spying the place out."

"What did they take?"

"Everything they could find. They were gone in fifteen minutes. Then I called the police."

"Thank you, Mr. Willis. I will be back in Chicago this coming weekend. I have a few things to take care of here, first."

"Want me to have someone clean up your apartment?"

"Yes, Mr. Willis, that would be lovely."

Clara was falling into a routine in Mexico. She slept gloriously late. She was served breakfast each morning by household servants. Usually it consisted of eggs—they were fresh, as the rooster crowing far too early each morning reminded her. Then there was fresh fruit and plenty of coffee. She hadn't had a drink of gin for several days and found herself feeling remarkably good. So she decided to keep on the wagon for a while as she cleared her head.

Newspapers were brought to her. They were from El Paso. By the time they reached her, they were at least a day old, but it didn't bother her. She was enjoying her new pace.

Though she didn't have the diary with her, she decided to write every day while she was there. She began to ponder how to use her story for good ends. Many of the movie and story magazines she loved to read contained tales that bore some resemblance to her real life. Maybe, she thought, she could one day write a book? Or better, maybe they'd make a movie about her someday? One that young girls could watch and learn from. It was the birth of a vision, just an idea at first, but she had a feeling that one day her idea might become the key to a secure future—without having to depend on some man to take care of her.

The news broke the next morning. Sam Blair's first mention of "Clara's Diary," was splashed on the front pages of Hearst newspapers from San Francisco to New York.

"Clara Smith Hamon, the girl accused of shooting Jake Hamon, Republican National Committeeman from Oklahoma, and who is being sought on the Mexican border, left a remarkable document warning other girls of the perils into which she fell and telling of her 'fight with the demon.' Her diary paints one of the strongest morals for girls ever published. Universal Service has secured the right to publish this remarkable document from the Chicago Herald and Examiner, which holds the copyright."

The first published installment covered Clara's diary entries from March 6, 1920 through the end of May. Her words captured the attention of the nation.

> *"Although I have dealt with a cunning, tricky devil—when my ship of happiness goes down, it will go down with colors flying. Before another day passes and ere my life is taken, I want to leave this word of warning to any other girl or woman who may be ready to embark upon the sea of companionship with a man. Let my poor, sad, broken heart—crushed hopes and blighted life—be a warning. Know your man when you give him your soul..."*
>
> *"The world may ask why I have never quit. I have given my ALL—ten of the choicest years of my life—my youth, health, and beauty. What would I have to gain now if I quit? No. I shall keep on until I am killed or die, hanging on to the vague hope that, some day, he may see the light and give me a new start in life."*

Georgia Hamon took a sip of coffee from the china cup and put it down on the table with a trembling hand as she listened. The caller, a dear friend from Chicago named Mildred Feeny, was breaking the news to her about the news that had already broken in the Windy City.

"I tell you, Georgia dear, it's just awful that they would print something like this. I feel so bad for you," Feeny said.

"Well, I'm grateful for your call, Millie," Georgia replied. Actually, she didn't know whether to be grateful or resentful. Mildred loved gossip, and Georgia was sure that her friend was enjoying every moment of the conversation. "Now read that part again to me, okay? The one you just read."

Mildred read the passage:

"I swear here before the all-knowing God that I would never have become his sweetheart if he had not told me—again and again—that he was going to get his divorce anyway, and he promised faithfully to marry me."

Georgia lapsed into silence for a lingering moment and then abruptly said, "Millie, I must go. I will be back in Chicago soon. Please save those newspapers for me, would you, dear?"

"Of course, Georgia. We miss you, and please know that all your friends up this way love you," Feeny replied.

After she finished talking to Mildred, Georgia called the operator. "Please connect me with Mr. Frank Ketch at his business office."

Twenty minutes later, Ketch was at the door of Georgia's suite. Olive let him in, and he went to a chair across from Georgia, who was lounging on a sofa with a distant look in her eyes.

"Did you know anything about this, Frank? Do you know who this Blair fellow is?"

"I've seen him around town. He gave Russell Brown a bit of trouble the other day in his office."

"What's his beef? What does he want?"

"Well, he's from Chicago, so ..."

"He may be from Chicago, but I've never heard of him. I don't read Hearst's rag. I read the Tribune, like most other intelligent people. It's a good Republican paper."

"I see," Ketch replied. "Well, I suppose the story will make it to these parts soon enough. But as of now, I haven't heard a thing from anyone." Ketch was lying. He'd been on the telephone for the better part of two hours prior to Georgia's call. He wasn't sure why he lied, but felt it better to keep Mrs. Hamon in the dark.

"Mr. Ketch," she said with a fierce look as she sat up, "I can tell you that none of this changes my mind about what I'm gonna do today. I got Mr. Harding's telegram, and I want you to make sure reporters are downstairs at two o'clock today. Is that Mr. Blair in town still, or did he hightail it back to Chicago?"

"I think he's still around. Staying here in the hotel, I believe."

"Well, Mr. Ketch, you make sure that snake of a man is front and center when I make my big announcement today."

"Yes, ma'am. Of course."

Because there were no Hearst newspapers for better than a hundred miles, Arthur Brisbane and Sam Blair ensured that hundreds of copies of that morning's Chicago Herald-Examiner were sent to Ardmore. They arrived on a train at just after one o'clock that afternoon, just in time for reporters to read the article before the now eagerly awaited press meeting with Georgia Hamon in the ballroom of the Hotel Ardmore.

Blair was a star.

He joined about thirty-five other reporters and about a hundred other local citizens and curiosity-seekers in the ballroom about five minutes before Mrs. Hamon was scheduled to appear.

"Hey, Sam, quite a scoop," said one older reporter who had never before seemed to be able to remember Blair's name.

"Thanks," was all Sam could manage in reply. He was overwhelmed by the newfound attention. But he was determined to leverage it into something even bigger. The diary, he thought, would begin to not only arouse curiosity about Clara, but even more, it would begin to build sympathy. He was determined to find Clara and champion her cause. He just didn't know where to start.

TWENTY-SIX

"...PUBLISHED ACCOUNTS OF IMMORAL RUMORS."

Mrs. Hamon showed up about five minutes late, but she made a grand entrance on the arm of Frank Ketch through the doorway in the back of the room. They walked through the crowd and toward a podium in the front of the room.

Ketch spoke first. "Hello, ladies and gentlemen. For those of you who don't know me, my name is Frank Ketch. I had the privilege of running the business affairs for the late Jake L. Hamon. He was also my dear friend. I have been asked by Mrs. Hamon to continue to look after things, which I will gladly do. Mrs. Hamon is a wonderful woman who has suffered a terrible loss. But she is determined to honor her husband's name and memory in a very specific way. Mrs. Hamon?"

Georgia came to the podium. "Thank you, Mr. Ketch. I appreciate your kind words and, of course, all of your help. I know that Mr. Hamon is looking down from above and smiling on this moment."

"Or maybe from below," one reporter cracked in the earshot of those around him. There was some instant laughter, which brought an angry stare from the widow at the podium.

"I am not sure what was so funny about that, but I want to talk to you today about my immediate plans. I will be returning to Chicago in a few days to get my things there in order, then I will be coming back to Ardmore. My plan is to buy a home here and become an active part of this community that my husband loved so much. Mr. Ketch is going to help me with these matters."

Reporters made a few notes, but began to look at each other with eyes that suggested they wondered why the big meeting just to talk about a widow's travel plans. That all changed with what Georgia said next.

Garrett placed a call to Seth B. Orndork, Sheriff of El Paso County, Texas. "This is Sheriff Buck Garrett from Carter County up in Oklahoma. Can you hear me all right, sir?"

"Yes Mr. Garrett, I hear you just fine. What can I do for you?" Orndorf replied.

"Well, Sheriff, I know you probably have the notice about being on the lookout for a gal named Clara Smith Hamon."

"Yes, yes. We haven't heard or seen anything," Orndorf said.

"That's fine, Sheriff, but the reason I was calling you is that this gal's parents reside right there in El Paso."

"You want me to go out to their place?"

"I'll tell you, Sheriff, if it'd be all right with you, I'd like for me and my deputy to talk with them. I was calling to clear that with you. Would that be okay?"

"Fine by me, Mr. Garrett. Fine by me."

"Great. Thanks. We're heading out in the morning. We'll come by your office when we hit town."

"Now for the real reason I called this here meeting," Georgia Hamon said. Several flashbulbs went off. "I was at my late husband's side early this year when we went from town to town meeting the good folks of Oklahoma during the race for the chairmanship of the state Republican Party. I saw how much everyone loved my husband. He was clearly the right man to lead the party. That was proven when Mr. Harding was elected a few weeks ago. As some of you may know, but others may not, Mrs. Florence Harding is my cousin. My late husband and I were looking forward to moving to Washington to help Warren." Her use of Harding's first name in such a casual way raised several eyebrows in the audience.

Georgia continued, "I want to devote the rest of my life to finishing the job Jake Hamon started. And I want to begin by letting you know that I'd be honored, and it would be an honor to the name of my late husband, to fill the office he loved so much by taking his place as a member of the Republican National Committee."

There were some murmurs from the back of the room, while the reporters wrote feverishly.

"I have here a telegram from the President-elect of the United States, which says, 'I EXPECT AND HOPE THAT MRS. HAMON WILL BE ELECTED AS THE MEMBER OF THE NATIONAL COMMITTEE FROM OKLAHOMA.'"

She said a few other things and then asked if anyone had a question. She looked directly at Sam Blair as if daring him to speak. He didn't—yet.

"Mrs. Hamon, Slim Murphy for the New York Journal. When did you receive the telegram from Mr. Harding, and can my photographer take a shot of it?"

"Yes, certainly. I received it late yesterday. I'll make it available to your photographer on the condition that you make the picture available to every other newspaper represented in this room," she replied with a smile.

There was some laughter and a smattering of applause.

"Yes, ma'am," Mr. Murphy replied.

"Sam Blair from the Chicago Herald-Examiner."

"Why, yes, Mr. Blair, I've heard about you."

Blair ignored the tease and plunged into his question. "Do have any comment on reports that your husband did not actually shoot himself but was instead shot by a lady named Clara?"

The room was instantly silent except for a lonely cricket hiding behind the baseboard on one of the walls. Georgia thought for a moment and then replied. "Mr. Blair, I was at Jake's bedside in the hospital, and he told me what happened. He shot himself by accident. Of course, my late husband had many enemies, apparently some who want to hurt him even after he is resting in the Oklahoma ground. So I'm not surprised that these enemies would try to concoct some salacious story."

"Well, apparently, some think there is more to the story than rumors. What do you make of the Carter County Attorney and the sheriff searching for this lady named Clara? If she is found and brought back and prosecuted, what would you think then?"

Georgia replied, "Well, if this woman is brought back to Ardmore, I'd be dead set against her prosecution, because there is no truth to the story that she was in any way connected to my late husband, other than as one of his stenographers."

222

"Mrs. Hamon, I'm Bill Monkton, with the Los Angeles Times."

"Good afternoon, Mr. Monkton," Georgia replied, clearly relieved to be finished with Sam Blair.

Monkton asked, "What would you say to others who might aspire to the same office you are seeking?"

"Mr. Monkton, I would regard it as greater than any marble monument that the State of Oklahoma could erect to my husband's memory. It would enable me to carry on his work and to do the things that I know he wanted to be done."

There was one other question. It came from a woman reporter, one of two in the audience. "Mrs. Hamon, I'm Betty Henderson and I'm with Woman's Way Magazine."

"Oh yes, I've read your magazine many times."

"Thank you very much. My question has to do with all this talk about how this Clara woman had a diary and how parts of it are being published in newspapers."

Georgia was very disappointed to be getting another such question, and the fact that it was coming from a woman hurt even more. "Well, um, I don't know anything about a supposed diary, but I do think that the young girls of this country are not well served by published accounts of immoral rumors."

With that, Mrs. Hamon left the platform. Frank Ketch caught up with her as she forced a pathway through the reporters and headed to the back door.

John Gorman looked at the beautiful Southern California sky as he sliced off the tip of his perfectly soft-boiled egg. He tore a piece of toast into strips and dunked one of the pieces into the egg. He pulled the yolk-covered bread out and devoured the entire strip in one bite. He took a swig of orange juice, then a sip of coffee before unfolding the morning edition of the Los Angeles Examiner. He saw the mention of Clara's diary and read the entire article. Meanwhile, his egg and the accompanying toast grew cold from neglect.

"Kansas City, Dec. 2. — Herewith is presented the absorbing diary of Mrs. Clara Smith Hamon, reflecting the heartaches, which preceded her slaying of Jake L. Hamon. The diary left behind by her in a trunk at Kansas City was found by Chicago Herald-Examiner reporters, who have, incidentally, found most of the facts thus far developed in the murder mystery surrounding the foremost political figure of Oklahoma."

Leaving his breakfast behind, he went into the house and to the telephone in the living room. He placed a call to his office. "Stella, fetch Mark for me, please."

"Right away, Mr. Gorman."

John L. Gorman was the founder and president of the motion picture production company bearing his name: GORMAN PICTURES. He was semi-successful in the business. His most popular film had been released a few years earlier. It was called "Corruption," and starred Helen Martin. Gorman was always on the lookout for a good story.

"Mark, have you read the Examiner this morning?"

"No, sir. Sorry, I haven't."

"Well, grab a copy. When I get in, we're gonna talk about this gal named Clara. Read all about it on page one."

"Pastor? Mrs. Hamon is here to see you," Alice Woodworth said. She was secretary at Ardmore's First Presbyterian Church.

"Any idea what she wants?" asked Dr. Charles Weith.

"No, sir. She probably wants to say thank you again for your work and words at Mr. Hamon's funeral the other day."

"All right, show her in."

Georgia Hamon, dressed elegantly, walked into the office.

"Mrs. Hamon, you're still in my prayers. I hope everything at the funeral was done according to your wishes. How are you holding up?"

"About as good as can be expected, Pastor."

"How can I help you today?"

Georgia opened her purse and pulled out a piece of folded paper. The minister recognized it immediately as something cut or torn from a newspaper.

"Are you aware of some of the stories being published in some cities in the country?"

"Ma'am?"

"Well, it hasn't hit the Oklahoma City or Ardmore papers yet, but there are some other big city papers sending copies to their representatives—those still hanging around and sniffing around for some kind of sordid story."

"Sorry, Mrs. Hamon. I still don't follow."

She unfolded the page in her hand and handed it to Pastor Weith. It was from the front page of the Kansas City Post. He put his reading glasses on and scanned the page. The widow sitting across from him saw his eyes widen as he grasped what he was reading.

"This is terrible!" he exclaimed.

"Yes, it is. I don't believe a word of it, Pastor. It's all a lie."

The minister had a sense in his gut that it wasn't a lie, but he knew he couldn't express that sentiment to Georgia.

"I'm very sorry you have to see things like this, Mrs. Hamon. It's hard enough to grieve, but this—this is uncalled for."

"I need your help, Dr. Weith."

"My help? How? What? Of course, I'm at your service."

"Surely you must have some minister friends in Kansas City, fellow pastors who may be able to talk to someone at that infernal newspaper."

Dr. Weith looked over the top of his glasses. "Um, well, yes—I imagine I do. But I don't know what—"

Georgia raised her gloved hand and interrupted. "Now, I know this isn't your bailiwick, Pastor, but I don't know who to turn to. Mr. Ketch says he can't help. Don't know how much I trust him, anyway. Can't you try to talk to someone?"

"I guess so. You know, I grew up in Kansas. Went to college in Lawrence, before I went out to Princeton Seminary."

"Of course, I knew that, Pastor. That's why my late husband liked you." She smiled.

"I was a few years ahead of Jake, back then. But we did enjoy swapping stories about the old days back home," he said. Then a look of momentary enlightenment came to his face, as if a light had come on—there was the flash of a thought. "Come to think of it," he said, "I went to school with a guy who is, I think, an editor at a newspaper in Kansas City."

"At the Post?"

"I'm not sure. Maybe. Let me look into this, all right?"

"Certainly, Pastor. And thank you so much for your kindness." She paused a moment, then added, "And your discretion."

"Of course, Mrs. Hamon. Of course."

TWENTY-SEVEN

"...IT WAS CLARA WHO BUILT JAKE'S EMPIRE."

The next day, Sam Blair packed his satchel and headed for El Paso, Texas. He was determined to be the one to find the famous female fugitive. He had learned about Clara's parents living in the city on the Mexican border.

Meanwhile, he filed daily installments from Clara's diary, along with other items of interest about the emerging case. Whether he intended it or not, Blair began to notice that his dispatches were having an impact on public opinion. More and more, it seemed that while sympathy grew for the mysterious missing woman, people began to sour on the image Jake's family and friends had tried to maintain.

An hour after he hit the streets of El Paso, he located the home of James and Margaret Smith. It was a short walk from the train station. As he came near the small home, he noticed two men leaving through the front door. The men tipped their hats to an old man and walked briskly down the sidewalk the other way. Blair recognized the men from Ardmore—Sheriff Buck Garrett and Deputy Bud Ballew.

Sam waited for the men to disappear around a corner in the distance, then he walked up onto the front porch and knocked on the door. A young man answered.

"Hi there, my name is Sam Blair, and I'm a reporter with the Chicago Herald-Examiner. Are you Jimmie Smith?"

"Yep, why do you want to know?"

"Well, I'm here about your sister."

"Which one?" the young man said smartly.

"Clara. Is she here?"

"Nope. Haven't seen her in a while."

"Are your parents at home?"

Jimmie opened the door as a gesture of invitation. Sam walked in and saw an old man and his slightly younger wife sitting in a room off to the left. He introduced himself.

"Don't know where Clara is. That's the same thing I said to the lawmen who were just here. Don't know anything else."

"I understand, Mr. Smith. But I want you to know that I am looking for her for different reasons than the sheriff."

"What do you mean, Mr. Blair?" Mrs. Smith asked.

"Well, I believe Clara had every good reason to defend herself against Jake Hamon. Whatever she did, she did to protect herself."

The elderly duo looked at Blair for a moment. Then Mrs. Smith said to her son, "Now, Jimmie, you go get this nice man a glass of that lemonade I made a while ago."

Blair smiled. The old man picked up a pipe and lit it. The reporter pulled out a cigarette.

"How the hell are ya, Chuck? Oh, sorry. You're a man of the cloth. It's been a long time," the man nearly shouted into the mouthpiece of the telephone on his desk. His name was Burris Jenkins, and he was the editor of the Kansas City Post. Pastor Weith had been right about his college friend being in the newspaper business in Kansas City. And he saw the fact that the man was editor at the very paper he and Georgia Hamon had discussed to be providential, since he didn't believe in luck.

"I'm doing very well, Burris."

"Let's see, last I heard you were preaching somewhere in Oklahoma."

"That's right. I've got a fine church in Ardmore."

"Ardmore? Ardmore," the editor said the words, while the pastor waited for his old friend to make the connection. "Ah, yes, that oil man who was shot by his girlfriend."

"Well, I don't know about that, but that oilman was a member of my congregation."

"Oh, I didn't know. It still pretty busy with the story out your way?"

"Yes, it is. And part of it is that something from your fine publication has made its way here."

"Oh, now I understand, you old hound dog. You're calling about that diary story."

"Yes, I am. You see, I conducted the funeral for Jake Hamon, and his widow came to see me a bit ago. She showed me the article in your paper. I thought I'd call you to intercede on her behalf. She is heartbroken over this, on top of her grief for her dead husband."

"Well, I'm truly sorry for her loss, Chuck, but news is news. Besides, I work for Mr. Hearst, and he is pushing this story."

"Burris, this kind of thing undermines the morals of our country. What about the young girls who might read it?"

"Now, you see, my old friend, that's where we part company. It's the 1920s. We're in the modern age now. Hell, the world just got over the biggest war in history. People need to blow off a little steam."

"Do you go to church up that way, Burris?"

"Um, no, I don't. Used to. But not anymore. No time for it. And frankly, no use for it."

"Sorry to hear that. I guess I've wasted your time and mine. Nice talking to you."

"Hey, hey, Chuck. Don't get mad. I'd like to help you if I could. But I can't. I got two daughters, so I get what you're saying. But this story has legs, and it's gonna walk around a while—maybe even run some."

"I hear you loud and clear. Have a great day, Burris," Weith said as he ended the call abruptly.

Having struck out at the Smith's house, Buck and Bud were on the next train out of town by the time Sam Blair was into his second glass of lemonade.

"I think they know exactly where she is," Bud said.

"You're probably right, but not much we can do about it. Sheriff Orndorf will get word to us if she shows up. Meantime, we'll get home and try to talk that jackass Russell Brown out of prosecuting the girl. You remember how Jake treated her at times. Clara worshipped the ground he walked on, but he just kicked dust in her face when push came to shove," Garrett reflected.

"Well then, it's probably for the best that she stay away for a good while."

"Hell, if she knows what's good for her, she should stay away from Ardmore forever."

"She from El Paso?"

"No. The Smiths lived over at Lawton. That's where she grew up, and that's where she met Jake Hamon. She was just seventeen, I think. Worked as a clerk in a store. But by the time Jake set up shop in Ardmore they were as thick as thieves. I tell you something, Bud. Lots of oil people will tell you that it was Clara who built Jake's empire. She was the brains of the thing."

"Then she probably felt like she deserved more than a few thousand bucks and a fur coat."

"Jake made a big mistake with that girl. She was a keeper. That widow woman is just trying to climb on top of Jake's body for her own glory. She didn't love him as a husband—at least she hadn't for years. Jake once told me that he asked her twenty times for a divorce, but she wouldn't budge."

"Religion?"

"Probably part of it. The rest was pure spite and greed."

Sam Blair spent the better part of four hours with the Smith family that day. He could sense that they liked him. They certainly liked that he seemed to be on Clara's side.

"Mr. Blair, whenever Clara shows up, I'll be sure to put her in touch with you in Chicago. She'll need friends," the old man said.

"I appreciate that, Mr. Smith, but I could help her now, if I could just talk with her."

"Well, I don't know how many times I can say it, we simply don't know where our daughter is."

Blair noted that every time Mr. Smith denied knowledge of Clara's whereabouts, Mrs. Smith looked down. He sensed that they weren't being honest. But he understood.

When he finally stood to leave, he asked if he could use the bathroom. As he walked down a hall, he noticed some papers on a table. Mr. Smith could see him all the way down the hall, so he couldn't stop and snoop. He did slow down, though, and as he walked by, he saw the words "Chihuahua City" on a page. After he was finished in the bathroom, he made his way back down the hall, Mr. Smith's eyes on him once again. He did not look at the table this time.

Jimmie Smith followed Blair down the steps from the house. "Hey, Mr. Blair, I want to be a reporter one day."

"Well, that's great, Jimmie. Maybe we can team up sometime."

The boy beamed. "That'd be so great!"

Georgia, with Olive Belle in tow, was on a late-night train just hours after her press conference. They were headed back to Chicago. Jake Jr. had gone back a couple of days earlier—just after his father's funeral. The long train trip gave Mrs. Hamon plenty of time to think more about her plans for the future. She also knew that when she arrived back in the Windy City, she'd be bombarded with questions from friends and the merely curious. Clara's so-called diary was the talk of the town.

She was able to pick up the Chicago papers when they changed trains in St. Louis. It was the first time she actually saw the articles by Sam Blair. Though she tried to dismiss the possibility of their truthfulness from her mind, she found her belief in the story Jake told her being shaken. At one point, she smiled and muttered under her breath, "Oh Jake, you lousy, lyin', son of a bitch."

"Did you say something, Mommy?" Olive asked.

"Oh no, dear, you just go back to your puzzle, okay?"

They arrived in Chicago in time to be back at their apartment before sunset. There wasn't much in the house to eat, so Georgia and Olive split a grilled cheese sandwich and a bottle of root beer before heading off to bed. The apartment was spotless, with not a single piece of furniture out of place.

As the week that began with the biggest funeral in Oklahoma history ended, Frank Ketch filed papers with the county court. It was a petition for his appointment as administrator of Jake's estate. The documents said that this was the wish of the dead man's heirs. The petition said that the wealthy oil man left no heirs and that his vast estate consisted of stocks, bonds, partnerships, oil leases, and railroad interests.

TWENTY-EIGHT

"...LAYING LOW IS WHAT I DO BEST,"

Sam Blair was back at his desk at the Chicago Herald-Examiner the next Monday. His daily articles had made him an office hero. The story of Clara was becoming the talk of the town.

"Sam, my boy, you've helped yourself to the big time. Reminds me of when I started out and got my big break. Did I ever tell you that one?"

Of course Arthur Brisbane had told him that one, but Blair was not interested in offending the man who gave him the biggest lead of his career. So he listened once more as Brisbane rehearsed his days in London and his writing about Jack the Ripper.

When he was done telling the story, Sam said, "Mr. Brisbane, I'm just overwhelmed that you trusted me with this. It's a fascinating story, and I think there's much more to it."

"Tell me about it, Blair," the editor replied. He then reached into his desk drawer and pulled a bottle out. "Care for a nip? It's colder here than in Oklahoma," Brisbane said with a smile.

"No, thanks, sir. I'm fine."

"Suit yourself. Now tell me what you mean by more to this story."

"Well, sir. I think I have a good idea where Clara Hamon may be hiding—or at least the city. Her parents wouldn't tell me where she was. Said they didn't know, though I think they were covering for her."

"Understandable."

"Of course. Yes. But I saw a paper on a table with the words 'Chihuahua City.'"

"Oh yes, that's south of El Paso. That's where Pancho Villa lives."

"The Mexican bandit that President Wilson sent General Pershing to capture?"

"Well, down in those parts, they call him a 'revolutionary.' They say he's retired now. He was given a large 25,000-acre spread down that way. Pretty nice. He's living high on the hog."

"Mr. Brisbane, I'd like to go down there and look for Clara."

"That's pretty risky business, kid. Expensive, too."

"I know the risks. At least, I think I do, and I'm willing to take 'em to find her and get this story."

"You really think there's more there?"

"I do, sir. I think she shot Jake Hamon in self-defense. My articles are influencing opinion down there. I think I can help her and help the paper."

"Let me check with Mr. Hearst. We'll see what he thinks. If he gets behind it, money won't be a problem."

"Gee thanks, Mr. Brisbane. I won't let you down."

"Well, you sure haven't yet, I'll give you that, Blair."

Perry Ross knew Sam Blair—at least he had met him once at a party in San Francisco hosted by William Randolph Hearst. Ross worked for Universal News Services, as did Blair. He had brought the afternoon paper with him into the dining room of the Gunter Hotel. He ordered a good-sized steak with all the trimmings and read Blair's latest prose about Clara Smith Hamon with a mixture of admiration and envy.

Ross was in San Antonio, just as he had been in Houston a day earlier, chasing another supposed "Clara" sighting. As he worked his way through the delicious steak—cooked medium-rare, just the way he liked it—his ears tuned to a conversation taking place the next table over from him. Two men—clearly men of means (he figured they were oil men)—were discussing the death of Jake Hamon. Since Ross didn't have anyone at his table, he decided to join them, at least with his ears.

He just about choked on a not-all-that-large bite of sirloin when he heard one of the men say, "Clara's still here. She's hanging around in hopes that she may be able to charter an airplane and cross into Mexico." One of the men noticed Ross was having difficulty.

"You okay, Mister?"

The reporter swallowed hard and cleared his throat. "Yes, sorry. Bit off more than I could chew. Thanks. My name is Perry Ross. I couldn't help but hear what you were just talking about. Didn't mean to eavesdrop, but did I hear that right? Is that lady who they say may have shot that Hamon fellow here in town?"

"Mr. Ross, I'm Lawrence Tillman, and this is my friend, James Leroy. Yes, that's exactly what I said."

"Pleased to make your acquaintance, Gentlemen. That's quite a story. I'm actually a reporter, and I've been chasing rumors about that lady for several days. You have any idea where I might find her?"

Tillman replied, "She's here in town. That's all we know. But we'd sure like to help the girl."

"You would?"

"You bet. We are, let's just say it this way, we were business competitors of the late great Jake. Didn't have much use for the guy. So the lady's a hero to us," James Leroy said with a laugh. Tillman joined in.

"I'll tell you what, I'd love to talk with her. I work for William Randolph Hearst, and I know the boss would love to hear her story. Could you help me?"

"I doubt it," Tillman said. "The lady just wants to hide. Not likely she'll talk to a newsman. Besides, we really don't know exactly where she is. We did hear, though, that she had been seen a couple of times at a store a couple of blocks from here. Might want to check some of places around here."

The next day, as Perry Ross wandered around town, asking this person or that if they had any idea about Clara being around, he went into a dry-goods store. He noticed a woman on the far side of the room. She matched the description of Clara Hamon. Their eyes met from a distance.

Then, just like that, she was gone.

Ross rushed over to where she was, only to see a blurred image moving through the door to the sidewalk. By the time he got to the door and exited, no one was there. He did, however, see an automobile racing around a corner a block away.

The reporter's automobile was parked on the street about a block in the other direction. He ran to the car and drove up the block, making the same turn the other car had made. But he saw no vehicle. He decided to keep driving along a state highway. He followed it for about ten minutes, then he noticed a vehicle stopped ahead. A woman was standing beside it. As he drew closer, he could see that she was crying. The car had a flat tire.

It was the woman he had seen in the store.

"Need some help, ma'am?" Ross said after he parked behind the other car and began to walk toward the woman.

"Oh my, I don't know what to do. This isn't my car. It belongs to a fine family. They live a few miles from here. What am I going to do?"

"Well, never let it be said that Perry Ross wouldn't help a damsel in distress."

"Why, thank you, sir. You're a blessing to a lady in need."

He looked at her several times and thought she indeed resembled the photographs of Clara he had seen, but he wasn't completely sure. He found the spare tire and jack and changed the tire for her.

"I don't know what to say, except thank you. You've been a savior."

He decided he needed to find out whether or not this woman was Clara. "My pleasure, ma'am. Like I said, I'm Perry Ross," he said. Then he waited for her reply.

She paused and said, "I'm Miss Smith."

"Well, Miss Smith, how about I follow back to where you're staying just in case that tire I put on doesn't hold?"

"Very kind of you, Mr. Ross. It's not far."

Ten minutes later they pulled up to a small farmhouse. She led him up the front porch steps and through a green screen door and into the living room. "Can I offer you a glass of lemonade, Mr. Ross?" she asked.

"That sounds wonderful." He looked around the room and saw that no one else was there. He raised his voice slightly, so the woman could hear him, "Where's the family that lives here?"

A few moments later, she appeared with two glasses of lemonade and a few homemade cookies on a china platter. "Here you go, Mr. Ross. They're in Dallas, visiting a sick relative. Should be back tomorrow sometime. I'm kinda watchin' the place for 'em."

"Thank you," Ross said. Then he added, "I mean, thank you ... Clara."

The woman looked at him and backed away. "Clara? What makes you think that's my first name, Mr. Ross?"

"Let's just call it a guess for now."

It didn't take but a few more minutes before the lady began to talk. "I am Clara. You're right," she said. She burst into tears.

The reporter pulled out a clean handkerchief from the front pocket of his jacket and handed it to her. "I'm a reporter, Clara. And I can help you tell your story."

"I killed him! There, I said it. He ruined my life. I killed him for Jack's sake. He's our son. Jake fooled me. He got all I had, forcing me to marry his nephew, from whom I was divorced a short time ago."

This sudden outburst was more than an acknowledgement, it revealed a part of the story that had not been known up till now. Was there a love child?

"Where is the little one, now?"

"He's with some friends back in Oklahoma. They promised to look after him for a while. I miss him so much!" She talked for the better part of an hour as Ross tried to keep up. He didn't want to get a word wrong.

"If twelve mothers find me guilty and the colonel free from guilt, I am willing to die a martyr for coming generations of my sex to profit by my experience and as a warning to other girls never to take a man's word on its face value."

"You keep calling him the colonel. Was he in the army?"

"Oh, that's just what he liked me to call him."

He wrote on his notepad and then asked, "How long did you know Jake Hamon, Miss Smith?"

"I have known him since I was seventeen. I was his stenographer. I was young, beautiful, and romantic and his golden tales of life were tempting. At last, I fell. We were so happy then, but alas—time has passed through the hourglass of despair, and I am a broken thing. Still, deep in my own heart, I hear an uttering that says: 'You were mistaken, but not to blame.'"

Ross asked her to talk about the night of the shooting.

"It happened at a hotel in Ardmore. After hours of lovemaking, wonderful caressing, and the thoughts of a happy married life, we left the hotel for a 'joy ride' that will forever last in my memory as the most beautiful hour of our companionship. He professed love for me, and treated me as a sweetheart until I allowed his attentions to reach the climax for which he planned for years. When the baby came, instead of making the colonel more kind and loving, Jack dear seemed to have sent a chasm which could not be bridged."

She broke down and wept. "I will tell you this, Mr. Ross. I won't return to Ardmore unless I can be tried by a just judge and a jury made up of twelve women. Please tell the authorities that if I don't have assurances about this, I will kill myself!"

Ross decided that was a good note on which to stop for the day. He had a story to write and send back to San Francisco.

As he left, he said, "Now, you just relax, Clara. I will look out for you. I'll be back in the morning to talk more. In the meantime, you get some rest, okay?"

Perry Ross drove back to town at a breakneck speed. He couldn't wait to write and file the biggest story of his career. And he couldn't wait to see her again and get more details about the shooting itself, something she seemed to be reluctant to describe to him in detail.

The woman calling herself Clara took a final swig of her lemonade and then reached for a cigarette. She watched from a window as Perry Ross's automobile raced away in a cloud of dust from the dry road.

"He's gone!" she yelled.

Two men, James Leroy and Lawrence Tillman, came into the room from somewhere in the back of the house. Tillman was carrying a bottle.

"You done good, honey."

"Thank you, Gentlemen. I thought I was pretty impressive," she said with a smile. "Now how's 'bout you pour a lady a drink and pay up?"

"Our pleasure, baby," Tillman said as he handed her a two-fingers of whiskey in a glass, along with an envelope containing a hundred dollars. She drained the glass in one swallow.

The lady's name, at least what she called herself at the brothel where she worked, was Peaches. She smiled at them and said, "I gave him plenty to write about. It'll keep him busy all night. But you never told me why you wanted to send such a nice young man down a wrong trail. I imagine he'll catch hell when they find out he's been had."

Tillman explained, "We're helping some friends have some friends. Just trying to muddy the waters a bit. Don't worry your pretty little face about that. Now you lay low, Peaches. It's important that the man not see you again."

"Why, mister, laying low is what I do best," she replied. They all had a good laugh.

The next morning, Perry Ross's story about his interview with Clara was on the front page of the San Francisco Examiner, along with more excerpts from the fugitive's diary, with commentary by Sam Blair.

"I thought you told me this Clara girl was down in Old Mexico. I've been trying to get the boss to swing some big expense money for you to find her," Arthur Brisbane barked at Sam. The editor chomped down so hard on his unlit cigar that Blair thought he was going to bite the thing in half. "Now, I read about her being in San Antonio and talking to that Ross fellow."

"Sorry, sir. I really don't know what to make of it. My information is very good. Possibly, Perry's mistaken."

"Mistaken? Hell, there's plenty of detail in the story. If it's wrong, it's not because he's been mistaken. It would be because he's been had."

"Sir?"

"Classic case of misdirection. Maybe, at least. So you're stickin' to the whole Mexico thing?"

Blair swallowed hard and then replied, "I am, Mr. Brisbane. I'd stake my job on it."

"You just did."

Perry Ross was shaving in his room at the Gunter the next morning when he heard a loud knock at the door. He opened the door and saw a man in uniform.

"You Mr. Ross?"

"I am. And you are?"

"I'm Deputy Sheriff Wilson. I need you to come with me."

"Where? What for?"

"My boss has some questions for you about the article you wrote for the paper."

"I didn't realize it would be in the San Antonio papers."

"It's not. But we got a wire from Ardmore, Oklahoma, to bring you in for questioning."

"About what?"

"They want us to hold you as a material witness until some man named Russell Brown can get here later today."

Ross sighed. "Okay, let me wipe my face and finish dressing. Give me a couple of minutes. I'll meet you in the lobby."

"I'll wait right here, Mr. Ross. Now, you hurry along, ya hear?"

Fifteen minutes later, Ross was in the sheriff's office. He was told that he'd need to wait for a few hours for Mr. Brown to arrive. The reporter sighed and hoped Clara would wait for him.

Of course, the woman he had talked to at the farmhouse was long gone. She took the money from the oilmen and hopped a train to Fort Worth. That night she was back in business at an establishment in the Hell's Half-Acre section of cowtown. The "business" was owned by the brother of the man she worked for in San Antonio.

When Russell Brown arrived, he hinted at all kinds of trouble for Mr. Ross for aiding and abetting a fugitive from justice. The reporter reluctantly agreed to take the Oklahoma attorney out to the farm to see for himself. When they arrived, an elderly woman met them at the door. While they introduced themselves, a man about her age joined her.

"Clara who?" the lady asked.

"Clara Smith Hamon," Ross replied. "I talked to her right here in your living room yesterday."

"What the hell was you doin' in my house, young feller?" the man asked indignantly. "You break in here?"

"No, sir. The lady invited me in."

"Now see here, we were up to Austin visiting my wife's sister for a few days. Got back about two hours ago."

Russell Brown pulled out a photograph of Clara. "You recognize this woman?"

"Sure," the man said. "I seen it in the newspaper. She the one who killed that rich guy up somewheres in Oklahoma?"

"That's what we think. We're just trying to find her. Very sorry to bother you folks this afternoon. Good day," Brown said as he tipped his hat.

Perry Ross was silent for the first few minutes of the ride back to town. The he spoke up. "You know, I should have realized it when she brought up that baby."

"Yes, you should have. Clara never had a baby. Besides, if she had one, she'd name it Jake, not Jack. Sounds like somebody sold you a bill of goods, Mr. Big Shot Reporter," Brown said. The he laughed out loud.

As for Ross, he just stared out the car window. He saw a tumbleweed roll in the distance and wondered where he was going to wander to when Mr. Hearst got wind that one of his up-and-coming reporters had printed a phony story.

"Sad about Perry Ross," said Hazel Faulkner, a reporter for the San Francisco Examiner. "He should've been more skeptical. Now he's out on his ass." She was talking to Morris Townsend, and she usually felt the need to include a bit of profanity when talking to the male reporters. She was a woman in a man's world. She may have been able to vote in the presidential election for the first time that year, but it was still the nineteenth century where she worked. That's the way Mr. Hearst liked it.

"Oh, I don't know, Hazel, that kind of thing could happen to the best of us. It's the luck of the draw," Townsend replied.

Just then, a lady came to Faulkner's desk. The visitor was wearing a long brown coat and a stylish duvetyne hat. "Are you Hazel Faulkner?" she asked.

"In the flesh. How can I help you, Miss … ?"

"It's Mrs. I'm Mrs. Hamon."

Hazel laughed and looked over at Morris Townsend. "Looks like we got another live one, Mo."

"I'm sorry?" asked the lady.

"You read the papers, don't you, honey?" Faulkner cracked. "Mr. Hearst has already been scammed by one phony Clara Hamon."

"My name is Ruth. Ruth Walker Hamon. I'm married to Frank Hamon, Jake's nephew. I have a story to tell if you wanna listen instead of cracking wise. I read your writing in the Sacramento Bee—that's where I live. But if you're not interested, I could take what I have over to the Chronicle."

Hazel straightened up in her chair and became all business. "Yes, of course. I'm very interested. Please, have a seat. Can I get you a cup of coffee?"

"No, thank you. Sorry to snap at you like that."

"I'm the one who's sorry, Mrs. Hamon. Please accept my apology."

Ruth Hamon nodded and said, "Like I said. Jake Hamon is, uh, was my husband's uncle. And there's part of the whole sordid story nobody seems to know."

"Well, you have my undivided attention."

"Where should I start?"

"How about the beginning? How did you and Frank Hamon meet?"

"We met in Arizona—we both worked in a railroad office out in Tucson. We were married two months later. I thought I had come to know him very well. But I guess I didn't know him very well, after all."

"What makes you say that?"

"Well, you see, about a month after we married, an envelope came in the mail from his uncle. I opened it, and it was a check made out to my husband for a hundred dollars. Frank was out of town then. When he came back a couple of days later, I asked him about the check. He looked frightened and then told me a story he should have told me before I said 'I do.'"

"What was the money for?" the reporter asked.

"It was a monthly allowance he received from his uncle."

"Allowance? Well, that's very generous. Were they close?"

"Not at all. Frank hadn't seen Jake Hamon in over a year. The money was payment for something Frank had done to help his uncle. You see, about a year before I met Frank, he had been married to another. Her name was Clara."

"Jake's Clara?" Hazel asked enthusiastically.

"That's her. Frank told me the story. Jake and Clara lived together like a husband and wife at a hotel in Oklahoma. But things got difficult when they traveled. Some hotels frowned on such things. So Jake came up with the idea of paying his nephew to marry Clara. He got $10,000 up front and a promise of $100 per month for life."

"Where were they married?"

"Weatherford, Texas. And they got a legal divorce a few months later, but Clara kept the Hamon name."

"Why are you telling us this?"

"Because Frank disappeared more than a month ago. He was mad at his uncle and obsessed with the idea that he should get more money from him. He wanted to confront him before Jake went off to Washington."

"Did he leave before or after Jake Hamon was shot?"

"He disappeared about a week before. Haven't heard a word from him since. I'm afraid for him. His always said that his uncle was as mean as a rattlesnake."

TWENTY-NINE

"WILL CLARA BE THERE?"

By the third week of December, there had been no breaks in the case. Newspaper coverage slipped from the front pages, but the story was still there, as if waiting for a fresh wind to blow.

Sam Blair was determined to see Clara, not to mention himself, back in the headlines. He knew that finding Clara would reignite the fire of curiosity and controversy. He was in Chihuahua City, but so far, the trail was cold.

Late one afternoon, he sat at a table outside a café. He was drinking a cup of very strong coffee. There was a man sitting at the table next to his. The man kept looking over at Blair. It made the reporter uncomfortable, so he left. The man followed him into the street.

"Excuse me, Señor, are you the man who is looking for the brown-eyed American girl?"

"Yes, I am. Do you know where she is?"

"No, Señor. I do not," the man replied, and then he briskly walked away.

Blair called after him, but the man disappeared around a corner. When Blair reached the corner, the man was gone. He was both upset and intrigued. But it was the first glimmer of hope in several days.

The next morning, as he walked through the lobby of his hotel, another man appeared. He was well-dressed and much older than the man in the street the previous day.

"Señor Blair?"

"Yes, I'm Sam Blair. Who are you?"

"I am a friend is all I can say. I have information about a beautiful señorita who is hiding in a lovely hacienda in our city."

"Where is she?"

"Patience, Señor. We must discuss business first."

Blair knew exactly what the man meant, and he was glad that his editor, with the generous help of Mr. Hearst, had sent him to Mexico prepared. "I understand, my friend. Let us sit down and talk about this."

"Gracias, Mr. Blair. I think we can come to an understanding."

The understanding would cost Blair and company $250. The reporter agreed and told the man to come back later that day for half of that. The balance would be paid when Clara was found. They shook hands.

The man returned later for the deposit.

"There is a park in the city called El Palomar. Do you know this place?"

"No, but I will find it."

"Be there tomorrow evening at nine o'clock. Near the fountain."

"Will Clara be there?"

The man smiled at Blair. "You are a funny man, Mr. Blair. You make me laugh." With that, the man left the hotel lobby with $125 of Mr. Hearst's money, and Sam had a sinking feeling in his stomach.

The newspapers Clara read were always a day or two old by the time they arrived at her comfortable hideout in Mexico. She was shocked at first when she saw her most intimate thoughts published on the front page, but then she found it somehow therapeutic to read the entries. They brought back a flood of memories—mostly bad, but a few of them brought smiles to her face as she read.

She also smiled—actually, she laughed out loud—the day she read the article published by Perry Ross about his encounter with the fake Clara. She seemed to sense that her story was becoming a national preoccupation. She saw the word 'Ballyhoo' in the paper one day, and repeated it several times. "Ballyhoo, Ballyhoo, Ballyhoo," she said while laughing.

The story about Ruth Hamon saddened her. She felt bad about her role in it. "Best to stay away from any man named Hamon," she muttered to herself as she read the article by Hazel Pedlar Faulkner.

She particularly liked the way the reporter Sam Blair described and dealt with her. He was respectful, sympathetic, and even a bit of an advocate—at least, that's how she saw it. By the time she got to the third published installment, she had made up her mind that if she ever went back to Ardmore, she'd want Mr. Blair to have exclusive access to her and her story.

Of course, Sam Blair wanted the same thing. Neither of them knew it yet, but they were indeed on the same page.

Sam Blair was curious as to why a group of lawyers wanted to meet with him, but he agreed to see them. He had just hit town at noon, having spent a few days back in Chicago. There was a handwritten message waiting for him at the front desk of the Hotel Ardmore: "Could you please come by office at 3:00 PM today? — James Mathers, Attorney at Law."

At three o'clock in the afternoon of Monday, December 13, Blair entered the office of James Mathers. There with him were his law partner, Charles A. Coakley, and two other attorneys, W. P. McLean and W. B. Scott, who told the reporter that they were from Fort Worth, Texas.

"We wanted to meet with you privately, because we've read your articles and have a hunch that you're on Clara Smith Hamon's trail," Mathers began.

Blair nodded. "Glad you're enjoying the writing. How can I help you gentlemen?"

Mathers continued, "We want to help Clara. All of us. We believe that she did what she did because she had to. And we want to make sure that she gets a fair shake."

"Mr. Mathers, you're the fellow elected to succeed Brown? Won't her prosecution become your responsibility when you take office?"

"I sure as hell am not going to prosecute her. In fact, I'm working behind the scenes to delay taking office so that I can defend Clara. That's how strongly I feel."

"Do you all feel the same way?"

"I sure do," McLean said.

"You the man they call 'Wild Bill' McLean back in Texas?"

The attorney flashed a proud smile and put his thumbs in his lapels and said, "Yours truly!"

"What's your interest in this? Why come all the way from Texas?"

"That's our business. Suffice it to say that Fort Worth is an oil town, and we have friends who are sympathetic to Clara. And if she gets in a courtroom, it'll be the biggest trial in a decade. What lawyer worth his salt wouldn't want to be part of that?"

"You men don't look like you come cheap. Clara probably doesn't have much money."

Mathers spoke for the group. "We wouldn't take a dime from her. If you find her, tell her that."

"Ah, so I guess there are some, shall we say, 'interested' parties who want to bankroll things?"

"Now, I don't know if you've spent much time reportin' round the courthouse up there in Chicago, but down here, we know when to talk and when to shut up," McLean said with a laugh.

"All right, Gentlemen. If I find Clara, I'll relay your kind offer. Anything else?"

"Just leave our names out of the newspaper for now," Mathers said.

"What names?" Blair replied with a smile as he donned his hat and turned to leave.

One evening, well into her second week at the comfortable hacienda in Chihuahua City, Clara took a walk on the grounds. She usually confined herself to the guest cottage—except for the meals with the family—but this particular evening, she was drawn to the house. The lights were off, but the main sitting room was illuminated by many candles, and several people were sitting around a table, as if in prayer.

Clara entered the front door and made her way to the sitting room. She counted eight people around a large table. As she drew near, she realized that they weren't praying—at least not in the traditional sense. It was more like they were in a collective trance. She was frightened. She'd heard many stories about strange rituals south of the border, but she assumed that they were exaggerations. Now, she wasn't so sure.

She stood there for a moment and then heard a young girl speak her name: "Clara. Clara. Is Clara there?"

After hesitating for a moment, she blurted out, "I'm here. I'm Clara."

Instantly, everyone at the table turned and looked at her.

"I'm sorry. I didn't mean to intrude," she said.

An animated conversation took place for the next few moments. Clara didn't understand a word. That is, until the girl who seemed to be in charge of whatever it was they were doing came to her and hugged her. The young lady pointed her finger at her own face and said, "Anita. You Clara?"

"Si," Clara replied. And with that the woman named Anita hugged her again. Anita couldn't have been older than sixteen or seventeen, Clara reckoned. She was barely five feet tall, with raven-black hair. But it was her piercing blue eyes that stood out.

Monday, December 20 was the day of destiny for Georgia Hamon's hopes to succeed her dead husband as the member of the Republican National Committee from Oklahoma. But not even a last-minute telegram on her behalf sent to key party leaders from Harry Daugherty, architect of President-elect Harding's run for the presidency could help her.

Every day it seemed that there was more news about the story. Jake Hamon's favor in the public eye was fading, while sympathy for Clara was growing. As for Georgia, she was beginning to look, and act, more and more like an opportunist.

The final nail to her own political coffin came in the form of a credible report that she had indeed known for years about Jake's relationship with Clara and was paid an allowance of $5,000 per month to look the other way.

A marriage of convenience hardly, in the eyes of most party stalwarts, merited any special consideration to Jake's widow. And when the votes were counted, she lost Jake's former seat on the RNC to a party loyalist named James A. Harris, forty-seven to twenty-seven.

Georgia left Oklahoma in a huff the next day, just in time to be far away for the media circus coming to Ardmore with the return of Clara.

The next evening, Sam Blair was in El Palomar Park a few minutes before the appointed hour of nine o'clock. It was a cool evening under a clear night sky. There were many people strolling about, notably couples in love. He heard music from a hand organ nearby. He stood near the fountain, as he had been instructed.

He heard the distant chime of a clock peal nine times, and he waited and watched. After a few agonizing minutes, two men appeared from a grove of trees nearby. Following them was a figure dressed in black—a lady—with a veil over her face.

It was Clara Smith Hamon.

They sat down on a nearby bench. After a moment, Blair looked around and noted that the two men who had accompanied her were gone.

"They're nearby," she said.

"Clara, I'm grateful that you've agreed to meet me. I don't know how much you know, but you and your story have become quite a sensation back home."

"I know, Mr. Blair. I've read every one of your articles. Are you the man who found my diary?"

Blair sheepishly replied, "Yes. I found it. I know it may seem to be a violation of—"

Clara put her hand up as if to stop him in mid-sentence. "Mr. Blair, I'm not a bit mad at you. Not at all. You were doing your job. I think you also wanted to help me."

"Yes. You're right on both accounts. And that's why I'm here now. I want to help you tell your story—the full story."

"Are Buck Garrett and Bud Ballew close to finding me?"

"Hard to say," he replied. "But if I found you, I can't imagine they're far behind."

Clara looked at Sam Blair. "Mr. Blair, I have to trust someone. The strain is killing me. My time here has been very good for my health and my heart."

"What would you like me to do?"

"I came away—came down here—because Jake Hamon and his friends wanted me to go. I didn't know when I left, however, that Jake was really going to die. I was only afraid of it. I'll go back with you, if you'll go bond for me and be sure that I don't fall into the hands of someone of small authority who will try to capitalize on the notoriety of my arrest."

"Actually, Clara, you have some powerful friends."

"Mr. Blair, Jake's associates may indeed be powerful, but they are not my friends."

"I know that. I'm speaking about other friends. You don't know this, but there are people standing in line to sign any size bond for you. And some of the most powerful lawyers in the country want to defend you. They believe in you."

256

"Really?"

"Yes, indeed. You know who James Mathers is?"

"Yes, I voted for him. He's a Republican and one of Jake's friends."

"Well, he may be a Republican, but he's not a friend of Jake anymore. He's willing to resign his new office to fight for you."

"My, my. I can't believe that."

"That, and there are some powerful lawyers from Fort Worth who want to help. You ever hear of W.P. McLean?"

"Wild Bill McLean? Sure. Everyone's heard of him."

"Well, Wild Bill is chompin' at the bit to see you beat any charges against you. You see, you have much sympathy. Your diary helped. People are seeing Jake as you've described him. Hard to believe, but a month ago, they were praising him, now they're burying the man all over again."

"Mr. Blair, let's go back to the hacienda where I've been staying. I want you to meet a wonderful family. There's plenty of room for you to stay over. We have much to talk about."

"Indeed we do, Clara."

Clara introduced Sam Blair to the Cabrera family—at least, she tried. The reporter spoke even less Spanish than Clara had picked up during her brief sojourn in Chihuahua City. But there were plenty of smiles after initial looks of fear when the stranger came in with her. The family allowed their guests some privacy, and Clara and Sam sat down on two couches in a cozy sitting room.

"So Sheriff Garrett will let me go to my parents' home before I surrender and meet me there?"

"Yes, I'm sure of it. He's on your side, too. In fact, most folks in Ardmore think the county attorney should just drop the matter."

"Is that possible?"

"Possible? Yes. But I wouldn't count on it."

"Then what?"

"Well, after you surrender to Garrett, he'll take you back to Ardmore to face the charges."

"Will he put me in jail? I don't think I could take that."

"I doubt very seriously that you'll spend a minute in jail. Like I said, there are many, many people ready to put up money or sign your bond, whatever the amount is. But it's up to you."

"I have found peace here in Mexico, but I know I need to go home. Please notify Mr. Garrett that I am ready to surrender. I'll be at my parents' place in two days."

"I will. Now, would it be possible to interview you for a story? I think the more people read about you and hear what really happened, the better your chances."

"I'm fine with that, Mr. Blair. I'm ready to tell my story to the world. Especially if that might keep me away from court—or jail."

THIRTY

"CLARA HAMON, SLAYER, FOUND"

"Clara," Sam said as he turned to a fresh page in his notebook, "start wherever you want. Just talk to me from your heart about you and Jake and what happened."

"For ten years he had dominated me. I hated him, and yet I loved him. Then came November 21, the day we were to part for good. His wife was coming in from Chicago soon. He had grown to be powerful, not only in business, but also in politics. Never mind that I had made him what he was," she said bitterly.

"That's fine, Clara. You're doing just fine," Blair said, trying to calm her down a bit.

"I'm sure you don't know this, but I was advised to kill him. That's right—by several of the biggest men in Oklahoma. He had many enemies," she said. Then she stared into the distance for a moment before continuing. "That bullet that killed him should've been fired ten years ago." She broke down and wept.

Blair just sat there, not knowing what to do. But then Clara composed herself. "He made his peace with God, you know. He told me so that morning in the hospital after he had said he was dying, and that I should go away and he would tell the world he had shot himself. He'd made peace with God, and I guess I forgave him that day. He told me that he'd see me in Heaven."

Sam Blair wrote feverishly, trying not to miss a single word.

"Every dollar he had, every bit of political influence he had, I helped him achieve. I say this now because I feel that I owe it to myself and to my family to protect my standing by giving out this information. And the men who surrounded him—who also became great and powerful because Hamon helped them—I picked these men for him and pleaded their causes. They don't know it, but I have saved many of them their opportunities for wealth. There is one man who is now biggest of all. I saved him. When Hamon had gone mad with rage and was preparing to turn this man loose from his staff, I again and again insisted that this man must stay. This man says he is my friend. I am prepared to believe that he is," she rambled.

"Clara, talk about the day you went to the hospital to see Mr. Hamon. The day after the shooting."

"Well, Mr. Blair, the day we said goodbye in the hospital, he told me I would be provided for, for life. He, of course, had said the same thing many times before. I have my family to think of, that's why I'm telling you this."

"Frank Ketch has been saying that Jake left no will."

"Well, I read those reports in the newspaper, but Frank is lying. That comes as no surprise to me. I'm telling you, Mr. Blair, there was, positively was, a will. I believe it still exists. I keep trying to convince myself that it will be found. I saw it. It said that he was leaving me one-fourth of his estate in the event of his death."

The next morning, Sam rose early and headed back to his hotel in town. He sent a wire to James Mathers, notifying the lawyer that he had found Clara and that she desired to turn herself in and that he would wire more details later. Then he went to his room and wrote an article for his newspaper. It was titled, "CLARA HAMON, SLAYER, FOUND."

Around ten o'clock the next morning, the telephone rang in Buck Garrett's office. Deputy Bud Ballew answered the call.

"The hell you say? Where is she?" the deputy asked the caller, James Mathers.

"I'm not at liberty to say, except that she wants to surrender voluntarily."

Buck Garrett got on the line. "Jimmie, this is Buck. Now we're gonna find out where she is, so you best tell us now."

"No deal, Buck. You need to let her do this the way we advise. That's the deal. I'll be back in touch tomorrow."

When the phone call was complete, Buck said, "Let's keep an eye on Mathers and Coakley. Get over to their office."

"Yep, on my way, Buck," Ballew replied.

About twenty minutes later, Bud returned. "Buck, I got bad news for ya."

"Don't like the sound of that," Garrett replied.

"Mathers and Coakley left town early this morning. At least, that's what the secretary over to their office says. He was already out of town when he called a bit ago. I think they took a train to Fort Worth. From there, they could be headed anywhere. "

"Shit!" Buck Garrett shouted.

"Jake saw himself becoming President of the United States by 1928. Did you know that?" Clara asked early on as they continued their conversation the next morning.

"He really said things like that to you?"

"Oh my, yes. He was always a dreamer. That was how he swept me off my feet back at Miller's Store in Lawton. Then, over the years, especially when he was in his cups, he'd look into the mirror in my room and sing his praises and his dreams. He said he was immortal and the idol of the state and, one day, would be the idol of the nation."

"There's a word for that kind of thing, Clara."

"What word?"

"They call it 'megalomania,' or sometimes a 'Napoleon complex.' Psychiatrists study things like that. I know one professor in Chicago who wrote a book on the subject."

"I'm sure Jake Hamon would make a good subject for such a book. You remember when Harding came to Oklahoma City during the campaign?"

"I read about it, sure."

"Well, a few days before, Jake was mildly drunk, and we had made love. Suddenly, he jumps up and says, 'Clara, I'm gonna be the biggest man in the United States. You wait and see. When Harding comes to Oklahoma, I'm going to have ten thousand men marching with torches. It will be Jake Hamon and not Warren G. Harding who will be the big man at that meeting.'"

"Did he ever talk like that when he wasn't drinking?"

"Sure he did. Lots of times. Like when President Wilson got back from Paris. I asked Jake about the big peace talks and all that, and he said, 'Why, if I could have gone over there, this thing would have been settled long ago. Wilson isn't smart. Just wait until I get in the White House. I'll show how I can make the world listen to my dictation!'"

Sam continued to make copious notes. His first article from south of the border would hit newsstands the next morning. He would be on the front page once again.

Clara's four attorneys, two of whom she had not yet met, checked into the Hotel Paso del Norte, located about a mile from the international border between the United States and Mexico. A telegram from Blair was waiting for them when they arrived. The reporter told them to be at 1119 San Antonio Street, the home of Clara's parents, the next day shortly after noon. Blair also instructed the attorneys to notify Sheriff Garrett and have him at that residence at 2:00 PM.

The lawyers enjoyed a quiet evening and looked forward to the big day coming up.

They also sent a wire to Buck Garrett, who soon boarded a train along with Bud Ballew. The lawmen arrived in El Paso on Christmas Eve, Friday, December 24, at 1:00 PM, giving them just enough time to get a shave and then head over to the Smith dwelling on San Antonio Street.

Clara's last evening with the Cabrera family was bittersweet. Sam Blair joined them for a dinner that was more of a feast. Then someone brought out a few bottles of something Sam had ever tasted. Tequila, they called it. They all joined in several toasts, even though the Americans could understand very little of what they were saying.

After an hour or so, the girl named Anita appeared, as if from nowhere. Clara was startled to see her, but smiled at her and raised her glass. Anita smiled back. Then the visitor engaged in what, to Clara and Sam, sounded like a very serious discussion with the family. The children were chased away, and Clara and Sam were invited into the sitting room, where that same table was again adorned with candles. Anita indicated that everyone should sit and join hands.

"What the hell?" Blair whispered to Clara.

"Mr. Blair, these are decent people. I'm not sure what is happening here, but I think it's some kind of ritualistic prayer from their religion."

"Are they Spiritualists?"

"Spiritual? What do you mean?"

"Not spiritual, but Spiritualists, you know, like in seances, things like that. I heard Harry Houdini debate a practitioner earlier this year back in Chicago at the Victoria Theater. He made a fool of the guy."

"Well, whatever they are or this is," Clara continued to whisper, "we're guests in their home, so we'll be respectful."

Clara and Sam watched as young Anita fell into some kind of trance, while others at the table whispered something over and over again in Spanish. Blair was both intrigued and uncomfortable. Clara shot an angry glance his way when he pulled out his pocket watch to check the time.

Then, all of a sudden, Anita was speaking loudly, though it seemed like her voice was distorted or altered once again. She said the same words Clara had heard on the other occasion: "Clara. Clara. Is Clara there?"

Not knowing what to do, Clara replied, "I'm Clara. I'm here."

Sam Blair began to wonder about that tequila they'd been drinking. He didn't feel drunk, but then, he wasn't much of a drinker. He wondered if there had maybe been something even stronger in their drinks.

"Clara, the barrier of death is terrible," Anita said, her voice still sounding different. It was deeper, almost guttural.

Clara started to tremble. "Is it Jake? Jake, is that you?"

The voice continued, "One who is dead is burdened with an obligation to those on Earth. I am trying, but I cannot reach you in any physical sense, or reach any of those who must decide upon your case."

Sam Blair released Clara's hand and reached into his pocket for his notepad. But she didn't notice. Her eyes were closed tight, as were those of everyone else at the table.

"I have been trying so hard, so hard that I want to tell them you must go free," the words continued to flow from, or through, young Anita. "I want to grasp them and make them feel the command I am seeking to issue from this side of eternity. But I cannot reach across the line of death. Clara, when you go into court, when the jury settles into its chairs, when your trial commences, I'll be there beside you. I'll be there with you. I'll be on the bench beside the judge; I'll be in the jury box. But, Clara, I know now that none will realize my presence. That is my present curse. I won't be able to make my presence known. I won't be physically able to get to the men who try you and demand that you shall be set free."

Then Anita looked up. Her face was dripping with sweat. She reached for a towel to mop her brow.

Clara said, "Anita, did you come here tonight because you knew there was a message from the other side from Mr. Hamon?"

The young girl stared at Clara with a confused look and then she said, "No hablo Inglés."

Sam Blair pulled his watch out again. It was almost 4:00 AM. Their train north was scheduled to leave in two hours.

In keeping with the tendency toward the sensational, William Randolph Hearst contacted the United States Department of State in Washington, DC to request that Clara and his reporter could be guaranteed safe passage across the border at Juarez. The newspaper mogul was assured that a man named Oscar Harper, who worked at the American consulate in the Mexican city on the border, would meet them and assist them.

Of course, all of this would enhance the story that would soon be on the front page of every newspaper in America— not just the Hearst-owned ones.

At the appointed hour, Sheriff Buck Garrett and Deputy Bud Ballew arrived at the Smith home. They placed Clara in custody, and the entire party, after tearful hugs, proceeded to the train station to travel back to Oklahoma.

"When do you expect us to arrive back in Ardmore?" Clara asked Buck Garrett.

"I think right about noon tomorrow, Clara."

"Well, that'll make for a merry Christmas Day, I guess," she said without a smile.

Saturday would indeed be Christmas, but holiday festivities were far from many minds in Ardmore as the news spread that Clara was coming home. Local real estate broker John Tucker had been busy for the past couple of days securing signatures, in petition-like fashion, from people willing to sign a bond for Clara.

"Yours will make sixty-five, Bill," he said to one of his neighbors.

"Well, I don't have much money, John."

"That's fine, hell, five of the names are from millionaires, so you won't actually have to put up a dime of your dough, my friend." The neighbor nodded and signed.

As the train bearing Clara, the lawmen, and her lawyers made its way toward, Ardmore, a steady stream of passengers, predominately women, made their way to her drawing room. One particular lady, named Harriet Almond, said, "Mrs. Hamon, I'm from El Reno, and I want you to know that all the gals in town are behind you completely. You fight for your rights. You're fighting for all of us!"

"Why, thank you, ma'am, very much. I hadn't realized so many people knew anything about me."

Several passengers asked her and Sam Blair to sign copies of newspapers bearing her image and details of the sensational story. As for Buck and Bud, it was easy duty. It was clear that neither man really thought of Clara Smith Hamon as a prisoner—certainly not a dangerous one.

At one point, Wild Bill McLean, peeked in. "Clara, could I speak to you for a moment, privately?"

Sam Blair got up and walked out the door. McLean sat down and said, "Now, we just met, but one of the things I want to do for you, Clara, is to make sure that if this thing ever gets to trial, we can put on the best case possible."

"I agree, Mr. McLean."

"I hope so, Clara, because I want you, from this point on, to be very careful what you say to that Blair fellow, or any other reporter for that matter."

"Sam Blair is on my side!" she replied defensively.

"I'm sure he is, Clara. But the more your words are in the paper, the harder it might be if and when you ever have to testify. Just think about that, okay?"

"Yes, Mr. McLean, I understand. But I will not be muzzled," she added.

THIRTY-ONE

"CLARA, CLARA, WELCOME HOME!"

Edith C. Johnson, society editor for the Daily Oklahoman, arrived in Ardmore from Oklahoma City, about an hour before Clara's train was scheduled to arrive. She noted the almost festive atmosphere, as a large crowd had assembled, even though it was Christmas Day. She had followed the story closely and had written several columns. Her prose dripped with sympathy:

> "In all the gamut of human emotion, life holds no agony comparable to that which such women as Clara Smith suffer. Nothing to them is a compensation—money, opportunity, pleasure, or even love itself. A love that overlaps all bounds and all bonds, brings in its train inevitable torment."

Because her picture was featured prominently whenever her column was published in the paper—one with the largest circulation in the state—many townsfolk, especially women, recognized her.

"You're Edith Johnson. I just love your writing. Isn't this exciting today?"

"It sure looks to be. Surprising to see all these folks out on Christmas Day."

"Well, Clara's our girl, and she's coming home."

"Do you know her?"

"Sure, I wait tables at the hotel where she lived."

"So you knew Mr. Hamon, too."

"Of course, but he was a nasty man sometimes. I wasn't surprised when he got shot."

"Were you surprised that it was Clara who shot him?"

"A little. But the more I thought about it, the better I understood it. The more I think about it all, poor Clara was caught in the black spider's web."

"What is your name, honey?"

"I'm Cynthia Smith—no relation," the lady said with a smile.

"Well, Cynthia, do you still work at that hotel?"

"The Randol? Sure do."

"I may come by to talk with you more in the next day or so, would that be all right?"

"Of course!"

Edith walked a few blocks from the station and marveled at how many people were milling about and waiting for Clara's arrival. This was Christmas, she thought, shouldn't these good people be at home with their families? Surely, there shouldn't be such a publicity circus on the day of Christ's birth? But then again, she admitted that she was part of that circus.

"Come in and have a turkey dinner, ma'am," one man said as she walked by his café. "We've got plenty and won't be serving again until three o'clock this afternoon."

She replied, "Well, you might see me then, but not right now."

"I understand," the restaurant man said. "I guess no one's hungry for food right now. This is the biggest thing to hit town since Ringling's circus came through a few years back. Elephants and all."

A few minutes later, as Clara's train pulled into the station, the crowd crept toward the end of the platform where the Pullman cars stopped. The lawmen made sure everyone else was off before escorting Clara into the station.

Buck Garrett stepped down from the train car first. Clara followed him, holding to tight to his hand. She was wearing a beautiful blue dress, and a fur rested on her shoulders. She was received like a movie star. One reporter made notes describing the woman in custody as a "slight, girlish, fur-cloaked figure."

"Clara, Clara, welcome home!" one voice said. It was joined by dozens of others. Edith Johnson thought it looked like a celebrity had arrived. In fact, movie cameras were on the scene, along with dozens of photographers capturing the moment.

Edith watched as the entire traveling party—looking more and more like an entourage—climbed into three waiting automobiles for the short ride to the courthouse. The reporter moved quickly to position herself where Clara might see her, in the hope of being recognized.

She wasn't disappointed. Clara saw her and recognized her from the picture that always accompanied her column. She had read the reporter's words of support and waved her over to the vehicle.

"Clara, thanks so much for stopping. I wonder if we might have a few minutes to chat later?"

"Why, Edith Johnson, I declare. What are you doing here on Christmas Day?"

"Came to see you, of course. Like everyone else," the reporter said with a smile.

"Tell you what, Miss Johnson, find your way over to the courthouse. I'd invite you to ride with us, but as you can see, there's no room. But after whatever it is they have to do with me there is done, I'd be honored to talk with you."

Then the party drove off. Edith scratched her head and turned to a man standing a few feet away.

"Excuse me, sir? Do you know the way to the courthouse?"

THIRTY-TWO

"...ALMOST LIKE A MOVIE STAR..."

About a half-hour later, there was a brief hearing at the courthouse. Several of Clara's relatives had been waiting there, deciding to avoid the scene at the train station.

"Not guilty," Clara said, when Judge Tom Champion asked her plea in reply to the charge of first-degree murder. She showed no emotion.

"Bond is set at $12,000," the judge said as he banged the gavel, declaring the brief meeting adjourned.

Jimmie Mathers brought four men forward to sign for her: Wirt Franklin, Max Westheimer, L.H. Love and T.A. Thurmond, all wealthy local citizens. As they signed, Mathers told those in the room, "We have sixty more names of people—good citizens of Ardmore—who wanted to sign for Clara. But these fine men will suffice. Clara, please know that you have many, many friends in this here town."

"Now, Mrs. Hamon, you are free to go wherever you like," the judge told her. "And I want you to know that we have but one intention—that is to be fair with you and ourselves."

Clara smiled at the judge and looked over at Russell Brown, the county attorney, as well as Sheriff Garrett, and said, "Oh, you all look like little boys having fun. I want to thank all the people who were willing to sign the bond for me. And I look forward to complete vindication."

Flashbulbs popped. And Clara, along with her entourage, walked out. Edith Johnson was waiting in the hallway. "Oh, Miss Johnson, we must talk. Walk with me, and we'll find a place."

"Thank you, Clara," Edith said as she joined the traffic flow.

Clara and Edith made their way to the law offices of Mathers and Coakley, where they sat in an office for the better part of an hour.

"What do you plan to do now, Clara?" was the reporter's first question.

"I'm going over to Wilson, where my sister, Mary Welling, lives. My older brother, Charlie, lives near there, too. I'll stay in Wilson for a while. Maybe I'll head back down to El Paso. My parents aren't well, you know."

"Do you have any idea when the trial might take place?"

"Mr. Mathers says that he's going to push for late January, but he says it may have to wait until March. I don't know all the details. I'm just glad to be home and free for now."

"I can only imagine."

"You know, Miss Johnson, I like your writing. I've been thinkin' about writing a book about my life. I can write so much better than I can talk. It's rather difficult for me to talk about some things, but I write easily, especially if I am in the mood. I'm a rather moody woman," Clara said, reflectively. "Yes, ma'am, when all this stuff"—she waved her hand—"is over, I intend to obey the impulse even when it comes over me in the dead of night. I will get up and write that story of my life!"

"I think you should, Clara. People are interested. We learned that when parts of your diary were published in the paper."

"Do you know Sam Blair?"

"I know who he is—I saw him with you today."

"Well, at first I was upset about my personal, private words been printed so everyone could read them, but then I realized that he was doing me a great service."

"Indeed he did. And you did the young girls of this country a great service through your words. They were great words of warning," the reporter confirmed.

"Oh, if only I could save other girls from the terrible experience I have passed through, if I could save only one girl, I would willingly be the martyr. My life should be a warning to every girl who knows my story."

"Your brutal experience, has it embittered you toward men?" Edith asked.

"By no means. I love men and I always will. But my main purpose now is to help my family. I need to be with them."

"Clara, you were received almost like a movie star when you got off the train. And look at you, adorned so beautifully, with jewels and fur. Have you ever thought you might like to actually be in the movies?"

Clara looked at the reporter and smiled coyly. "That's a question I cannot answer until after my trial. I can say this, though, I have received offers."

"You have? Already?"

Clara smiled again. "Miss Smith, thank you so much for talking with me. I must find my sister. I'd like to go to Wilson in time for a nice family Christmas dinner."

"Thank you, Clara—and Merry Christmas!"

When Buck Garrett walked out of the courthouse after the brief hearing, several young boys were waiting for him. They were all about ten years old, or so he figured.

"Howdy, Sheriff. You have to fight off any bad guys to bring that lady back to Ardmore?"

"Not now, boys. It's Christmas. You get on home to your folks. Probably time for dinner."

"Had our dinner early," one boy said. "On account of the big doings."

"I see, well, I ain't had my supper yet, so I'll catch up with you another time," Garrett said as he walked briskly away. Of course, the boys followed him like a pack of loyal puppy dogs.

The sheriff decided to duck into the drugstore, but they followed him in. So he decided to tell them a story they'd never forget. "Yes, siree, boys, that lady was sure glad to see me when she crossed over from Juarez. Why, the poor thing had been shut up in a dungeon down there in Mexico."

"She was?" one of the boys asked.

"Sure as shootin' she was. You see, it was this way: She left town after she shot old Jake Hamon and went across the river into Old Mexico and fell in with a rich man down there, a close friend of old Pancho Villa, himself. This fellow's the one who put her in the dungeon. Kept her there for two whole days. Turns out, it was some kind of secret club down there."

"A secret club?"

"Yes—you boys've heard of those, right?"

They all nodded affirmatively.

"Well, these Mexicans, it turns out, liked to pray all the time," he said with a smile.

It was then that one of the boys spoke up: "Oh, he's just talking bullshit, as my pappy says."

"Now you watch your tongue, young feller, and all of you now, scat. Get home before I round you up and take you to the jail."

The boys ran away, screaming.

"Nice story, Sheriff," said a man who had been watching his encounter with the boys. "Would you have some time to tell me what really happened down there? I'm with the Kansas City Post."

Buck Garrett looked the man over and said, "How many of you birds gonna circle around this old corpse of a story?"

"Sheriff?"

"Hell, just leave me alone. If you want to interview me, come by my office on Monday. But I can tell you now, I won't have much to tell you that you don't already know."

Garrett saw that it was just after three o'clock, and he went over to the café across the street. He was mildly surprised to see Bud Ballew in the place. The deputy used his boot to push out a chair. "Come join me, Buck. Merry Christmas."

Buck tipped his hat and sat down. Both men enjoyed a fine Christmas dinner and rehearsed the highlights of their trip.

Shortly after six o'clock that evening, Clara sat with her sister's family and her brother's family around a dining room table in Wilson, Oklahoma, and enjoyed a Christmas dinner of ham, turkey, and all the trimmings. It was topped off by homemade cherry and apple pies. Mary played the piano, and everyone sang the songs of the season.

The next morning was Sunday. She sipped coffee as she lounged on some large pillows in her bed in the guest bedroom at the Welling home, while her sister's family headed off to church. She decided to get her sermon that day from Edith Johnson's column about her in the Daily Oklahoman.

"Ever since she was 17 years old, Clara Smith has been dominated by Jake Hamon, one of the most dominant men of this state. A woman need not live as much as ten years with a man of Jake Hamon's powerful personality, his stubbornness, his overbearing nature, to have her will broken, to be his shadow and reflection, in a word, almost his slave. Unless she is a woman of extraordinary strength of character, she is going to become more or less colorless in point of character and personal independence. In fact, she actually loses all faculty for independent thought and action. And when love, even though it be abnormal in some of its phases and expressions, is an overpowering factor in all her thinking, all her feeling, she is not the free agent that she once was, that under healthier conditions, she might be today.

I am no more inclined to condone or overlook the sin in the life of Clara Smith now than before I went to Ardmore and became somewhat acquainted with her. I do feel a profound pity, however, for a woman who occupies the most tragic situation I ever have witnessed, and I do want to see her build a new and better life."

She took another sip of coffee and smiled. Her smile had a devilish curl to it, like a cat after it had grabbed the proverbial canary. But the smile disappeared from her face when she turned the paper to the next page and saw a large advertisement.

That evening, on the last Sunday of 1920, there was a sermon of a different kind at Ardmore's First Presbyterian Church. Dr. Charles Weith had officiated Jake's funeral a month earlier. He had also tried, on Georgia Hamon's behalf, to persuade at least one newspaper editor not to publish "Clara's Diary."

Now, the minister was going to deal with the issue the best way he knew how—he was going to preach about it. Notices were placed in the Ardmore newspaper, as well as a few other papers in neighboring towns:

"Dr. Charles C. Weith will speak on the subject, 'Clara Smith and the Morals of the Nation,' this Sunday evening at 7:00 PM. First Presbyterian Church, 223 W. Broadway Street, Ardmore, Oklahoma."

Dr. Weith walked from a side door onto the church platform a few minutes after the service started. The crowd was singing the hymn "Faith of Our Fathers," and the sound from the large church organ filled the room. The minister looked over the crowd and was momentarily stunned. He thought he might have a better than usual Sunday night attendance for his special sermon, but this was a standing room only kind of thing. In fact, he couldn't remember seeing so large a group in church on any Sunday morning. The only time in recent memory anyone had seen that many people in the building was for Jake Hamon's funeral.

After the music, announcements, and other preliminaries were finished, Dr. Weith came to the pulpit with his Bible and several pages of notes. He put his glasses on and spoke in his best stentorian Presbyterian voice:

"About a week ago, in a business house in our city, I saw a very attractive girl speaking across the counter to a young man, and in the course of the conversation, she handed him a great bunch of clippings stating that these were the clippings of the Clara Smith diary, and all the other news concerning her which she had read and carefully saved for him. That's the moment I became aware that girls were thinking of these things, and I feared sometimes to their detriment. This is why I am preaching on this subject tonight."

He had the complete attention of every person in every pew. Some were there out of curiosity. Others were showing support for the preacher they saw as courageous. But a few— and these were among the wealthiest and most influential church members—were outraged. Not by the Clara story, but by the fact that their minister was, as they saw it, getting down into the gutter with the dregs of society. They saw Weith's sermon as sensational, sordid, and beneath the dignity of what they thought their church stood for.

"It is a well known fact that women condemn their own kind when guilty of the crime of immorality. A woman who has transgressed in this manner cannot come back, for her own sex will not receive her. This makes it impossible for fallen women ever to reform. This is wrong. If women would give their own kind the hand of encouragement and lead them back to a clean life and not ostracize them, there would be an opportunity for a woman to come back."

There were a few murmurs in the crowd. This was not quite the message many expected. They were hoping for John the Baptist, or Jeremiah, but they seemed to be hearing someone talk like ... Jesus.

"More than that, the double-standard of morals between men and women is wrong. A man ought to be as clean as his wife. Why should a husband demand purity from his wife, while he lives like a libertine?"

This prompted several rare "amens"—rare because conservative Presbyterian congregations tended to endure sermons in somber silence. But the outcries were also rare because they came from unlikely sources—women. "Let us come back to sanity!" Dr. Weith thundered. And there was a smattering of applause—the first such outburst anyone could ever remember in the stately auditorium of First Presbyterian.

"I am credibly informed that thousands of girls go to Los Angeles trying to break into movies. There seems to be an inordinate desire on the part of many girls to break into the limelight. The ordinary humdrum life no longer appeals to them. They love to feed on the sensational, and right here, I want to sound a note of warning to parents to guard well your own daughters."

Maybe it was the presence of so many visitors, but at that moment, the crowd turned "revivalists," with more "amens" and applause.

"Make it a point to know where they are every hour of the day. It is a very serious mistake to permit young girls to go to movies and other places of amusement unchaperoned, and to allow young schoolgirls to roam our streets until eleven o'clock."

Several young ladies in the crowd crossed their arms and glared at the preacher for the remaining minutes of the sermon. Then Dr. Weith prepared to close:

"Mrs. Hamon and her family expect to make a home here in Ardmore, and in our beloved congregation. Let us give them a royal welcome. Let us make the atmosphere as kindly and friendly for them as possible. Let us get this disagreeable incident and these depressing circumstances out of sight as quickly as possible."

It was a noble effort. But the matter was out of the minister's hands. The lid was off, and every indication was that Ardmore, Oklahoma, would become the focus of national attention in the coming new year of 1921.

THIRTY-THREE

"...PROCEED AT ONCE TO THE CITY OF ARDMORE..."

Not having a wife or even a regular girl at the time, John Gorman persuaded his secretary, Stella Fabian, to attend the New Year's Eve party with him—not that it took any arm-twisting. After all, it was being held at the home of the biggest man in movies—literally and figuratively—Roscoe "Fatty" Arbuckle. He had recently purchased it from another big name—Theda Bara, Cleopatra herself.

Stella used every dime she had saved to buy a dress for the occasion. She just knew that all the other big stars would be there, too. As for John, it was to be just another night on the job, though in much finer clothes. He was always trying to drum up support for his fledgling movie company. What he needed most was ready cash to use trying to figure out how to bring the Clara story in the news to the screen. It had the makings of a great movie, he thought. But he didn't dare give too much of it away. Not in that room, at least. It could be stolen in a Hollywood minute.

"Oh, Mr. Gorman," Stella said on first sight of the spacious Tudor house on West Adams Avenue, just off Figueroa. "Think that other funny man, what's his name—oh yeah, Charlie Chaplin. Think he'll be at the party?"

"Sure, sweetheart. I'm sure they'll all be here. You make sure to meet 'em all, but stay out of my way. I've got business to conduct before I head to Oklahoma next week."

"Okay, Boss. Whatever you say."

The party was a big hit. Chaplin was indeed there. So were Gloria Swanson, Lillian Gish, and the strikingly handsome Tom Ince. Of course, Prohibition was nowhere in sight. The booze flowed, and the revelers partied until dawn on January 1, 1921.

Stella woke up that next morning in a strange bedroom all alone. She was naked, and she felt very ill. She ran to a trash bucket and threw up and wondered what had happened the night before. After splashing some water on her face, she looked around the room for the first time. She saw that her clothes were strewn across the floor. There were also some garments that obviously belonged to a man, including a rather large pair of trousers.

She tried and tried to remember how she got to the room, but it was all a blur. All she was sure about was that she drank an awful lot of gin. And her head and stomach verified that fact.

She quickly dressed and left the room. When she entered the kitchen, a servant offered her a cup of coffee and some orange juice. Stella asked her where everyone else was.

The servant replied, "No telling."

As for her date, well, John Gorman had abandoned Stella a few minutes after the partiers slurred their way through the lyrics of "Auld Lang Syne." He and two potential investors dropped into a speakeasy nearby, then headed over to the

Beverly Hills Hotel, where one of the wealthy men maintained a suite.

And before dawn, Gorman had talked them into providing some significant seed money for his next project, which he told them was a big secret, but would be the biggest movie of the year. The hint of mystery actually helped swing the deal.

Or that, too, may have been the gin.

As the new year got well under way, there was much talk around town about the upcoming trial. Jimmie Mathers had made it clear that he wanted to be part of the defense team for Clara. The problem was that he was scheduled to begin his term as county attorney, replacing the outgoing Russell Brown on the sixth of January.

Mathers decided to appeal to a powerful friend and political ally. He took a train to Oklahoma City that week.

"Thanks for meeting with me on such short notice," Mathers said to Oklahoma Governor, James Brooks Ayers Robertson.

"Not at all, Jimmie. I've been following the story, and I half expected to be hearing from you. I'm pleased that you came in person. Face-to-face is always better than that damned talking contraption."

"So you're aware of my problem?"

"More than aware, Jimmie. I'm prepared to help," he said. Then he reached for a sheet of paper and grabbed his reading glasses. "Here, let me read this to you. Tell me what you think.

"TO THE HONORABLE S. P. FREELING, ATTORNEY GENERAL OF THE STATE OF OKLAHOMA: I am informed that the Honorable James Mathers, who was elected to the office of Carter County Attorney last November, has been employed by Clara Smith Hamon for her legal defense in a matter being prosecuted by that office. To my mind, owing to the widespread notoriety that has been given to this case, it seems that the best interests of the state require that your office be required to appear in and take charge of the prosecution. In my opinion, the people require from those charged with the enforcement of the law, some effort looking to the orderly procedure of this prosecution. This, therefore, is to order and direct you personally, if possible, to proceed at once to the city of Ardmore and take full and complete charge of the prosecution of the case of the State of Oklahoma vs. Clara Smith, and to do any and all things needful in the premises. — Respectfully, J.B.A. Robertson, Governor."

"How's that, Counselor?" he asked.

"I wouldn't change a word, Governor," Mathers replied.

"That's good to hear, seeing as I sent it over to his office this morning and over to the newspapers about an hour ago," the governor said while flashing a big grin.

A few days later, there was a knock at the door of the Welling home in Wilson, Oklahoma. Mrs. Welling answered it and faced a very well dressed man who smiled and said, "Hello, ma'am, my name is John Gorman, and I'm the president of a motion picture company out in California. I know this may seem forward, but I've been following your sister's story and would love to talk with her about it."

The lady was stunned and speechless. A moment later, from somewhere out of sight, Gorman heard a voice say, "Who's at the door?"

The visitor replied, "It's John Gorman, from John Gorman Pictures in California. Is that you, Clara? I tried to send a telegram, but was unable, so I thought I'd just drive out here and try to meet you in person."

Clara appeared from around a corner, still standing a few feet back from the door in the hallway. Gorman could see her image, but barely. "What can I do for you, Mr. Gorman?"

"I ask just a few minutes of your time, ma'am, and I promise I'll be on my way."

Clara hesitated. Then she came closer to the door, sizing the man up. Finally, she said, "All right, fine, come in."

A short while later, John and Clara were having an animated conversation, and her sister was bringing refills of coffee. "I've seen some of the movies you mention, Mr. Gorman."

"Please, call me John."

"Okay, well, John, I've seen them, and I'm sure I've read your name in a magazine somewhere. That movie "Little Miss Nobody," that was one of yours?"

"Indeed it was."

"So, you really think this sad and pathetic story of mine would make a good movie?"

"I most certainly do. I've got a gut sense about these things. All I need is for your permission to write it up like it would appear on the screen."

"A script?"

"Exactly!"

"Yes, well, my lawyers have made it pretty clear that I shouldn't talk with anyone about anything, so I don't see how I can help you now."

"I understand perfectly, Clara. Besides, the trial coming up would have to be part of it, so we need to let that play out. All I'm asking for now is an understanding that once everything reaches a conclusion and you're a free woman, you'll give me first crack at it. No strings attached for now. We can bring the lawyers in later."

"And what do I get in return?"

"You'll become famous."

"In case you haven't noticed, John, I am already famous."

"Ah yes, your name is known, but that infamy will fade away with the headlines. As for a film, well, that'll last forever."

"Fine by me. You have my word," she said, extending her hand to Gorman. He kissed it and then shook it. She smiled and blushed slightly, then asked, "Will you be staying around?"

"I plan to spend a lot of time in these parts over the next couple of months. I think we were meant to meet."

"You mean, like fate?" Clara asked.

"Well, the governor may want to stick me front and center in the middle of this mess, but I have a trick or two up my sleeve," Oklahoma Attorney General Prince Freeling said to his secretary. "Get me Tom Champion down in Ardmore on the telephone."

The secretary placed the call.

A few moments later, Champion was on the line. "Yes, Mr. Freeling, how can I help you?"

"Tom, now listen to me. I need you to handle this business with Clara Smith or Hamon, or whatever the hell her name is, for us. You're the man for the job. I'll oversee things, but you need to handle the courtroom. Can I count on you?"

"Sure, all right, Mr. Attorney General. I'll do it, but I'll run the trial my way. No meddling? Can we agree on that?"

"Tom, if you get this thing over with and off the front pages, I'll let you do an Irish jig in court every day for the rest of your life."

"I doubt I'd be interested in that, Prince. In fact, I doubt anyone would. I also doubt that anything short of the Second Coming could keep this trial out of the headlines. But I'll sure do my best on that score."

Over the next few days, the process began to take shape. Judge Champion appointed a special prosecutor to step in for Jimmie Mathers. He chose Ardmore attorney H.H. Brown, who happened to be the brother of outgoing county attorney Russell Brown. He called the new prosecutor, "one of the greatest lawyers of the entire Southwest."

That raised a few eyebrows, but not for long, especially when the judge then appointed his identical twin brother, J. B. Champion to the defense team.

Judge Champion's biggest challenge would be how to manage such a big trial in a courtroom that only had room for about 200 seats. Some advised him to move the whole thing to the convention hall. But he had some time to ponder the logistics.

The trial was set to get under way on March 10, 1921.

Meanwhile, John Gorman became a regular visitor to the Welling home in Wilson over the next several weeks, but this fact was kept from public notice. In fact, Clara shielded it from her attorneys. It was a family secret. Clara and John began to work together on a script for a movie with an exciting name—FATE.

She was lonely, despite all the public interest in her case. No one came to call on her other than her attorneys and John, never at the same time, of course. Clara was beginning to see the producer's presence in her life as more than luck. He was becoming a friend and confidant with an always-ready soft shoulder.

This was just fine with Gorman. He had been intrigued with Clara from the moment he saw her picture in a Los Angeles newspaper. And he knew that somewhere along the way, intrigue had turned into infatuation for him.

They talked, sometimes for hours on end, sitting on a front porch swing drinking iced tea or lemonade, then in the home's parlor over coffee. He became a fixture at the dinner table with the family. And though it was a small town, and a very small house, John and Clara were growing a big dream together.

He wondered if Clara was falling for him, but he didn't ask.

In fact, she was already in love with the movie man.

With six weeks to prepare for the biggest courtroom drama that Ardmore—in fact, all of Oklahoma—had ever seen, there was frenetic activity behind the scenes. Lawyers for both sides prepared their cases. More than 150 potential jurors were rounded up. And nearly 200 subpoenas were issued to potential witnesses.

Prominent on the list of those expected to testify in March were Frank Ketch, Dr. Walter Hardy, Dr. A.G. Cowles, E.W. Sallis, Sam Blair, and Bob Hutchins. Buck Garrett and Bud Ballew spent a great deal of time traveling and serving papers. And they got press notice wherever they went. The duo quickly became—for a brief time—the most famous lawmen in the country. A rumor was even started that Buck was related—a nephew some whispered—to Pat Garrett, the man who shot and killed William Harrison Bonney, better known as "Billy the Kid." Buck never commented on the rumor, content to let it become part of his own legend. But he knew it wasn't true.

At one point, Clara traveled to Fort Worth to meet with Walter Scott and Wild Bill McLean, two of her attorneys. She spent two days at the Westbrook Hotel—her residence of choice while in Cowtown. What the lawyers didn't know was that John Gorman was also staying at the Westbrook. They were, of course, registered in separate rooms, but spent most of their time in the room under his name.

By Valentine's Day, their business relationship and friendship had blossomed into a full-grown love affair. But they were discreet. Clara knew that such a thing would be much more than merely scandalous on the eve of her trial; it could be catastrophic. Of course, she already had an abundance of experience in such matters.

THIRTY-FOUR

"I AM NOT GOING TO HARDING'S INAUGURATION."

More coffee, Mr. O'Brien?" Georgia Hamon asked.

"I'm fine, Mrs. Hamon," the man replied. James C. O'Brien was al'do Chicago prosecutor who had volunteered his services to Jake's widow knowing the publicity wouldn't hurt as he ventured out into the world of criminal defense. He had two nicknames. One was "Red Necktie" because of his trademark scarlet and scarf-like tie. The other moniker was not nearly as benign. He was called by some "Ropes." This was because of his effective record as a prosecutor sending the guilty to the gallows.

"Cousin Florence won't talk with me at all?"

"Sorry to say, ma'am, but no. I've talked to Jess Smith again and again about this. They simply don't want you to attend Mr. Harding's inauguration."

"So much for family."

"Yes, well, I'm sure the soon-to-be First Lady of this land doesn't want the goings-on out in Oklahoma to become part of their big day next week when the president-elect is sworn in."

"I guess I understand. But it hurts so much. Yet another way that rascal of a husband continues to haunt and hurt me, even from the grave."

"My advice to you is to somehow get your story out. You are every bit the victim that Mr. Hamon was."

"I'd say more, Mr. O'Brien. Much more."

The attorney nodded in agreement. "If I may again suggest that you make some kind of statement for the papers, the ones here and those out west. I'm sure anything you say will be picked up by the wire services. I'll do all I can to make that happen."

"And if Olive Belle and I travel to Ardmore, will you be with us?"

"At your service, ma'am. You can count on it."

"All right, let's work on that statement right now."

"Great. You tell me what's on your mind and heart, and I'll write it up."

The next morning, newspapers across the country read the fruit of that process. It was sent as a telegram to one of the prosecuting attorneys, H. H. Brown, and it was released to the press at the same time:

"Chicago, Illinois, February 28, 1921
H. H. Brown, Attorney
Ardmore, Oklahoma
Please publish in tomorrow's Armoreite that I am not going to Harding's inauguration. I am almost in nervous prostration over my husband being killed. I helped my

husband prove up our farm and drove farm horse and buggy. My husband owned no automobile then, we were poor twelve years after we were married. I am not saying unkind things about Clara Smith. — MRS. JAKE L. HAMON"

The news was welcomed with relief in Washington. In Ardmore, people wondered whether the real Mrs. Hamon would attend the trial.

Of course, she would. She had already been subpoenaed by the state.

During the first week of March, with the biggest trial in the history of Oklahoma set to begin, Ardmore was rife with rumors and gossip about how the prosecution would go about making its case against Clara. Some of the scuttlebutt had to do with a relatively new morsel of speculation—that Jake Hamon was being blackmailed by an unnamed business or political adversary.

Another story being noised about had to do with Jake Hamon telling two different stories from his deathbed, one that Clara shot him accidentally, the other that she did it out of spite. And then there was a persistent rumor that the trial would reveal that Clara had purchased a gun in Oklahoma City just two weeks before the shooting. This, of course, would tend to support the idea that what she did was premeditated and that Clara could face not only incarceration, but even the death penalty.

Of course, Clara already owned a gun, one given to her by Jake, himself. Now, though, some were saying that she had once pointed it at Jake in anger, and he had taken it away from her.

On the eve of the trial, one Oklahoma newspaper published an essay that seemed to crystalize what the story had become. It said, in part: "Once it was wine, women, and song. Now it is petroleum, paramour, and politics. But the same triangle, nevertheless, in slightly different garb. Jake Hamon was rich and politically powerful. Clara Smith was the woman—the other woman—clever enough to hold the man for ten years. He decided to cast her off. She killed him, she says, in self-defense. History is full of the thing."

March 4, 1921 was a sunny day in Washington, DC, but the temperature hovered a just few degrees above the freezing mark. Warren Gamaliel Harding chose George Washington's Bible for his left hand as he raised his right hand during the oath given to him by Supreme Court Chief Justice Edward D. White.

In his address, the new president droned on long after the attention span of his audience had been exhausted. He promised an era of "normalcy" and service, with words such as: "Service is the supreme commitment of life. I would rejoice to acclaim the era of the Golden Rule and crown it with the autocracy of service. I pledge an administration wherein all the agencies of Government are called to serve, and ever promote an understanding of Government purely as an expression of the popular will."

Sitting on the platform with all the dignitaries were members of the new president's Cabinet. Among those was Albert Fall, the new Secretary of the Interior. He oversaw vast portions of land in the American west, land rich with oil. That was the job Jake Hamon had been promised.

There would come a time in the not too distant future when Mr. Fall would find himself envying Jake. Dying at the hand of a scorned mistress was surely better than dying a thousand public political deaths in one of the most infamous scandals in the history of the nation.

One hundred eight-two men were summoned to make up the jury pool for Clara's trial. Witnesses made their way to town from all across Oklahoma and Texas. Both sides speculated that the big trial would take no more than one week. The Carter County court docket was completely cleared, though there were fifteen or so cases pending at the time. The lawyers were ready.

A teletype machine was installed in a jail cell adjacent to the courtroom to enable journalists to transmit news from Ardmore to America and the world. Dozens of major publications sent journalists to cover the story.

Georgia Hamon, along with her daughter, Olive Belle, and attorney O'Brien hit town on March 9. All hotel rooms in the city were filled. And for a few days, all the eyes of America would be on Ardmore. It was already being described as "the most sensational homicide trial known to the criminal annals of Oklahoma."

By now, many were referring to Ardmore as "Clara's Town."

"I'll be in the courtroom every day, my dear, but it will be hell not being able to talk to you," John Gorman said to Clara.

"I don't know what I would've done these past several weeks if you hadn't shown up on the front porch," she replied. "You saved me, Johnny."

"Well, you get through this trial—and I know you will—and we'll head out west and start a new chapter in the story of Clara. A story the whole world will see and admire."

John and Clara had spent most of their time together, at least recently, dreaming big dreams. He talked about movies and stars, and Clara drank it all in. He showed her his notes about the movie he wanted to make about her life.

All he needed was the ending.

He hoped it would be happy. What he didn't tell the woman who had fallen helplessly and hopelessly in love with him was that he planned to make a movie about her story with or without her.

Of course, it would be better with her.

Meanwhile, in Washington, DC, President Harding was enjoying the first days of his presidential honeymoon. He was the talk of the town and the nation. His administration was already a breath of fresh air, but then, Woodrow Wilson was hardly a hard act to follow. The now-former president had been a virtual recluse, and when he did appear in public for the inauguration, people were shocked at how he looked. The man was a shell of his former self.

"Jess, now you make sure the First Lady doesn't come across any newspaper articles about that business out west," Harding said to his assistant, Jess Smith. They were at a breakfast table in the residential area of the mansion.

"I'm on it, Boss. I'll keep a lookout."

"And while you're at it, Jess, find us a place somewhere near here where we can gather for some off-hours recreation, if you know what I mean," the president said with a sinister smile.

"I'm working on that one, too, sir. Got a line on a place just a few blocks from the White House."

"Great. They call this the White House, but it already strikes me as something of a glass house. I need some privacy. And sooner rather than later."

THIRTY-FIVE

"YOU PRESENT YOUR CASE, AND WE'LL PRESENT OURS."

Promptly at 9:00 AM on March 10, 1921, Clara Smith Hamon entered the courtroom. She wore a blue tailored suit, with a hat to match, along with black silk stockings and patent leather shoes. She was surrounded by five attorneys.

Fifteen correspondents sat at a press table off to one side. They watched and made notes. Sam Blair was there. He was the star of the group, and everyone went to him for details and background. Edith Johnson was there, too. Sam and Edith became an odd couple of sorts; the young city room reporter and the lady who looked more like a spinster librarian than a journalist.

Also in their company was a corpulent man whose attire seemed to be in perpetual disarray. What was unusual about this particular man was that he didn't represent a major American newspaper. In fact, he wasn't even American—he was British. Gilbert Keith "G.K." Chesterton, a famous writer in England, but not as well known in the United States, happened to be traveling through the region at the time of the trial. He was fascinated by the story and the surroundings and decided to stick around and send dispatches back across the pond.

Clara and her attorneys, particularly Jimmy Mathers, whispered back and forth in an animated manner for several minutes.

At 9:13 AM, a bailiff called out, "Oh Yes, Oh Yes, the honorable district court of Carter County, Oklahoma, is now in session." Everyone in the courtroom stood as Judge Thomas Champion entered the Carter County courtroom and took his place at the bench. He banged the gavel.

"Please be seated. I call these proceedings to order. Are all parties ready?"

Attorney General Prince Freeling replied: "The prosecution is ready, Your Honor."

"The defense is ready, as well, Your Honor," attorney James H. Mathers declared.

"Now, I want to be clear. I want no one under the age of sixteen in this courtroom for the duration of this trial. I ask that Sheriff Garrett enforce this rule." The judge looked over at Garrett, who was standing in a corner. "That clear, Mr. Garrett?"

"Yes, sir, Judge."

The first order of business was jury selection. Most observers believed that this process would take more than a day, maybe two. The pool of 182 had been whittled down to 35 men in the run up to the trial. Both sides had ten pre-emptory challenges.

So it surprised nearly everyone in the room, and became the first bombshell from the trial, when the prosecution used only one challenge and the defense used none. The jury was seated before lunch that first day. A tailor, four merchants, a dairyman, a banker, a grocer, two farmers, a barber, and a retiree would listen to the lawyers and sit in judgement on Clara.

Only two of the men on the panel were under forty years of age.

Georgia Hamon entered the courtroom shortly after three o'clock. She was accompanied by James "Red Necktie" O'Brien, her flamboyant Chicago attorney. Dressed in black and wearing a heavy veil draped from a hat, the widow made a dramatic, head-turning entrance. She took a seat in the first row just behind the prosecution table. Also with her were Jake Jr., Olive Belle, and her father, Jasper Perkins from Chicago.

By this time, a minister, the Reverend Crayton Brooks of Ardmore's First Christian Church, was seated behind the defendant. He was there to support the defendant. Clara stared at Georgia for a short time. But when Georgia noticed her gaze, Clara looked away, and soon both women were engrossed in the proceedings. Clara even took notes, as she would through the entire trial.

Before court adjourned for the day, the state asked that reporter Sam Blair and Mrs. Jake Hamon be excused as witnesses. The defense did not object, but they asked that Clara's mother be excused, as well. Judge Champion granted the requests.

Attorney General Freeling rose to address the judge. "Your Honor, the proof in this case will revolve about, and we desire that the jury be taken to the hotel room to view the scene."

"We have no objection, Your Honor," McLean said.

"Well then, we'll gather here in the courthouse tomorrow morning at 9:00 AM sharp. Then the jurors will walk over to the hotel, led by Sheriff Garrett. However, the attorneys will remain here at the courthouse." Champion then banged the gavel. "Court adjourned."

Everyone noticed that the temperature had started to drop. What had started out as a mild pre-spring day with temperatures in the sixties, was giving way to a cold front blowing in, one that would make the next day much colder.

Freeling saw Mathers walking with Wild Bill McLean about twenty yards ahead.

"Jim, Bill, that was a hell of a surprise, not objecting to any of the jurors," the attorney general said.

"Well, that was the general idea, Prince," McLean replied sarcastically.

"Point taken. Some of us were wondering if we could meet tonight to discuss some unofficial ground rules for testimony and cross. Not giving anything away to each other, but to work together so as not to have this thing become a circus. Not to mention, we don't want to tick off the judge. We worked pretty well together on tomorrow's excursion."

Mathers and McLean stopped in their tracks and looked at the attorney general. There was a pause, then McLean spoke up, "Hell, what do we care if it becomes a circus? That'll be your problem, Prince. You present your case, and we'll present ours. How's that sound?"

Prince Freeling turned and walked away without uttering a word in response.

The next day was Friday. Just after calling court to order, Judge Champion called a recess with the instruction that the jurors examine rooms twenty-eight and twenty-nine at the Randol

Hotel. It was, as had been anticipated, a bitterly cold day, and the delegation walked in formation the few blocks to the hotel.

Clara was allowed to personally arrange the furniture as she recalled it from that November night. She moved a rocking chair, some pillows were shifted, and a table was adjusted. The door connecting the two rooms was opened. She broke down at one point, collapsing on a bed and weeping.

"Now, Clara honey, we need you to gather yourself. We have a job to do here," Sheriff Garrett said as he sat down next to her.

"Oh, Buck, it's just so hard."

"I know, I know."

Clara soon composed herself and left the room. Sheriff Garrett then led the jurors, one at a time, through the rooms. No questions or comments were permitted from the twelve men. After about a half-hour, the delegation bundled up and headed back to the courthouse.

Following opening statements by Freeling for the prosecution and Mathers for the defense, the first prosecution witnesses were called. A steady stream of Jake's former business associates testified that Jake was good to Clara, but that she had a volatile side. Mike Gorman, a vice president at an Ardmore bank, told the court that he had once entered Jake's office and witnessed what he thought was Clara pointing a pistol at the oil man. This in turn led to testimony by several that Clara had purchased a pistol in early November at an Oklahoma City sporting goods store. The defense did not challenge the testimony, conceding that fact.

The stage was then set for the most compelling and dramatic testimony in the first stages of the trial. The prosecution called Dr. Walter Hardy, the owner of the Hardy Sanitarium, where Jake died. It was Hardy who had treated Jake's wounds.

Dr. Hardy was the star witness for the state. The prosecution was counting on his testimony to make even the thought of Clara's acquittal seem impossible.

THIRTY-SIX

"THE STATE CALLS DR. WALTER HARDY..."

Dr. Walter Hardy was fifty years old. He began his career in Ardmore as its first doctor in 1901, establishing his Hardy Sanitarium on the second floor of the Ramsey Drug Store at Main and Caddo Streets. It had ten beds, a small laboratory, and even one of the first X-ray machines in the region. Hardy had earned his medical degree at Washington University in St. Louis.

Eventually, he needed more space, so he moved to a building at 212 First Avenue Southwest in 1911, and that space was expanded in 1917. Hardy was the first physician to own an automobile and was a pioneer in medical aviation, with his own ambulance airplane just after World War I. He also acquired Ardmore's first radio station, first for the sanitarium, and later given to the community.

His hairline was receding, but he sported a stylish moustache. He wore wire-rimmed glasses, and looked every bit like a civilized city doctor.

"The state calls Dr. Walter Hardy to the stand."

The physician made his way to the front of the courtroom and raised his right hand, swearing to tell the whole truth. Everyone in the room had heard this or that about that fateful November night when Jake staggered into Hardy's hospital, but the good doctor had been silent on the matter.

Until now.

"Dr. Hardy, did you take Jake Hamon for treatment on Sunday, November 21, 1920?" Prince Freeling began.

"Yes, I did."

"What time was that?"

"It was about 8:30 PM."

"Was Mr. Hamon brought to your hospital, or did he come by himself?"

"He walked into the hospital alone."

"How was he dressed?"

"He had on an overcoat and full dress suit."

"And what was the condition of his face with reference to being pale or white?"

"It was white."

"Doctor, did you speak to him first, or did he speak to you?"

"I spoke to him."

"What did you say?"

At this point, James Mathers rose and said, "Objected to as incompetent, irrelevant, and immaterial."

The judge replied, "Overruled. Answer the question, Doctor Hardy."

"I asked him what was the matter."

"What did he do then?"

"He threw his arms around my body and kissed me on the forehead."

McLean spoke up, "We object to this love affair being related."

There was a small amount of laughter in the room, and the judge used his gavel to warn against any crowd response.

Freeling replied, "We object to the remarks of counsel and move that they be stricken."

Champion agreed, "Objection sustained, let the remarks of counsel be stricken from the record."

Returning to his witness, Freeling continued, "Now, Doctor, as he kissed you, what did he say to you, if anything?"

"He said, 'I am shot by Clara Smith. I am going to die. I am very weak and want to go to bed.'"

It was then that the prosecution introduced two exhibits into evidence: a blood-marked union suit and a shirt, also heavily stained with blood. At that moment, both Georgia and Clara burst into tears. They sobbed uncontrollably, almost violently.

James Mathers shouted, "We object to this display of bloody things. It is prejudicial to the rights of the defendant and tends to inflame the jury."

Georgia buried her head into the shoulder of her son, Jake Jr. After a few minutes, the widow fled the courtroom.

Clara quickly regained her composure.

Freeling resumed his questioning. "What happened next, Doctor?"

"I helped him walk to the elevator, and Jake said to me, 'Doctor, take my right hand. I want your promise that you'll never reveal how I was shot, except in open court. I want this promise for the sake of my wife and children.'"

Hardy described undressing Hamon. He then held up the suit and shirt and touched his finger to a hole. "Here is where the bullet bore through into his body. And here is where the bullet came out."

"Did you give him any medicine?"

"Yes. I gave him a quarter of a grain of morphine."

"Did he say anything else?"

"Yes. He said, 'I want Frank Ketch.'"

When it came time for cross-examination, the defense was represented by McLean. "Now, Doctor, I will stand here and you stand here (pointing). Now show the jury where the bullet hit and where it lodged. You stand over there, and show it with this pencil. Make a mark on my shirt if you want to."

Hardy made a mark on McLean's white shirt.

"What was Jake Hamon's position, where was he when he was wounded?"

"He told me that he had been lying on his bed."

"All right. Now, Doctor, if Jake Hamon had been lying on the bed, I want you to take me and put me in position there on that floor as he claimed he was and show the jury how the bullet would come."

"I don't know what position he was in."

"Well, I mean on that bed. He told you 'here is the way I was lying in bed.' Put me in that position. Where would Clara be?"

"She would have to be out to his left."

"Would have to be on his left and shoot across his body, wouldn't she?"

"Well, partly across."

"Partly across. Isn't it a fact the bloody holes went in straight from the front?"

"No, sir."

"Well, we got his clothes here, Doctor."

"Yes, it appears that the bullet went straight in the clothing. In my opinion, Mr. Hamon was lying on a bed when he was

310

shot. And this is what he told me. He told me that Clara came to him and lay next to him. She stroked his head tenderly with one hand and shot him point-blank with the other."

"Objection!" thundered Wild Bill McLean as he jumped to his feet. "This is pure speculation!"

"It is not," Freeling replied. "Dr. Hardy is qualified to bear witness to certain medical facts as well as the utterances of a dying man."

"Objection overruled," the judge said.

"Now, Dr. Hardy, did Jake Hamon have any other health issues, anything that might hinder the potential for recovery from such a wound?"

Hardy paused before answering the question. "Yes, he had a chronic condition."

At this mention, there were murmurs in the courtroom, prompting Judge Champion to once again warn the gallery about outbursts.

McLean pressed. "What was this chronic condition?"

"Cirrhosis of the liver."

More crowd noise was followed by yet another loud gavel.

"That's caused by the constant and heavy drinking of whiskey, isn't that right?"

"Yes."

"Doctor, but for the cirrhosis of the liver and but for his being on a spree, that bullet wouldn't have killed him that afternoon?"

"I cannot say that. It's too speculative. It don't do a man any good to be drunk."

By the time McLean was done with his questions, it was time to adjourn for the day. But Judge Champion said that they would have a rare Saturday session the next day.

When court resumed the next morning, they heard testimony from several witnesses, including W. B. Nichols, the former police chief of Oklahoma City, and Frank Ketch, Jake's business manager.

Ketch said that the first question out of Jake Hamon's mouth the morning after the shooting was, "Where is she?" Hamon asked Ketch to get her away before Georgia and the kids hit town. He instructed the business manager to give her money. He testified that when he saw Clara he said, "Clara, I have never interfered in yours or Jake's business before, but I am going to do so now. You have got to get away."

Also on the stand during the Saturday session was the Reverend Dr. T. J. Irwin of Lawton, one of the clergymen who had helped with Jake's funeral. He told the court that before he died, Jake had prayed and repented of his sins. He added for emphasis, "if Jake Hamon's soul was not saved" his would be lost, too. The minister also testified that Jake told him that three times he had tried to buy Clara off and that the killing was a frame-up.

Court was adjourned at noon.

The Monday session was filled with testimony from E. W. Sallis, the driver who had escorted Clara on her circuitous travels right after she left Ardmore in the immediate aftermath of the shooting.

By the time the state rested its case at the end of the Monday session, there was a sense in the courtroom that they had done a good job establishing that Clara had indeed shot Jake.

Following adjournment that day, McLean told some reporters that Clara would take the stand as the trial moved into its fifth day.

THIRTY-SEVEN

"THE DEFENSE CALLS CLARA SMITH HAMON..."

By the time Judge Champion entered the courtroom a couple of minutes after nine o'clock Tuesday morning, March 15, the place was packed. It was standing room only. Of course, everyone had heard that Clara was going to testify. So there were whispers of disappointment, though barely heard out of fear of the gavel, when McLean called Ella Walling, Clara's sister, to the stand first off.

"Mrs. Walling, when did you first learn of the true nature of your sister's relationship with Jake Hamon?"

"I learned about it a little more than a year ago, when my father came to Ardmore to kill Hamon. He had just found out about how Mr. Hamon had treated Clara. But he was disarmed by Sheriff Garrett before he could do anything. Daddy is ill. He has tuberculosis, and that is why he is not here to testify himself."

"Objection!" H. H. Brown, one of the special prosecutors, shouted.

McLean insisted that it was a proper question. How Clara's family processed the whole matter of a rich and powerful married man taking advantage of her was relevant. The judge agreed. Freeling's reply, though, set off the first fireworks of the day, and the most significant demonstration of the trial to date. He said, "Fine, Your Honor. The state is willing for the jury to know how they took it, the old woman and all."

McLean was livid. "We ask the court to instruct the jury to pay no attention to this remark. That old woman, as he calls her, is, in my judgment, as good a woman as has given birth to any lawyer in this case!" This was met with loud applause throughout the courtroom.

"Order! We'll have order in this court!" Judge Champion shouted, but to no avail. Finally, after a minute or so, he demanded that the court be cleared and be in recess for thirty minutes.

When court resumed, Clara's mother was called into the courtroom and testified briefly, but it was little more than an attempt by the defense to capitalize on the previous insult to garner sympathy for their client. Mrs. Smith testified that Clara showed up at their house on Thanksgiving Day, and she was bruised from a beating.

Then came fourteen year-old Phyllis Walling, Clara's niece. She twisted a little ring on her finger as she spoke lovingly of her "Aunt Clara."

After a lunch break, it would be Clara's turn.

"The defense calls Clara Smith Hamon to the stand." All eyes were on the defendant as she rose from her seat at the defense table and walked slowly toward the witness stand. She was wearing a charcoal grey suit and stylish hat. She seemed calm and confident as she put one hand on the Bible and raised the other to accompany her oath.

She answered a few preliminary questions from Wild Bill McLean, then the attorney encouraged her to testify in a narrative way, describing the events on the fateful Sunday the previous November.

Clara began and spoke in low and dramatic tones:

"At about two o'clock, Mr. Hamon came in, and we had a pleasant conversation. He laid down on his bed to rest, but only stayed a short time, perhaps less than an hour. He said he was going back to the office and that later he had a dinner planned in the hotel dining room with some friends, including Mr. Harding's right-hand man.

"I began packing. We had agreed that I was going to leave for California the next day. He expected Mr. Harding's man to bring an offer to join the Cabinet as Secretary of the Interior. Mr. Hamon wanted this very much because it would give him control over vast oil-rich territory. I was disappointed at this, but I had come to accept it. Mrs. Harding wanted Mr. Hamon to bring his wife and family to Washington. They are related, you know.

"Later, I decided to go out for a drive in my car. A last look around for a while. I guess that was about six o'clock. When I got back to the hotel, Mr. Hamon was entertaining his friends with a feast of duck. I looked into the dining room and he saw me. I saw Frank Ketch near the door, and I walked over to him and told him to tell the boss that I was going back upstairs and I went back up to the room.

"I called down for some ice water, and soon there was a knock at the door. It was Bill, the porter, with the water. But behind him was Mr. Hamon. He was drunk. After the porter left, he grabbed me, choked me, and shoved me down on the bed and began to curse at me. I asked him not to use profane language. I was afraid of him. He had a look of hate in his eyes. I struggled to get up and managed to. But he choked me again and backed me up against the window. He twisted the skin on my hand and nearly broke my fingers by bending them back. Then he reached for a knife on a nearby table and yelled, 'I will cut your throat!'

"I reached for my purse and found my little gun."

At this, McLean took charge, it was a predetermined point in the story they had gone over many times. He said, "Now, Clara, what did you do with the pistol when you got hold of it?"

"I held it on him and said, 'Let me pass,'" she replied.

"And what did Mr. Hamon do?"

"Well, he did actually back away a little behind a chair. So I started to try to pass by him to get out of the room. I got to the door, and it was locked so I had to unlock it with one hand while holding the gun in the other hand. The next thing I remember is that Mr. Hamon struck me with a chair, and the gun went off. I pulled the trigger or something as he hit me, I don't know, but the gun went off. I didn't mean to shoot him," Clara said, and then she began to weep and sob into a frilly handkerchief.

"Your Honor, could we ask for a ten-minute recess?" McLean appealed to Judge Champion. The judge granted the request.

When court resumed, McLean asked Clara, "Now, after the gun went off, did Mr. Hamon say anything?"

"Yes, he said, 'You hit me.' And then he showed me a large spot of blood on his mid-section."

"Did he say anything else?"

"Yes. He said, 'Clara, I will say it was an accident.'"

"Now, the next morning, before you left town, did you go to the hospital to see Mr. Hamon?"

"Yes, I did. Mr. Hamon held out his arms and pulled me down and kissed me and asked me to forgive him. He said it would never have happened had he not been drunk."

"One more question, Clara. Over the years, did Mr. Hamon ever talk to you about leaving his wife and marrying you?"

"Yes, many times. Countless times."

"Your witness," McLean said to Attorney General Prince Freeling.

"Now, Clara, isn't it true that when you came back to the hotel after your ride, that you interrupted Mr. Hamon's dinner and made a scene?"

"I don't remember doing that. I remember seeing him with his friends, but I only spoke to Mr. Ketch."

"You mentioned marriage in your testimony, can you describe for the court how it is that you claim Jake's last name when you have never been married to the man."

"Objection!" thundered Jimmy Mathers. "Irrelevant."

"Overruled. I'll allow it. The witness will answer the question."

"Well, Mr. Freeling, some years ago, Mr. Hamon arranged for me to marry his nephew, Frank. But it was only for a few months, and this so I could legally claim the Hamon name when we traveled together."

"You mean so you could share rooms in hotels as man and wife?"

Mathers was on his feet. "Objection, Your Honor!"

"Withdrawn," Freeling said with a smile before the judge could rule. "I have no more questions."

"Redirect, Mr. McLean?"

"No, Your Honor. The defense rests."

"All right, seeing as it's after four o'clock, we're going to adjourn, and we'll hear closing arguments tomorrow. I'll have instructions in the morning. Court adjourned." Down came the gavel.

THIRTY-EIGHT

"...IT'S FORTUNATE THAT GUN WENT OFF THAT DAY..."

Attorney General Prince Freeling spoke for more than two hours, painstakingly reviewing the evidence. By this time, he knew he was fighting an uphill battle. He knew there was wide-spread sympathy for Clara as a victim. His goal—his job—was to try to get the twelve men in the jury to make their decision based on facts and reason, not emotion.

He had his work cut out for him

"Gentlemen, you are all decent men. You have the capacity for compassion. Most of you are married. Some of you have daughters. And there is much in this complicated case that resonates with husbands and fathers on a certain level. But your sworn duty is to the law and the facts.

"Based on these, you have no choice, no matter what you may or may not feel on a personal level about the defendant, or even the dead man, you have no choice but to find Clara Smith Hamon guilty of murder. She bought a gun. She had a grievance. She was a woman scorned. Did the deceased treat her right? No. But he didn't deserve to die for it. She told a powerful story about how she was attacked and the gun went off in self-defense. But the physical evidence indicates that she shot the man while he was lying down. You remember Dr. Hardy's testimony. If he was lying down, he wasn't attacking. And the good doctor said that Mr. Jake Hamon told him—a dying man—that Clara Smith Hamon came to lay next to him, and she stroked his head with one tender hand and shot him with the other.

"Are you going to believe the testimony of one of the finest citizens in this part of the country, or are you going to believe the contrived and convoluted ramblings of a woman desperate to avoid the consequences of her pre-meditated act?"

Though McLean had carried the ball during direct testimony and cross-examination, the defense team knew that James Mathers would be a better fit for their closing argument. He was well known in Carter County and had recently been elected as the county prosecutor. Everyone knew that he had delayed taking up his new duties as a prosecutor because of his belief in Clara's innocence.

Mathers sensed that the state had failed to make its case, but he wasn't going to take any chances. He decided to use his time to undermine the confidence of the jury in the very facts that Freeling had reiterated.

"Now, let's look at the wound itself. It was from the front. Direct from the front. Clara is right-handed. For her to lay down behind the man and stroke his head with her left hand, the right one presumably holding a pistol, hen to somehow place the pistol in a position to fire directly into the body from the front, well, this would be quite a feat.

"Also, let's not forget that Dr. Hardy, the star witness for the prosecution, testified that Mr. Jake Hamon was suffering from a life-threatening disease, cirrhosis of the liver, brought on no doubt by the chronic abuse of liquor—which is illegal these days in these United States.

"Had Jake not been a drunk, he'd likely still be alive, and would have long ago recovered from a wound he clearly wanted to hide.

"No. It should be clear to everyone in this courtroom. His relationship with our client had undermined his chance for the kind of political power that megalomaniacs like him crave. And like all would-be tin horn Napoleons in the world, when he couldn't get what he wanted, he sought his revenge. He couldn't take it out on Harding or Coolidge or the Republican Party of Oklahoma. But he could use poor Clara as a punching bag one more time.

"Frankly, it's fortunate that gun went off that day. If it hadn't, you twelve men might be serving right now on a jury sitting in judgment on a fallen political power-broker. A man who had beaten a woman to her death."

Mathers turned and walked back to the table. It was a masterful presentation.

But would it be enough?

Judge Thomas Champion then gave a lengthy list of instructions to the jury—more than thirty elements. Several members of the panel seemed to be particularly interested in point number eleven: "You are instructed, Gentlemen of the Jury, that homicide is excusable when committed by accident or misfortune in the heat of passion, upon any sudden and sufficient provocation, or upon a sudden combat, provided that no undue advantage is taken, nor any dangerous weapon used, and that killing is not done in a cruel or unusual manner."

At 4:30 PM the jurors filed out and retired to a room to deliberate. Forty minutes later, they were back. The foreman, B. C. Loughridge, a seventy-three-year-old retired merchant, responded to Judge Champion's question: "Gentlemen, have you reached a verdict?" Loughridge replied, "Yes, Your Honor." He then handed a slip of paper to the clerk, who announced:

"NOT GUILTY."

Clara dropped forward in her seat. Her brother, Jimmie, came up from behind and was the first to hug her. "Jimmie," she said, "I am the happiest woman in the world."

Georgia Hamon was not in the courtroom for the reading of the verdict.

Oklahoma Attorney General Prince Freeling's first words when the verdict was announced were, "of course." He had sensed the inevitable for several days and found himself angry at the governor for putting him in that position.

Edith C. Johnson had been in the courtroom for every session, sending tidbits and articles back to her paper in Oklahoma City. Her article about the verdict seemed to articulate what so many felt had happened: "Clara Smith, ostensibly tried for the murder of Jake Hamon, was not tried for murder at all. The trial was based on the lack of virtue in the slain man."

Within minutes of the verdict, and while the courtroom remained the scene of celebration, Clara had disappeared. She was secreted out a side entrance and on her way back to her sister's home in Wilson. John Gorman had been in the courtroom and left immediately. He was at the Welling home when Clara arrived.

"Clara, we have our happy ending. Now we can make our movie."

"Oh, Johnny," she said as she threw her arms around the producer and kissed him passionately. "I can hardly wait!"

"And I have the perfect title for it."

"What is it, Johnny? Tell me."

"We're gonna call it, 'FATE.'"

THIRTY-NINE

"BUT SHE UNDERESTIMATED THE BACKLASH..."

At that moment, Clara Smith Hamon was the most famous woman in America. And she was determined to leverage her fleeting celebrity into something durable and long-lasting. Ever since John Gorman had knocked on her sister's door in January, she had been nursing, then nurturing, an ambition.

She wanted to be a star.

She had also fallen in love with John Gorman. Some in her family wondered if she was putting herself into another Jake-like relationship, but Gorman presented himself as a gentleman. Even Clara's folks took a liking to him. John wanted to make a movie about the whole story.

All he needed was money—Clara's money.

Meanwhile, Clara wanted to work on her image. She wanted her story to be one of redemption and a cautionary tale. So the Sunday after the trial ended, she made her way to the Ardmore's First Christian Church. She asked the pastor, Dr.

Grayton Brooks, to baptize her. The parson had been following the trial, and he had counseled Clara on occasion since Jake's death.

She confessed, professed, and declared her faith and her renewal, surrounded by family and church members. She wore a white robe, which raised some eyebrows. Some in the church were suspicious of her motives, but they liked the fact that their little church was momentarily famous across the country. And, of course, they knew that the gospel and the church were supposed to be about forgiveness, redemption, second chances, things like that.

A few days after her dip in that sanctified water, Clara's name made the newspapers across America once again. This time, it was for the also very public immersion in the movie business. She signed a contract with Gorman's company—a two-year deal—to make movies.

Or at least one. Then they would see where they went from there.

The idea of "fifteen minutes of fame" was still decades away, but that is what Clara was determined to leverage. Her longtime fascination with movies and stars of the big screen made it hard for her to resist that particularly seductive limelight, no matter how unrealistic her ultimate success would be—as many in her life vainly whispered in her ear. Her mind was made up.

And her Johnny was going to make it happen.

Clara failed to see that her lover was becoming the new Jake—a man who promised to her the world in exchange for her soul. And like Jake Hamon, whatever real feelings he may have had for Clara, they were trumped along the way by his own unbridled ambition and skillful manipulation.

Several weeks later—it was May 1921—Clara met with Frank Ketch to sign some papers. Long gone were the high-powered and similarly priced lawyers who made up the dream team that orchestrated her acquittal. They had earned much more than their fees. Each one would go on to leverage their involvement in Clara's trial with great success, particularly Wild Bill McLean. A few years later, he found himself in another great murder trial—this time he would join the prosecution in an attempt to put a famous preacher in the Texas electric chair.

But McLean and all the rest of her attorneys were nowhere to be found at a moment when Clara was vulnerable and really needed them. Not that she would have listened. Probably not. Her mind was on other things.

So she was no match for the crafty Frank Ketch. She signed the papers as he instructed her. And in return for dropping any other claims on Jake Hamon's estate, she received a cash settlement as well as some modest oil royalties.

She could have held out for more—that's what the lawyers would have advised. But she was convinced that big money was in her future—her movie star future. She was ready to put Ardmore behind her.

Next stop, California.

A few months later, Clara showed up at another Christian church, this one in Los Angeles. She wasn't there for a baptism, or even a Sunday service. She was at the Wilshire Boulevard

Christian Church to marry John Gorman. And the Reverend M. Howard Fagan was happy to officiate.

There were a few "B-list" movie-types in attendance, friends of John. It was his world—and she was just starting to find her way.

They postponed the honeymoon. Too much work had to be done. John promised her a big trip to San Francisco for the world premiere of their movie.

Back when she signed the contract with Gorman, the publication, Motion Picture World, hinted that Clara would be making $1,000 per week and that any motion pictures in which she appeared would bear the trademark, "Clara Smith Hamon Pictures, Inc." But this was all hype orchestrated by John Gorman.

In fact, Clara wound up putting $75,000 of her own money—most of what she received when she signed that settlement with Frank Ketch—toward a $200,000-budget to make FATE. She would be the star—playing herself in a thinly-veiled story based on the true life of Jake and Clara. The film was produced at Warner Bros. Studio on Sunset Boulevard in Los Angeles that summer. Clara hoped FATE would make her a star.

But she underestimated the backlash and ignored the warning signs. A group of theater owners in New York City issued a statement saying that they were, "emphatically opposed to the exploitation of criminal sensationalism."

They were not alone.

All that remains of it all is found mainly in footnotes from the early days of Tinseltown. By the time of its opening in September 1921, the movie had already been swallowed up in controversy and censorship. Then came that moment in San Francisco, a city which, as it turned out, was not the best venue for the film. Police seized all the reels for FATE from the projection booth. They also arrested one of the producers—a forgettable fellow named W. B. Weathers. The charge was indecency.

Weathers was released on $250 bail, and brought to trial a couple of weeks later. He insisted that all eight reels of FATE be screened in the courtroom. At issue was whether or not the film "was adapted to excite vicious and lewd thoughts and acts." A jury of twelve women actually found the defendant "not guilty."

But even that small victory did not help. The movie was already doomed. Dead on arrival. Movie houses across the country refused to screen it. It was shown a few times in Oklahoma over the next few months—but not in Ardmore.

Clara's story by then was being overshadowed by what is now widely remembered as Hollywood's first scandal. Roscoe "Fatty" Arbuckle was accused of rape in San Francisco. Whatever happened occurred that fateful weekend when Clara's movie was seized. Events that Labor Day weekend in San Francisco in 1921 became a perfect storm. The devastation left behind would impact the film industry for decades to come.

It wasn't so much that Arbuckle's troubles hurt the roll out of FATE. At the time, it was actually quite the opposite. Clara's movie was actually far more damaging to Hollywood than the big man's famous scandal.

But that's not how things are remembered these days. Clara Hamon and her movie disappeared in Arbuckle's monumental shadow. No prints of FATE survive to this day.

Clara's "fifteen seconds" were over.

She divorced John Gorman in 1924, about the time that Jake's name was back in the news. Harding was gone. His own fate was determined also in San Francisco, where he died of food poisoning. Some wondered, though, if his misdeeds had caught up with him and maybe The Duchess had seen enough and decided that Clara had the right idea when it came to a cheating man.

The reason for briefly renewed interest in Jake Hamon a few years after Clara shot him to death in their room at the Randol Hotel, was a series of hearings in Washington, DC.

There was a big and quite famous investigation involving a major scandal about oil leases in many places, particularly one spot called Teapot Dome. And the man who got the job Jake Hamon wanted and had paid big money for was on his way to prison. A Secretary of the Interior named Albert Fall.

Some wondered out loud if things might have been different had Jake Hamon lived and been in charge over at Interior.

Probably not.

THE END

AUTHOR'S NOTE

This book is based on a true story. All the characters are real. But because I have invented dialogue, this book falls into the category of historical fiction. Please know, however, that the conversations and situations I have constructed are based on extensive reading and research about the characters and their history.

Why write historical fiction? Why not just stick with history itself and write a nonfiction account of something? I mean, David McCullough's books aren't so bad, and some say they read like novels. But here's the thing—what about great stories, real ones, from history, where there is not enough material in the records to fill in all the blanks?

This is, I think, the greatest service the historical fiction writer can provide for readers. Sometimes the only "story" we have exists in fragments. The DNA of a broader narrative is there, but it's not easily seen, and it must be carefully reconstructed with informed imagination.

Enter the practitioner of the craft of historical fiction. The writer builds a superstructure from a few fragile fragments, but always with an eye on all other relevant facts and materials extant. It's sort of like how they build dinosaur skeletons from a small assortment of scattered bones.

The late Irving Stone was a genius at this. Writing in the preface to one of his great books, "The President's Lady: A Novel About Rachel and Andrew Jackson," he talked about this kind of research and writing. He said it was, "as authentic and documented as several years of intensive research, the generous assistance of the historians and librarians in the field, and literally thousands of books, magazines, pamphlets, newspapers, diaries, public records, correspondence and collections of unpublished memoirs and doctoral theses can make it."

Then Stone dropped the other shoe: "The interpretations of character are of course my own; this is not only the novelist's prerogative, but his obligation. Much of the dialogue had to be recreated, but every effort has been made to create it on the basis of individual character, personality, temperament, education, idiosyncrasy, as well as recorded conversations and dialogue, memoirs, diaries, letters, and published accounts by relatives, friends, associates, even of detractors, and enemies."

To my mind Stone struck the right balance, setting a standard for all who dare to reimagine the past.

David R. Stokes
Fairfax, Virginia
November 2015

ACKNOWLEDGMENTS

I want to express my gratitude to several people who have helpedalong the way. Laura Bailey and Cyd Allen, two proud residents of Oklahoma, unearthed archival material from Ardmore, Lawton, and Oklahoma City. This included newspapers, magazine articles, and court records. Holly Slater did the same for me in San Francisco—paying special attention to the original newspaper coverage in William Randolph Hearst's San Francisco Examiner.

I am also indebted to a number of people who helped whittle away at the flaws of the original manuscript, from a gifted copy editor named Melissa Gray, to proof readers Tracey Dowdy, Holly Slater, and Al Donaldson.

Mark Moorer, a senior producer for the CW television network, created the excellent art for the cover.

The idea for this book came to me several years ago when I was writing, "The Shooting Salvationist: J. Frank Norris and the Murder Trial that Captivated America." Among the attorneys involved in that famous case from 1926-1927 was a Texas lawyer named W.P. "Wild Bill" McLean. By the late 1920s, he was one of the most well known and sought after lawyers in the American southwest. The Clara Smith Hamon case, years earlier, gave him his big break.

I also want to thank my Hollywood representatives, Alexia Melocchi and Alexandra Yacovlef, with Little Studio Films. They believed in this story from the first moment I shared it with them. And they are passionate about seeing it developed for film. Stay tuned.

Finally, but really first and foremost, I want to thank my wife Karen and my daughters, Jennifer, Deborah, and Brenda. They are the shining lights brightening every day of my life. Oh, and then there are my seven grandchildren...but don't get me started on that.

– DRS

RESEARCH

I have written both fiction and nonfiction, and I can tell you that the research for a novel—especially one based on a true story—can be as involved as that required for a work of strict nonfiction. For this book, I have drawn detail and color from the following resources:

NEWSPAPERS
The Ada Evening News
The Ardmore Statesman
The Chicago Tribune
The Daily Ardmoreite
The Los Angeles Examiner
The Morning Tulsa Daily World
The New York Times
The Oklahoma City Times
The San Francisco Examiner
The Washington Post

PERIODICALS
The Chronicles of Oklahoma (December 1941 & October 2009)
Distinctly Oklahoma Magazine (August 1912)
Texas Monthly (January 1985)

BOOKS

Adams, Samuel Hopkins. "Incredible Era—The Life and Times of Warren Gamaliel Harding." New York: Capricorn Books, 1964.

Allen, Charlise Foust. "Images of America: Ardmore." Chicago: Arcadia Publishing, 2009.

Anthony, Carl Sferrazza. "Florence Harding: The First Lady, the Jazz Age, and the Death of America's Most Scandalous President." New York: William Morrow and Company, Inc., 2008.

Bagby, Wesley M. "The Road to Normalcy and the Presidential Campaign and Election of 1920." Baltimore: The Johns Hopkins University Press, 1968.

Brownlaw, Kevin. "Behind the Mask of Innocence—Sex, Violence, Prejudice, Crime: Films of Social Consciences in the Silent Era." Berkley and Los Angeles, 1990.

Burns, Eric. "1920: The Year that Made the Decade Roar." New York: Pegasus Books, 2015.

Chesterton, Gilbert Keith. "What I Saw in America." New York: Dodd, Mead, and Company, 1922.

Daughtery, Harry M. "The Inside Story of the Harding Tragedy." New York: The Churchill Company, 1932.

Dorman, Robert L. "It Happened in Oklahoma." Guilford, Connecticut: Morris Book Publishing, 2006.

Hinshaw, David. "A Man From Kansas: The Story of William Allen White." New York: G.P. Putnam's Sons, 1945.

Houts Marshall. "From Gun to Gavel: The Courtroom Recollections of James Mathers of Oklahoma." New York: Morrow, 1954.

Lewis, Jon and Smoodin, Eric. "Looking Past the Screen: Case Studies in American Film History and Method." Durham, NC: Duke University Press, 2007.

McCartney, Laton. "The Teapot Dome Scandal: How Big Oil Bought the Harding White House and Tried to Steal the Country." New York: Random House, 2008.

McGalliard, Mac. "Reporters Notebook." Ardmore: Sprekel Meyer Printing Company, 1973.

McInnes, Elmer D. "Bud Ballew: Legendary Lawman of Oklahoma." Guilford, Connecticut: TwoDot, 2008.

Mee, Charles L. Jr. "The Ohio Gang: The World of Warren G. Harding." New York: M. Evans and Company, 1981.

Quinby, Ione. "Murder For Love." New York: Convici Friede, Inc., 1931.

Pietrusza, David. "1920: The Year of Six Presidents." New York: Carroll and Graf Publishers, 2007.

Russell, Francis. "The Shadow of Blooming Grove: Warren G. Harding in His Times." New York: McGraw Hill, 1968.

Stokes, David R. "The Shooting Salvationist: J. Frank Norris and the Murder Trial that Captivated America." Hanover, NH: Steerforth Press, 2011.

ABOUT THE AUTHOR

David R. Stokes is a *Wall Street Journal* best-selling author.

Three of his books are under review for development in Hollywood: "CAMELOT'S COUSIN: The Spy Who Betrayed Kennedy," "NOVEMBER SURPRISE" (sequel to "Camelot's Cousin"), and "CAPITOL LIMITED: The Forgotten First Kennedy & Nixon Debate in 1947."

His first book, "THE SHOOTING SALVATIONIST: J. Frank Norris and the Murder Trial that Captivated America," a narrative nonfiction thriller and true crime bestseller, is also being considered as a six-part television miniseries.

An ordained minister since 1977, David speaks every Sunday (9:00 & 10:45 a.m.) at EXPECTATION CHURCH, a non-denominational ministry in Fairfax, Virginia, with more than 30 nations represented in its congregation.

He has hosted his own national satellite radio talk show and is a regular guest-host for talk shows around the country. David has also produced and hosted podcasts for The Cold War Museum and Richard Nixon Foundation.

David has been married to Karen since 1976 and they have three daughters and seven grandchildren. They live in beautiful Northern Virginia. His personal website is:

www.davidrstokes.com

CPSIA information can be obtained
at www.ICGtesting.com
Printed in the USA
FFOW01n1940161215
19393FF